MAGPIE'S SONG

Allison Pang

Published by Outland Entertainment LLC
3119 Gillham Road
Kansas City, MO 64109

Founder/Creative Director: Jeremy D. Mohler
Editor-in-Chief: Alana Joli Abbott

ISBN: 978-1-954255-29-6
EBOOK ISBN: 978-1-954255-30-2
Worldwide Rights
Created in the United States of America

Editor: Danielle Poiesz and Double Vision Editorial
Cover Illustration: germancreative
Cover Design: Jeremy D. Mohler
Interior Layout: Mikael Brodu

Printed and bound in the United States of America.

Visit **outlandentertainment.com** to see more, or follow us on our Facebook Page **facebook.com/outlandentertainment/**

— A WORD FROM THE CRITICS —

"Pang delivers a fascinating storyline, strong character development, and plenty of plot twists which will draw readers into the first book of the IronHeart Chronicles and leave them eagerly anticipating the next tale in the series. Maggy is a plucky and loyal character that will fascinate readers but what makes this novel so enthralling is the relatable and carefully drawn characters coupled with vivid imagery throughout every scene."

–4 Stars – *RT Book Reviews*

"Allison Pang's *Magpie's Song* is exactly the sort of thing I love to read most. Beautiful prose, interesting characters that I want to know better, a carefully crafted world of that is both mysterious and almost inevitable. It's rare that a book surprises me on so many levels. Powerful stuff with enough surprises to make me smile and enough twists to keep me on my toes. I can't recommend it enough!"

–James A. Moore
–author of the *Seven Forges* series and the *Tides of War* trilogy

"Vivid, thrilling, clever, and imaginative, *Magpie's Song* is a genre-bending gem built around a kickass heroine and a compelling, beautifully-wrought SF/fantasy world you'll want to explore further. Allison Pang's talent is on every page. Fans of Pierce Brown and Wesley Chu will love *Magpie's Song*."

—Christopher Golden,
New York Times bestselling author of *Ararat*

"Pang has crafted a beautiful world with a ticking mechanical heart and a story that flies with fast-paced action. Utterly enchanting!"

—Laura Bickle, critically acclaimed author of *Nine of Stars*

"Maggy is an unlikely heroine, but Pang makes it easy to root for the foulmouthed scavenger.... [U]nique worldbuilding and impressive character work.... Readers will be eager to know what comes next."

—*Publishers Weekly*

— ALSO BY ALLISON PANG —

Comics, from Outland Entertainment
Fox & Willow: Came a Harper
Fox & Willow: To the Sea

The Abby Sinclair Series
A Brush of Darkness (Book One)
A Sliver of Shadow (Book Two)
A Trace of Moonlight (Book Three)
A Symphony of Starlight (Book Four)
A Duet with Darkness (a prequel short story
in the *Carniepunk* anthology)

The IronHeart Chronicles
Magpie's Fall
Magpie's Flight (forthcoming)

Standalones
"Respawn, Reboot" (a short story in the
Out of Tune, Book 2 anthology)
"The Wind in Her Hair" (a comic in the
Womanthology: Space anthology)
"A Dream Most Ancient and Alone" (a short story in the
Tales From The Lake Vol 5: The Horror Anthology)
"A Certain TeaHouse" (a comic in the *Gothic Tales
of Haunted Futures* anthology)

To Lucy, Moon Child of my heart.

'Ware IronHeart's breath and IronHeart's claws
For when IronHeart roars, Meridion falls.

They calls me Raggy Maggy
But I have no song to sing.
I've a ghost for a shadow
And a sparrow on the wing.

— CHAPTER ONE —

"**W**ell, it's certainly not from *here*." I smirk, eyeing the tiny dragon with a raised brow.

Beside me, my clanmate Sparrow snorts and pushes a lock of pale hair from her face. "Obviously. You can tell because there's no rust on it."

And there isn't. The dragon is about the size of a robin and perches on a nearby barrel, its metallic body gleaming beneath the sodium light with the golden glitter of an oil-coated pearl. Tiny cogs whir and click in miniature perfection, nestled inside a shiny glass belly full of steam and smoke. A red-hot ember flares in a rhythmic pulse in the chambered center of its chest.

In the entirety of my nineteen years, I've never seen anything like it. Its exquisite appearance is at odds with the severity of our surroundings, making the BrightStone junkyard seem even more haggard than it is. And that's saying something.

"So where do you think it came from? The Upper Tier...or the *upper tier*?" Sparrow points up to the sky with an exaggerated flourish and rolls her eyes. For all that she's five years younger than I am, she has enough cynicism for the both of us. Living on the streets as we do, a sense of humor is a necessity. Sometimes it's the only thing we have.

I gaze upward to search through the hazy fog of the slag heaps, straining to see the emerald glass of the shining towers of Meridion in the distance. The floating city looms above BrightStone as it always does, its secrets dense and seemingly without end.

It's all bones here below, a graveyard of corrosion and twisted metal, the castoffs of Meridion sprawled in haphazard fashion like the burial grounds of elephants I once saw in a picture book. The junkyard sits outside the crumbling ruins of BrightStone's lower quadrant, which is now nothing more than a maze of cobblestone streets and empty buildings. It probably had a name once, a proper one, but these days we just call it the Warrens.

I move closer to where the dragon sits until I'm only a few feet away, and I glance back at Sparrow with a shrug. "Too finely made, even for the BrightStone jewelers in the Upper Tier. No, some spoiled Meridian brat probably lost her precious toy out the window of a wind balloon. Or down the garbage chute."

"Still pretty, though." A hint of longing threads its way through Sparrow's voice, her dark eyes suddenly pensive. She's a tiny thing, but there's a boldness that belies her small stature, a subtle cheeky disposition that's part humor and part defense mechanism wrapped in BrightStone's drab hand-me-down rags.

"Aye," I say softly, studying the delicate webbing of the dragon's wings, the golden membranes overlapping like the mocking sweep of an exotic bird's feathers.

A Meridian would call it beautiful, no doubt. A wonder of engineering. But all I can see is night upon night of hot meals and the promise of a real bed with blankets, a roof, and maybe a bath in something that doesn't resemble pig swill. Maybe even a shiny hammer and a new wool coat.

Toy or not, this dragon could be sold. Melted down. Ripped apart.

It turns toward me, catching my gaze with its jeweled eyes.

I wonder for a moment if it will startle, but I shake away the absurd thought. After all, it's merely a toy. And yet, there's an odd sensation of recognition I don't understand as it maintains eye contact. My heartbeat clatters in my chest, as though reminding me why I'm here.

Sparrow and I have a certain weight of scrap we need to collect—anything that could be sold or traded. For those of us living in the Warrens it's the only legal way of making enough jingle to survive. But whatever our individual supplementary means of subsistence might be, every member of the clan is required turn in their scrap at the end of each day or earn their keep in some other fashion.

Sliding my hammer from my belt with a careful hand, I nod at Sparrow. "I'm short my quota. Halvsies and such?"

"Aye." Her coat flaps in the breeze, and she shifts. The dragon snakes toward her, its steaming breath hissing like an angry teakettle.

I see my chance and close the distance with a scuff of boots. I carefully press down on the back of its neck until it touches the lid of the barrel. The dragon squirms, nearly sliding through my oiled fingers, and I turn my battered hammer so that the clawed fork traps its triangular head.

"Oy, look at it wriggle," Sparrow says, eyes wide.

"Help me put it in the bag." My knuckles strain as the dragon lets out a shriek. "Mine's mostly empty." Sparrow struggles with the drawstring, forcing me to adjust my stance to allow her better access. "Quit moving, beastie, or I'll take the hammer to you," I warn.

A disdainful sniff puffs from its intricately carved nostrils, but I don't hesitate to take a firmer grasp behind its head and thrust it into the bag once Sparrow has it opened. The dragon lets out an indignant rumble, but Sparrow's already tightly tying the bag shut.

She hands it to me with a shrug. "So now what? Not exactly like we're going to be able to fob it off at the scrap-trader's." She purses her mouth. "Be a shame to destroy it, though."

A sigh escapes me. I know she's right. Not about destroying it so much as having it traced back to us or our clan. Something this fine... People would take note.

"We'll have to be careful about it," I admit.

"We could turn it over to Rory..."

The thought makes my stomach twist. "No. Not that. We'd never see a penny." Rory acts like a liaison between our clan and the rest of BrightStone. Our *leader* might be what he calls himself, but he's nothing more than a bully with a slight edge over the rest of us.

"That leaves us with smelting it, then," she says.

"Maybe. But I bet Archivist Chaunders could tell us how much it's worth. Then we can take it to Molly Bell over at the Conundrum. She might not give us full price, but at least the profits would be ours."

It's a risky venture at best. Molly Bell deals in black market goods and information and has an extensive clientele of BrightStone elites and underworld lackeys alike. Approaching her is a bit like swimming with a shark: sooner or later, she always takes her pound of flesh.

Sparrow cocks her head at me. "Oh, aye. That's brilliant. You really think Rory will let it slide if we start dealing with Molly Bell behind his back?" She scoffs. "I don't trust her any farther than I can see her. And not even then, Mags."

"Well it's not like we can just walk into Spriggan territory to try to sell it ourselves, now can we? Besides, what Rory doesn't know won't kill him."

The words sound hollow even in my own ears. As excuses go, it's paper-thin. But what of it? I've never found anything of real value before. Rory won't hesitate to dole out punishment for coming up short, but the temptation is so strong I can taste it.

"Might kill *us*, though," Sparrow mutters.

A shadow passes overhead, the darkening pall of an Inquestor air patrol, its sails spread wide on either side of its narrow hull. It's one of their scout ships, drifting upon invisible currents of fog and steam. From below it looks like a silver hummingbird, darting in and out between the buildings.

I throw the bag over my shoulder and slide my hammer into my belt. The ship's sudden appearance only serves to make me uneasy. Inquestors tend to stay out of the Warrens, abandoned as they are. A patrol out at this time of day would be looking for somewhat.

Or someone.

I don't want to be either.

Sparrow and I have been on the receiving end of their searches before. Last time I'd been stopped, they took nearly a full day's worth of scrap for no reason except that they could. Rory had beaten me senseless when he found out, the arrogant bastard.

Still…

Short my quota or no, the dragon in my sack troubles me. The longer we hold on to it, the more likely we'll be discovered. And the more likely we'll give up any chance of a profit. I shift the strap of my bag so it's sitting more securely on my shoulder. "Let's just head toward the Conundrum now. The sooner we dump this, the better off we'll be. Maybe I can make up for my missing scrap tomorrow."

Sparrow lets out a disbelieving grunt. "Come on, then. I'll split my takings with you, and we'll say the patrols chased us out of the junkyard. Wouldn't be the first time."

I cast a wary eye at the shadow, but the air patrol is heading toward the lights of BrightStone's Upper Tier and away from us.

"And good riddance." Sparrow sighs with relief.

We slink our way to the borders of the junkyard, pausing when we discover the remains of an ancient carburetor, its innards slowly leaking out in inky streaks. I pick off the bolts, but they jangle miserably in Sparrow's sack with every step she takes.

At the outskirts of the Warrens the fog thickens around us in a cloak woven of soot and ancient rust. The coverage is deceptive, making it seem as though the lower bowels of the city are cleaner than their wont. But like a diseased whore, all it takes is a stiff breeze from the fetid bay to remove the illusion, its skirts lifted to reveal the rotting core beneath.

Oily puddles stinking of fish guts and damp shit cover the cobblestones in layers of filth that make it hard to walk. You get used to the smell the way you get used to never being warm or having a belly that never stops biting.

In the distance, the dull clang of the Mother Clock thumps out the hour, the sound burrowing its way through the crevices of shutters and chimney tops, crumbling brick and slick-packed cement. Something crunches beneath my foot, and I wave away the fog, blinking in surprise when I see a metallic hue.

More scrap?

I kneel, my fingers digging through the muck without hesitation.

"Mags?" Sparrow's voice is a whisper from the gloaming.

"Hush. There's somewhat here." I feel hard metal. Oil, slick... and warm? I pull a lightstick from the inner pocket of my coat and tap it softly. It blazes to life, illuminating the alleyway in a putrid piss color. Enough to get a better idea of what I'd stumbled over, at least.

Sparrow mumbles a swear above me.

"Hells." The metal glints beneath my foot, and I realize it's another dragon, just like the one in my sack, but its wings are a shattered mess of coils and springs and no ember beats within its broken glass chest. An uneasy feeling churns in my gut.

But really, it isn't the metal so much as the blood pooling in a large depression in the cobblestones. And it's not from the dragon.

I trace the sluggish crimson rivulets to the source—a body sprawled in a haphazardly ungraceful position. Death being the great equalizer, it clearly has no time to stop for dignity.

The man's head is cracked; something spongy leaks from his ears, and his jaw hangs open like a door knocked off its hinges. Death isn't a new thing for us by any stretch, but that's not what makes me pause. I glance at Sparrow, nestled deep in her coat, and she swallows.

"His face…" she says, barely a whisper.

"I know." I carefully prod his cheek. Even beneath the yellow luminescence of my lightstick, his skin seems to shimmer.

He's a Meridian. A real, gods-be-damned Meridian.

I've never seen one before, and as far as I know, neither has Sparrow. These days they keep to themselves in their floating city, using the specialized techniques of their red-robed Inquestor squads to keep the rest of us in line—BrightStone citizens and half-breed Moon Children alike.

Moon Children like me and Sparrow.

"I always thought the glowing-skin thing was bullshit." Sparrow tugs at a lock of her hair. "Too bad we don't glow. It'd be a lot handier in the dark."

"Or make us easy targets," I retort. "At least now we know what that air patrol was looking for." I touch his face again, marveling at the way it glitters, almost like a hint of frost upon a windowpane.

"We should get out of here," she says. "This is bad news."

"In a minute." I look up at the Meridian towers. Had he jumped or been pushed?

I shuffle forward, patting down the ruins of his fine wool coat until I discover a credit chit. I nearly toss it. The chits are Meridian currency, but they find their way to BrightStone from time to time. The shops here only take credit chits from Inquestors and BrightStone citizens of the Upper Tier—noble gentry who wouldn't deign to rub shoulders with gutter rats like us if their lives depended upon it.

Still, the thought of leaving money behind rankles. I pocket the chit on the off chance I can trade it for something later.

"Mags," Sparrow hisses at me again. I frown at her. Scavenging is first come, first serve. If I don't do it, then someone else will five minutes from now.

"Nearly done." I snag a few loose odds and ends that can be melted down if I can't sell them, and oh...a parcel of dried tobacco worth more than everything I have on me put together.

Sparrow leaves me to clamber up the brickwork of the nearest building, her fingers expertly digging into the rotting cement. "There's a ground patrol coming. I think they're looking for him." She melts into the shadows of the rooftops only to reappear a moment later. "Half a block. They're being quieter than usual."

"They're a tad late, don't you think?"

Something about the raggedness of his coat nags at me, and I run my hands along the lapel as I lower my lightstick. I feel the wound before I see it. Holes upon holes and shattered bones and cooling viscera. "He didn't just fall," I say. "Poor bastard's been gutted right under the ribs."

She exhales slowly. "Come on. They're nearly at the corner."

Now that she's pointed it out, I can hear the telltale thudding of heavy boots from somewhere behind us. "Time to go."

I pocket whatever is left of the second dragon's body and narrowly avoid the less than pleasant bodily fluids leaking from the soft parts of the man's flesh. No sense in leaving a trail.

I reach the far end of the alley, Sparrow silently flanking me up above. She whistles sharply twice, and I freeze.

Not one patrol but two.

And I've run smack into one of them.

It's a contingent of at least ten by the quick count I make, all dark-crimson trench coats and oiled mustaches, white gloves and brass buttons. Definitely not the normal caliber of the BrightStone watch.

No, these are Inquestors.

Shit.

It's said that Inquestors were Meridians once, before they came to BrightStone, but I don't know if it's true. They certainly don't shimmer from what I've seen. The leader of this particular patrol glares at me in disgusted recognition. Inquestor Caskers is a beanpole of a man wrapped in sallow skin and bristling black hair, his squared jaw set like that of a bulldog. The brass star on his breast indicates his rank of lieutenant, and his mustache is freshly waxed.

He cuffs me when I don't move out of his way. My cap falls off into the dust, and my white hair tumbles past my shoulders in the guttering lamplight, the mere presence of which earns me another stinging slap.

"Oy. A Moon Child. Raggy Maggy, is it?"

I taste blood on my lips, but I keep my face down and my hands in my pockets. "Yessir."

He pushes my hair out of the way to check the brand on the nape of my neck, letting him know which of the three Moon Child clans I belong to. My clan, the Banshees, resides within the Warrens while the Spriggans have taken what's left of the merchant districts and the Twisted Tumblers have the run of the Theatre Quarter. The rest of BrightStone is a no-man's-land of uneasy truce and feigned ignorance, but it gives us the semblance of having power over ourselves. Getting caught outside your territory by an opposing clan, though, is usually grounds for a beating, often of the more fatal sort.

I swallow, unable to keep from peeking up at him. If I'd run when I first saw them I might have managed to elude them long enough for them to decide I wasn't worth the trouble of chasing down. But there's no point in making a fuss now. He's got real evidence of who I am and that I was here.

Inquestor Caskers's dark eyes rake over me with a familiar bent, narrowing when they see my sack. I let my mouth go wide and scared, making myself appear as harmless and uninteresting as possible.

He grunts, fixing me with a hard gaze before tugging on the bag at my shoulders. "Seen anything worth reporting this evening? Anything untoward we should know about?"

It's asked in the mildest of tones, but the threat lingers all the same. It takes everything I have to simply stand there instead of jerking away. In the end, I simply shake my head. "Nothing," I mumble.

Caskers stares at me a moment longer and lets go of the sack. "Indeed. I don't have time for you now. Get out of my sight before I change my mind."

I dart low to retrieve my cap as they shove past me. I still have a few moments before they discover the body and decide I'm involved somehow. Which they will. And I'm not going to stick around to see what happens when they do.

I don't dare glance up at where Sparrow might be hiding, but I start to hurry down the alleyway.

"Hold up, Lieutenant!" one of the Inquestors shouts. "We've a man down here…"

"That's that," I mutter, wincing as their shouts of alarm echo off the bricks.

"Oy! Stop her!" Caskers orders.

My sack bobs against my back as I run, the hard weight of the dragon slamming into my hip. A hand snatches at my arm, fingers curving like iron around my elbow.

Bastards left a guard at the end of the alley.

I snarl at my captor—this one slightly bowlegged with a face of jowled blubber. "Not so fast, girl." A lightstick hangs from his belt, and he frowns when he sees my hand. "You've blood on your sleeve."

My heart sinks. *Stupid, stupid, Mags.* I reach into my pocket in desperation and fling the broken dragon parts at his face, escaping as he covers his eyes.

I whistle shrilly as I pelt away, and Sparrow answers me with a whistle of her own. As coded messages go, it's a rudimentary thing but it gets the job done. Easy to hear, hard for outsiders to understand, and for Moon Children, sometimes that's the difference between life and death.

I whistle again, looking for the best route. *Which way?*

Two short blasts followed by a long hold in response. *Two up, one over.*

I yank the hammer from my belt as I sprint the next two blocks, the heavy steps of the Inquestors pounding in pursuit. I leap upward, snagging a low-slung metal beam hanging across the street. It gives beneath my weight; the rusted edges wail as I whip forward so it hurtles from the brickwork, landing behind me with a clunk. A bang and a sharp curse follow suit, indicating my venture to trip my pursuers was successful, albeit only temporarily.

The end of the street materializes in front of me, the brassy-gold shine of the lanterns reflecting off a drainpipe.

Almost there.

Heavy breath follows me, but it's winded. If I can get to the rooftops, they won't dare come after me. My fingers clutch the drainpipe, and I dig my boots into the mortar to shimmy up and up.

My teeth slam shut hard, the vibration ringing in my ears, as I'm yanked sharply down. One hand on my boot and another on my bag, pulling it from my shoulder.

Not the dragon!

I kick out, making contact with something soft as I wriggle out of the shoulder strap.

Without bothering to aim, I swing the bag by the strap, hurling it up into the darkness to land on some distant rooftop. I catch the dull clank of metal against stone. Good enough. With any luck I'll find it later, once I get out of this mess.

Another pull and I drop farther down the pipe. I spare a glance below only to see Caskers emerge from the shadows, his face sputtering with fury as he commands my obedience. "You *will* attend me, Moon Child."

I should. Every instinct I have tells me I should turn myself over to them, but something inside me snaps. I spit at him and swing wildly at my captor with my hammer. My first attempt merely blemishes the side of the wall, but my second…

A wet gurgle and a groan come from the Inquestor as the hold on my ankle slackens. I scramble away, the hammer slipping from my grasp. Above me, Sparrow holds out her hand. I grab it, and she hauls me to the first bit of landing.

"Had to drop my fucking hammer," I grunt.

Sparrow's dark eyes are wide pools of fear. "We've got bigger issues, Mags. Come on." She dashes away, her feet slapping on the rooftop. I swear as I stare down at the scene below.

The unfortunate Inquestor I just hit sprawls on the cobblestones, a red stain pooling around her head. Her legs twitch like a pipe beetle after it's been lanced on a stick, but she's got her hands clamped over an eye. Her lips are pulled back in agony, and I realize I've impaled her.

Click.

Now the pistols are drawn, aimed in my direction. My gaze meets that of Caskers, and somehow my hand rises to salute him. His brows knit in single-minded concentration, the report of the gun snapping off the walls of the alley, cement shattering right above where I'm standing.

My ears ring as I flee. From behind me comes the rattle of the drainpipe, but I keep going. I skip over the tops of the buildings, my knees bent for balance. My lightstick is long gone, and it's safer to take my chances in the fog without it anyway. I pause to get my bearings, and Sparrow's form materializes beside me.

"We should split up. Less chance of them tracking us," she says. Another bullet whizzes by, and I duck beneath the buzz of it, fire blooming over the right side of my scalp. It only grazed me, but there's a dark dampness on my fingers when I gingerly test the spot.

"Go!" I give her a shove as the dull rumble of an air patrol roars to life above us, the engine fans thrumming like a half-mad metronome. Not a mere scout ship this time but an actual Interceptor. Sparrow lets out a squeak and tears across the rooftops. I take off in the opposite direction, away from the Warrens.

I skid down a rough embankment made of half a toppled chimney, and I head for the old industrial quarter. My ears are pricked for the sounds of an alarm until the textile mill looms out of the mist, its familiar broken windows peering at me jaggedly.

Inside, there are squatters, but it doesn't surprise me in the least. Most of the BrightStone citizens living in the Warrens are outcasts adrift in their own private hells. Some unfortunate animal roasts on a spit, and the scent of greasy meat roils my stomach.

My hair is already becoming matted with blood, and I lean against the arc of a broken pipe, ignoring the dull throb of pain. If the flap of skin on my head is any clue, I'm going to need stitches.

Out of habit, I run my fingers over my breastbone to the copper panel resting between the curves of my nearly nonexistent breasts. I let out a sigh of relief. My heart continues beating the way it always has, a comforting *tick-thump, tick-thump* vibrating softly below my touch. But I'm not totally in the clear yet. Most patrols give up after a few minutes, but the last look Caskers gave me had been intensely personal, my eventual demise reflected in the depth of his beady rat eyes.

"You're a marked woman, Mags," I whisper to myself. Rory might very well Tithe me for this...and that hardly bears thinking about.

My thoughts churn, but I have to trust Sparrow has found her way home by now, or at least a good place to hide. My only consolation is that she wasn't involved. Even if the Inquestors catch her, they have no reason to think she has anything to do with the dead Meridian.

A cockroach scuttles over my face. I flick it off and crush it beneath my thumb. Hunching forward, I tuck my scarf in around my neck to soften the sudden chill creeping through my patched overcoat. My scalp burns as blood drips down my cheek. I need a bonewitch to stitch it before I do anything else. My ears strain in the darkness, but there's no sound of a patrol, no gunshots in the distance.

All clear for now. With a sigh, I uncoil from my perch to creep along a narrow ledge and then downward, my fingers digging into the ancient brickwork for purchase.

"Piss on me, piss on you. Piss on all the Meridians, too." I singsong the familiar children's rhyme, letting the words drift into the fog as I head for Surgeon's Row, my bloodstained hands shoved deep in my pockets.

Time's heartbeat flickers faint
To the cadence of the walking dead.
Consuming all and producing naught
Crushing my bones to make their bread.

— CHAPTER TWO —

H old still, Mags," the bonewitch orders.

I wince as the needle slides under my hairline and stare out of the tumbledown shack that serves as the bonewitch's surgery. The stool I'm perched on is spotted with rust, but the needles are clean and that's all that really matters.

Outside, the evening crowd shuffles past, but no one pays us any mind. Here on Surgeon's Row, it's better to not look at anyone too closely anyway. It's located in the heart of the trade district, and its patrons wind around a haphazard display of vendors and a tent slum made of beggars and thieves who can't quite bring themselves to live in the Warrens.

The bonewitch tsks at me. She's a stout teakettle of a woman, with fat fingers that have no right to be as nimble as they are. I've often wanted to ask how she ended up here, since she clearly knows what she's doing, but there's no point. Most of the bonewitches on Surgeon's Row were doctors once—the real kind employed by the Salt Temple or private hospitals—but the Rot struck hard and fast when it first appeared twenty years ago and left its mark on victims and survivors alike.

None of us knows where the plague came from, but we all know how it ends, contained in a prison of necrotizing tissue and putrefying organs and a brain that slowly loses its own sense until all that's left is an empty shell. The Salt Temple priests like to preach about sin and punishment and the righteousness of a disease sent to cull the unworthy, but I've never really understood it.

Undoubtedly, the bonewitch lost a family member to the plague, and once she was touched, no respectable patient would dare visit her for fear of being "tainted." Moon Children are the least respectable patients of all—and more importantly, we're immune to the Rot. Not that such a thing seems to mean much in the eyes of the BrightStone citizens. They still call us *sin-eaters*. Sacred scapegoats, I suppose, whose legacy is nothing more than to be viewed with superstition and fear. The salt priests claim we are a necessary inconvenience, absorbing the sins of the city and keeping the Rot from taking more than it does, but it's always sounded like bullshit to me.

Scared people are just easier to control, is all.

The bonewitch gives me a sour look as she ties off the catgut. "How many is this now? Four? Five?"

"What can I say? I like living dangerously." I wink at her with a cheekiness I don't quite feel.

"Foolishly, you mean," she retorts, irritation flickering in her narrowed eyes.

"Same thing." I squirm when she rinses the area with warm water. "Nearly done yet?"

She grunts something noncommittal and pulls out a little tray of inks. "As soon as I leave my mark."

"Can't we skip it?" My stomach rumbles with impatience.

"Rules are rules, Mags. If you don't like getting tattoos, don't get injured so much. Might be simpler for you in the long run."

She squints in concentration as she lightly tattoos her mark beside the stitches. It's a simple thing, a curved line with a dot below it. In a few weeks, no one will see it beneath my hair anyway. But the bonewitch is right. I've got three other marks of hers, one on my thigh and two on a calf. The former is courtesy of a slippery pipe, the latter due to a rather brief knife fight. Not that there isn't a one of us similarly marked. The Inquestors insist all surgical doctoring be accompanied by a mark—the better to track who's doing what to whom, even here in Surgeon's Row. Not that everyone obeys, but every once in a while a bonewitch is reinstated to doctor status and I suspect that has a lot to do with the levels of compliance. If nothing else, the marks are a remembered history of my life.

No markings accompany the heart-shaped panel on my chest, though, leaving its creation shrouded in mystery. But bonewitches come and go here, and I have no memory of when I got it, only that it protects the clockwork heart that keeps my blood flowing.

"There now. Finished. That will be two shillings."

"I've only got one." I pull my cap down over the sore spot. It stings, but the bleeding's stopped.

The bonewitch snaps her fingers and holds out her hand. "Two shillings, Mags."

I pull one from the purse tucked deep in my coat pocket. "You know I'm good for it." I press the coin into her palm. "I'll pay you the rest tomorrow."

She chews on her lower lip, rolling the disc between her fingers, and then nods. "Aye. And maybe if you find anything worthwhile in the slag heaps, you might consider bringing it to me?" She gestures to her meager tray of tools with a weary shrug. Medical supplies are hard to come by, but sometimes I find a battered syringe or a scalpel mixed up with the rest of it.

"Well and good. See you tomorrow, Doc." I bow at her mockingly as she shoos me out the door.

Surgeon's Row is packed this evening, but I catch the rhythm of it easily enough, slipping into the crowds without notice. It always seems to come and go in waves. Tension tends to build up in the worst parts of BrightStone, held in quiet check by the city guard and the Inquestors, but even they can't stop pockets of violence from breaking out. Too many hungry bellies to feed, and with winter coming, it only leads to greater despair. But it gives the bonewitches work, so at least some good comes of it.

My newly mended wound aches beneath the tightness of the stitches, and I fight the urge to rub it. Most people are too busy with their own issues to mind me much. Whimpers of pain emerge from one leaning shack, and the sound turns to a shriek that's abruptly cut off.

A shudder ripples through me. The only anesthetic here comes out of a bottle, and it's rare to find patients who can afford that much.

A fruit vendor huddles on the corner, hawking fresh apples from a wheeled cart, but they look pretty damned wizened to me, their skin wrinkly and brown.

I eye the apples. Leftovers from Lord Balthazaar's estates, most likely. The Inquestors might provide us with some of their stores from time to time, but most of our food is sold to us by Balthazaar, the richest man in BrightStone.

I purposefully stumble on the cobblestones, catching myself on the corner of the cart. The vendor swears at me, but I only nod and apologize, pocketing two apples as I stand up. The old man continues to berate my clumsiness until I round the corner, and then it doesn't matter anymore.

The apples are wormy things, but they take the edge off what's been a long evening and I scarf them down as fast I can. I wipe the sour juice from my mouth with sticky fingers and head for Blessing Bridge.

I'm sure it was named long ago; for all that the salt priests have a temple nearby, the only thing that's a blessing about the bridge now is that you can use it to leave the Warrens. Sparrow and I tend to use it as a meeting place. If she's managed to get away from the Inquestors, I'll find her here.

Before long I'm standing at the center of the bridge, watching the sluggish waters of the Everdark River drift below me. An oil sheen so thick I could probably walk on it ripples over the surface. Rumor has it the water is clean at its source in the Frostfell Mountains, but as it tumbles down the mountainside to cut a swath through BrightStone, it swallows everything in its path, growing swollen and black and full of corpses, only to finally vomit its guts into the sea at the mouth of Bloody Bay. It's also caught fire at least once a year since I was ten.

I lean over the rusting rail and spit, my heart sinking when I see no sign of Sparrow. Though I do catch a glimpse of another Moon Child scratching something into the rocks at the base of the bridge.

Penny.

I whistle a hello to her and she glances up, pausing in her artistic endeavors to wave me over. There's a set of rusty pipes embedded in the column beside her and twisted into a primitive ladder, so it's easy to clamber down. I grimace as the stink of the water hits me. It could knock a man over from ten paces; being this close to it is nearly unbearable.

A rat floats by, gnawing at something fleshy, and I shove it away with a pole that was lying on the shore.

"Oy. Just who I was looking for," Penny mutters, pocketing her screwdriver as she finishes up. Penny's short for a Moon Child, with fat calves and a thick waist, her pale hair braided to hang over one shoulder. With her ability to read and write making her an invaluable resource to our clan's survival, Penny is Rory's second-in-command. She's a few years older than me, and though we tend to butt heads, even I have to admit she's never been anything but fair in her dealings within the clan.

"Aye." I choose to ignore the ominous implications of her words and peer over her shoulder at the carving, only recognizing the word *Meridian*. "What's it say?" I ask.

A snort escapes her. "'Spriggans are Meridian suck-tits.'"

"A work of living poetry, to be sure." I pause. "Don't suppose you've seen Sparrow flitting about?"

Penny yawns, absently rubbing her crippled left hand over her brow. Somewhere along the way, two fingers were sliced off when she was caught in Spriggan territory, but she's never seen fit to share the details.

"I should have known she'd be in the thick of it with you," Penny says on a sigh. "But aye, she made it home a short while ago. You might want to get back to Rory about that. And sooner rather than later seeing as he won't let her leave until you return."

"There's nothing quite like blackmail to keep one's clan in check," I snarl. Inwardly, relief washes over me. At least Sparrow is safe.

"If it works," Penny agrees, her mouth compressing into a thin line. "The Inquestors paid us a visit. Seems they're demanding restitution for the loss of one of their number."

A jolt races through me. "Did she die?"

Penny spits. "Near enough. They wanted Rory to turn you over to them, but he's put them off for the moment. I suspect if we pay them enough, they'll forget all about it."

It's on the tip of my tongue to ask about the dead Meridian, but something makes me pause. Penny hasn't brought it up, so perhaps the Inquestors have not chosen to share that information, either. Better, perhaps, to leave it alone until I know just how much trouble I'm in.

"I don't suppose they were good enough to bring back my hammer?" A humorless smile rolls over my lips. "Last I saw, it was stuck in the Inquestor's eye socket."

"That was poorly done, Mags," Penny snaps, losing patience with me. "Thanks to you, we'll be under heavy scrutiny for weeks." Her eyes fill with bitter humor. "I wish I could have seen it, though." I sigh, and she gives my arm a squeeze. "Go on and take your lumps. The sooner you do, the sooner Rory will move past it."

"Hopefully right over a cliff," I mutter darkly, resting one hand on the pipe ladder.

Her lips quirk up in a ragged grin. "An improvement either way."

Blood fills my mouth as Rory backhands me across the room. "Do you have any idea what you've started?"

I stagger to my knees, the taste of copper on my tongue. "I didn't mean to hurt anyone. They were trying to take my scrap."

Not entirely true, but admitting anything else would only lead to a bigger beating, and I'm not going to volunteer for that.

Rory paces, prowling in tighter and tighter circles until he has pushed himself nearly against me. He's tall and robust, with knuckles as gentle as packed ball bearings. He's older and better fed than the rest of us, and it shows in the muscles rippling beneath his ill-fitting shirt. His coat snaps out behind him as he moves, and his pale hair is tucked neatly beneath his cap in a queue.

The only thing in his eyes is rage.

The center hall of the Lady Slipper Hotel that makes up the Banshees' home base is octagonal—a wide open courtyard, flanked on all sides by the crumbling ruins of pillars and stone hallways. Crowded around the upper levels, other Moon Children stare at us, their faces hollow, tinged with fear. A thread of guilt weaves its way through me. The tiniest hint of rebellion on my part and my clan is reduced to being punished for it.

Sparrow crouches at the far corner, her mouth pinched tight. My lips sting, and I glare at Rory. "What would you have me do?"

He snatches my jaw, still aching from where he hit it. "You crippled one of his soldiers, Mags. Blinded her eye. By rights, I should take one of yours." He stares at me, his gaze half-lidded and cruel. "After all, you don't need two to survive in the Pits. I've half a mind to Tithe you right now."

Hatred grips my gut, cutting at my innards with cat's claws. It's not an idle threat. The Pits lie past the Warrens, the remains of a salt mine that gleam like a forgotten portal to the Hells. And we've all seen the Tithes, the plague bearers shrouded in white as they trudge through the streets led by pale-haired Moon Children and flanked by Inquestors and gray-cloaked salt priests spouting their empty platitudes.

At least one Moon Child is chosen by clan leaders to be taken for each Tithe, to escort the infected into the Pits to watch them live out their final days and care for the dying.

And the Moon Child never comes back out.

"You wouldn't dare." I dance away from him as he steps toward me. "I'm one of the best scrappers you've got..."

"And that is the *only* reason I haven't Tithed you yet, Mags. But it won't save you forever."

My nostrils flare wide. He hasn't mentioned anything about the Meridian body; either the Inquestors haven't told him or he doesn't want it blabbed to the rest of the clan. I dig through my coat pocket and flip him the Meridian credit chit, desperate to find him something else to focus on. "I found this."

He snatches it out of the air without taking his eyes off me, and I notice a bruise blooming on his temple beneath the fall of his hair. He scowls at me when he sees where I'm looking, but holds the chit up to the flickering light of the lanterns.

I shift my hips, my legs preparing to run if makes another move on me.

His mouth curls into a sneer as he tosses the chit back to me. "You are going to off-load that at Molly Bell's tonight. Tell her to credit it to my account. Every penny," he warns. "We'll pay the Inquestors restitution via their own money, and none will be the wiser."

"Aye." I pocket the chit again when he dismisses me.

Sparrow gives me a pained smile as she rises from her corner and we fall into step. The others disperse into the shadows to find some other distraction for the evening. It will be subdued, though. I've stirred up enough trouble to last the rest of the week.

Run-down staircases lead up to the second and third floors, and we take the closest one, pushing past several younger Moon Children, their eyes saucer wide. As best we can tell, the Lady Slipper was once a well-appointed hotel but was abandoned in the bowels of BrightStone's Lower Tier when the plague hit. At least the hotel has rooms for all of us, even if running water and heat are nonexistent. Superstition—or fear—keeps people away these days. I guess being immune to the Rot has its advantages.

Sparrow and I share a space at the top of the third landing with a broken window and a couple of rag-filled mattresses. None of the doors have locks. None of us have anything worth stealing, anyway, and anything of value goes to Rory, one way or the other.

Sparrow shakes her head as I sink onto the mattress. "Be glad you weren't here earlier," she says, tossing her sack onto the floor. "The Inquestors... They hit him, Mags. They came in and forced him to his knees. Threatened to shoot him on the spot if he didn't make it right." She bites down on her lower lip, as though to keep it from trembling.

The vision unfolds in my mind, and I can't keep the smirk off my face. "I'd pay a bit of jingle to have seen that."

She shakes her head at me. "No, you wouldn't. I know the two of you hate each other, but he's the only protection we've got. If something happens to him..."

I sigh. Sometimes I forget how young she is. "I'm not sure it would be that bad, frankly. With him out of the way, Penny could take over. At least she wouldn't beat us as much."

"Don't you get it?" She whirls on me, shoving me against the wall. "He was going to Tithe you! He told the Inquestors as much! The only reason he didn't was that stupid chit."

"I'm sorry," I murmur, squeezing her shoulder and trying to ignore the chill rippling over my spine at her words. My panic won't help her. "I didn't mean to make light."

She wipes at her face and turns away. "I know. I didn't know where you were, and then the Inquestors showed up...and I'm not sure I can see a way out of this. Why couldn't you have just left the body alone?"

"What's done is done," I remind her.

"So what are you going to do?" She paces to the broken window to stare down at the alley below. The remains of a fire escape cling to the crumbling brickwork, a thick vine of weeds roping around the iron like the skin of some dead reptile.

I rub the stitches on my head. "I'll take the credit chit to Molly Bell's, but I want to look for my bag before we go. I threw it on one of the rooftops, and assuming we can find it, we'll off-load it as quick as we can." I look at her sharply and lower my voice. "Did the Inquestors mention anything about the dragon?"

"No. And they didn't mention that you found a Meridian, either. Just that you injured one of them."

"Probably for the best."

What I'll do with the money from selling the dragon, I don't know. Such an amount might be enough to bribe a way out of the city entirely, but it would have to be planned so very carefully. I've never really thought about it before. I've never had the jingle to even consider it.

But now...

Sparrow says nothing when I stand beside her to look out at the city. The lights of BrightStone's Upper Tier sparkle like a bauble, waiting to be plucked.

I tap Sparrow on the shoulder. "Let's go."

The place where I found the Meridian is still crawling with Inquestors when we near it, airship patrols buzzing to and fro with a disgusting regularity.

"Tch," I grumble. I can't risk being caught again, and both Sparrow and I know it.

She tilts her head toward the foundry as if in question. I nod, and we race across the crumbling rooftops until we reach it. We sit down without words and stare up at the night sky. Not that there's much to see—the perpetual fog surrounding BrightStone never really leaves, even as high up as we are. Every once in a while, a shaft of silver slices through to light up the rusting drainpipes, blurring everything into a crystalline softness.

"Well, that was a waste of time, aye?" Frustration heats my face, the window for this potential opportunity at freedom slipping through my fingers.

"Maybe tomorrow, then." Sparrow pulls out a cigarillo from her coat and lights it with a snap of a lucifer match, puffing it slowly. She offers me a drag, but I wave her off.

"Maybe." I shift in my wool coat, stretching out to cross my arms behind my head. The damp of the roof seeps into my skin. I ignore it, the same way I ignore the constant rumble in my belly and the lump of concrete digging into my calf.

Meridion's shadow drifts above us, a floating monstrosity of luminous glass, and the pale sphere of the moon crests the spire of its highest cathedral to taunt us in seductive mockery. On the clearest nights the bottom seems to glow silver, like a polished shilling. I've never been able to make out any real details as to what makes it hover, though a series of massive black chains anchors it far offshore beyond the docks. Perhaps to keep it from floating away like a balloon.

"Do you think you can see the ocean from atop it?" Sparrow asks the question without her usual cheer, a wistful longing in her voice as we stare up at Meridion. She obsesses about the sea. Always has.

But not me. My heart lies above us, wrapped in the promise of Meridion. *Freedom.* The chance to fly away from here, or even just be lifted so far above that I can't see the ugliness on the ground.

Not that the great floating city pays its fallen Moon Children any mind. The old tales say the Meridians come from some far-off land, fleeing the decay of their own civilization. It's a pretty story, painting them in a romantic light, but isn't that always the way with history?

For all the insistence that each Moon Child is the unwanted progeny of a Meridian father and a BrightStone mother, I'm not sure how it's really possible unless Meridians are sneaking down to seduce BrightStone women in their sleep. My own mother died when I was young, so I'd never gotten the chance to ask her where I'd come from. Like nearly every other Moon Child I've known, somewhere around the age of twelve I woke up with silvery-white hair and an immunity to the plague, only to be rounded up and sold to a clan.

I glance at Sparrow, her hair glimmering as white as my own. It's pulled into a loose bun, ringlets bordering her narrow face. She's a tiny thing, her bony frame lost in an oversized coat and trousers two sizes too big. Her body never seems to stop moving. But tonight, her dark eyes are glassy and blank, lost in thought.

"Probably," I say finally, taking pity on her. "Perhaps if the mist is gone. It'd be something, though, wouldn't it? To be up there so high with the whole world stretched out before you..." A soft exhalation escapes me. "I'd give anything to see it, just once."

She sighs. "My mam used to tell me stories of the ocean before she died. Like a great mirror as far as you can see, sparkling green and blue. Nothing like the nasty waters of Bloody Bay, aye? But the sea… Mam said you could sail away on it to a better place. Like magic."

"Anyplace is better than here," a gravelly voice rumbles at us. It startles me into sitting upright as Ghost emerges from behind the shadows of a rotting chimney, his naked feet as silent as his namesake. He's a lanky fellow, a few years older than me, with high cheekbones and dusky skin a few shades darker than mine. His graceful limbs slip past us, shrouded in patched trousers and a loose coat, and the shaggy cut of the pale hair beneath his wool cap declares him a Moon Child, same as us. Silver hoops glitter from his ears.

Sparrow and I exchange a look. Ghost doesn't deign to speak with us often, and for good reason. He's clanless, one of the few Moon Children without the protection of a gang. Rumor has it he keeps house within Molly Bell's establishment, perhaps under her employ, but it's nothing I've ever been able to confirm. None of my business anyway.

He crouches beside me, his toes blackened with soot. I watch them curl into the grooves of the roof, calluses thick and hard. "And Meridion isn't made of magic. Just men who think they are." A snort escapes him. "There is a difference."

"Like you'd have any idea," I scoff, waving my fingers in a little flourish. "Everyone knows they glitter like starlight and dance with an angel's grace upon currents of wind. Science or magic, it's all the same."

He shrugs. "The Warrens are full of patrols this evening… looking for somewhat." He says it casually, like he already knows why. Sparrow stiffens beside me, and I nudge her. His eyes narrow, but his mouth kicks up in a cynical smile. "Keep your secrets, then."

"There's nothing to keep." I turn to face him. My arms hang over my knees, fingers playing with the laces of my thin-soled boots. "And if I was involved, it doesn't really concern you, now does it?"

"As you say." He rises and strolls to the edge of the roof, a hand lightly trailing behind him for balance. He pauses, tipping his chin toward me and shrugging off his coat. "You might want to keep better track of your things, though."

I freeze as he slides the strap of my bag off his shoulder and tosses it at my feet. It clinks with a heavy thud, but no movement comes from under the cloth. My heart sinks, but I don't let it show on my face.

"Thanks," I mumble. No sense in being ungrateful.

On the other hand, what if he had looked inside?

I glance over at him, but he's already sliding his coat back on, absently peering into the fog. The silence stretches out for a span of minutes, and then a weak hissing emerges from the bag. Almost as one, our heads swivel toward the sound.

A sardonic gleam lights up Ghost's eyes. "You'll forgive me if I wish to see what that's all about, aye?"

Shit. Our gazes meet, my fingers clutching the drawstring tightly as I measure my options. Take the bag and run, or fight him for it. Neither feels particularly appealing, especially since he's given it back to me. "Fine. But it's mine," I say hotly. "I found it."

"Did you?" He crosses his arms. "I'd say you lost it."

I stare at him a moment longer, and he finally acquiesces with a little nod.

I tug at the drawstring, easily undoing the knot. The burlap falls open as a golden rush of metal erupts from between my hands. The dragon retreats a few steps before whirling to face us. One wing droops, slightly bent.

Ghost lets out a slow whistle, and there's something half-admiring about it when he crouches to get a better look. The dragon's mouth opens to reveal a glittering set of pointed teeth.

"Don't touch it," I snap, my arm raised to shove him.

"Wouldn't dream of it," he says disdainfully, rolling his eyes. "Where did you find it?"

"The slag heaps." My upper lip curls. "I didn't steal it, if that's what you're asking."

"It's not, but that little piece of wonder right there? It's Meridian made, no doubt. If you're caught with it…" He glances up at the floating city, as though to ward off some secret attack.

Sparrow steps forward for a closer look at the dragon. *"'Ware IronHeart's breath and IronHeart's claws, for when IronHeart roars, Meridion falls.'"* She intones the familiar nursery rhyme, almost seemingly out of habit, and then her eyes widen, sparkling. "Do you think it could be? IronHeart, I mean?"

Even Ghost snorts at this. "Doubtful. It might be a dragon, but it doesn't exactly look large enough to bring down a city."

"Size isn't everything," Sparrow says sourly.

On the surface, I suppose she's right, though the whole idea is ridiculous. Nursery rhymes aside, I don't know anyone who truly believes a massive metal dragon named IronHeart lives in the belly of the floating city. Only the Meridians would know for sure, and they've never said anything about it. Then again, having a generation of citizens raised on songs that wish for your demise probably isn't anything to be proud of.

"There was another one," I say suddenly. "A broken one. Beside the dead…man I stumbled over this evening. I threw some of the pieces at an Inquestor."

A slow sigh escapes Ghost, and he stills. "Don't suppose you'd let me have it? Not to keep," he hurries on. "But I know someone who might be able to help."

"Not unless you've got a buyer in mind," I tell him bluntly. "All I want right now is to sell it, preferably without any way of tracing it back to me."

"And then what?" he asks.

"What do you care?" His questions suddenly feel far too intimate for my liking. I scowl at my hands, rubbing the rough skin of my palms. Blisters upon blisters beaten into a thickness from years of dancing upon the rooftops. "That's my business." I glance at Sparrow. "*Our* business, aye?"

"All right, then," he says stiffly. He crouches and sighs again. "If you're serious about selling it, meet me atop the Conundrum in about an hour. I may know someone willing to meet those requirements."

"If you mean Molly Bell—"

"I don't." Before I can ask him anything more, he leaps and the wiry muscles of his legs hurtle him into the darkness. I hear the slap of his feet against the far wall, the drainpipe swaying with his weight as he disappears.

"Show-off," Sparrow mutters.

I snort. "Aren't we all?"

A tiny laugh bubbles from her and scatters her previous melancholy. "So what do we do?"

The dragon is currently attempting to scale the chimney, cement crumbling beneath its golden claws. I stoop to give it a boost up, wincing when it jumps onto my shoulder instead. An odd little chirrup escapes it.

Sparrow grins. "Well it certainly seems to like you, anyway. What are you going to do with it? We can't stroll the streets with it on your shoulder."

"Tempting, but no. We'll have to put it back in the bag."

She eyes the dragon dubiously but retrieves the bag from our feet. It snarls at her, loud in my ear.

"Sorry—" I tug it off my shoulder "—but we can't let you be seen."

It lets out another grumble, but I'm already pushing it into the sack. Pain lances through my thumb, and I jerk my hand away, ignoring the drop of crimson beading on my skin.

"Ungrateful thing," I snap at it, knotting the drawstring shut. "Be still," I warn it. If it decides to shred itself a hole while we are at Molly's... Shit.

A sulky creaking rumbles from the sack, but it goes silent a few seconds later.

Sparrow's mouth curves into a smirk. "Next you'll give it a name and let it fetch your wee slippers for you in the morning."

I stick out my tongue and slide the sack over my shoulders as we scramble to stand, the younger girl only a few inches shorter than me.

"You think Ghost will come through?" she asks. She scuffs the roof, and I can tell she doesn't want to get her hopes up.

"No idea, but we should hear him out. We've got some time to kill, though. We'll trade the chit to Molly Bell before we meet with him, but let's snag a bit of shepherd's pie first. I never haggle particularly well on an empty stomach." I purse my lips at her. "And I've three coppers in my pocket that says I'll beat you to the Cheaps."

"Deal." Before I even officially start the race, she spins and launches herself off the roof, her hands snagging a jutting bit of pipe. With a twist, she vaults to the other side of the alley; her fingers scrabble the brickwork for purchase as she lands.

"Cheater," I call after her. She fades into the fog, and a moment later, I follow. The air drags at my coat as it rushes past, but I don't mind. Sparrow and I both know I'll win if I set my mind to it. At least this way it doesn't feel like charity when I give her the money.

Not that I won't make her work for it.

I speed up. My vision narrows so that all I can see is the heady mosaic of walls and roofs, brittle stairs and ancient lampposts. My hands are numb to the scrapes, the pull on my flesh as I grasp and release, the momentum of my body swinging me forward. I smile as I land next to Sparrow and we take off again.

The copper shingles blur beneath our feet like the glittering waves of a metallic sea. For a moment, we fly.

Tick tock, tock tick
The three blind mice are bound
In wax and blood and an empty tub
Trapped in darkness where I drown.

— CHAPTER THREE —

The Cheaps aren't much more than a series of tumbledown fishing shacks perched around the docks, but they are a good place for gossip and a constant source of drunken revelry. As a former port city, BrightStone had once been a major trading hub on the Merrow Coast, but with the rumors of the plague, the ships have long since stopped sailing into port. That and the embargo set by the Inquestors. Nothing comes in or out of BrightStone without their say-so.

The fisherfolk here are allowed to ply their nets and lines a short ways out, but Inquestor airships keep a close watch on the tide. It's a risky venture for the run-down boats, even so. These days the damn things might just as easily capsize as float, and dying in a rusted oil bucket ranks fairly low on the ways to go.

My measly pennies buy us each a fish pie and a pint of piss-flavored ale that does nothing more than wet my throat. Not the lamb I'd been hoping for, but it fills the belly and that's good enough. The two of us find a couple of empty casks to perch on, wiping our greasy fingers on our coats after we shovel the food into our mouths.

I sip my ale slowly, but there's nothing to savor about it. At least if you look busy, people tend to leave you alone. The flames in the streetlamps dance in the breeze, illuminating the docks in a hazy reddish hue that gives Bloody Bay its name—though the only blood that's spilled is from sailors scuffling and the occasional gutting of some hapless drunk who's been too careless with his coin.

In the better parts of BrightStone, the streetlights are steam powered—real electric. But here no one can be bothered to maintain the mechanisms. And that's assuming they wouldn't be disassembled and melted into scrap within hours.

The salt stink of the bay hitches a ride on the evening air, but it does little to eliminate the scent of the unwashed masses parading before us. Desperate people, clinging to a few moments of forgetfulness in the bottom of a bottle of ale.

I pick a bone out of my fish pie and watch as a rat runs off with it. Mad Brianna saunters her swayback hips down the quays, snatching at hands and demanding coin for the promise of a future that doesn't end in a gutter. As fortune-tellers go, I suppose she means well enough, but Sparrow and I roll our eyes anyway. There's always at least one person who takes her up on it, but I've yet to see her twisted words become anything more than a passing fancy. I avoid fortune-tellers myself. I already know how my life is going to end.

A steam-powered automaton clinks its way past us, its metal fingers tightly clutching a small, wax paper–wrapped package. It's a base model, created with a rudimentary structure to appear humanoid, a walking skeleton made of copper and brass. Its cogs whir in a clear ball of a glass brain. Sometimes the BrightStone gentry in the Upper Tier will use them for deliveries, but tech of this caliber is difficult to come by, even for those who can afford it. Either way, it's rare to see one sent to this part of town.

This one stands tall, and its electric orbs swivel suspiciously over the crowd. It pauses, its metal brows furrowing as Mad Brianna wobbles her way in front of it, cane thrust out for balance. "Tell your fortune, Metal Man?"

A steam-powered sniff whistles from its jaw. "Surely not… madam."

"So polite," she cackles, but her mouth curves into a sly smile, one of her street urchins materializing from beneath her cloak to snatch the package from the robot's grip. The boy yips in triumph and ducks into the writhing mass of people before the robot has time to react.

It lets out a startled creak and cranes its head. "Thief!" It lurches into the crowd amid mocking laughter.

Mad Brianna might be blind and insane, but she also runs a well-disciplined thieves' guild. The package will be handed off to a plant about ten seconds after the theft, and whatever is in that box will be long gone before the owner ever finds it. The real rub is when the automaton finds itself in a dark warehouse somewhere, only to be brutally dismantled.

I should know. I was raised by her.

Sparrow and I both were. We were orphans by chance, until whatever made us Moon Children awakened in our blood. Sparrow lost her mother when she was five, crushed beneath the wheels of a horseless carriage in an accident, and I don't remember my mother at all.

As the drama unfolds before me, I study the myriad children dashing about. Which ones carry the blood of Meridion? At younger ages, it's hard to tell. Half-breeds generally look like their BrightStone mothers, until about the age of twelve or so, and then…

I'm a skinny thing, all elbows and scabbed knees. A pair of greasy pigtails, torn trousers, and shoes stuffed with rags so they don't slip off my feet.

I notice small changes at first: A few strands of hair here or there. A slight alteration in the tint of my eyes. A heightened sense of awareness. Shadows once too dark to creep inside become sanctuary, and before long, I am one of the top pickpockets in the guild.

Mad Brianna's mouth pinches when she sees me, but she says nothing. When the whispers start up, I ignore them, but it's coming. Five others have turned in the time since I've lived beneath her roof, so I'm not surprised when I wake up one morning to discover I look like I've bathed in a moonbeam, and even less so when Rory appears a few hours later to claim me.

Or my skills, rather. And a few years later, Sparrow's.

"Oy." Sparrow's voice pulls me from my woolgathering. She drains the last of her ale, wiping her mouth on the sleeve of her faded brown coat, and tugs at her green crystal necklace with a nervous twitch. "Come on, then. Maybe afterward we can stop at the sweetshop? There's usually stale pastries in the bins for a ha'penny."

"If we're successful with our sale, I'll buy us something straight out of the oven, aye?" I slide off the barrel, done with lingering. We slip into the crowd briefly but stick closest to the shadows. Our hair gives us away for what we are, though to most people, we don't warrant a second glance. To see us is to acknowledge us, and that means admitting the realities they'd come here to forget.

If the Inquestors have been looking for me, they haven't seen fit to mention it to the general populace. Uneasiness fills my belly with flies until a hand snatches at my coat.

"Rags. Mags. Come to visit?" Mad Brianna clutches my wrist tightly, her body rocking side to side.

Sparrow sighs as I extricate myself from the madwoman's bony fingers. The touch of her skin is corpse cold, and I shake myself to stave off the prickle.

Brianna clucks at me. "Aw, no love for yer auld granny? I know what you are, lass." She licks her shaking lips, her milky eyes peering at my sack. "I know what you carry. I can hear it with every step you make. Always could, you know."

"Do you now?" I ask with the raise of an eyebrow. The dragon hasn't moved since we arrived at the docks, but no sense in taking chances. Besides, insane as she is, the woman has an uncanny way of seeing through me, blind or not. She's been the closest thing to a mother I've ever known, too, so I tolerate her madness as best I can, though it's clear she's grown much worse over the last few years.

She pats my chest, fingers tapping the clockwork heart panel. Inwardly I breathe a sigh of relief. Nothing about the dragon.

"Secret, secret," she mumbles. "Tick tock, tick tock, blind mice up the clock. Striking time and half past nine..."

"We've got to go, Brianna," I say gently. "We're Moon Children now."

She blinks blearily at me and points up to Meridion. "But I know what you want. You'll do more than get there, lassie..." Her mouth opens in a choking gasp that's supposed to be laughter, but it's the sound of dust inside a coffin and it burrows into me with barbed needles. "They've bred their own fate, Moon Child."

"Enough." I tug on Sparrow's scarf, and we immediately head for the nearest alley, drifting into the fog like ghosts. Brianna's mocking voice escorts us for nearly half a block, squalling mad cat cries of doom.

I hunch my shoulders against it. "They'll kill her for saying such things." There have always been those who proclaimed the collapse of Meridion, but whispering in the back rooms of a tavern is far different from spouting prophecy on the street corner.

Sparrow sighs. "I don't think she cares."

I shake my head against the thought. Nothing I can do about it anyway, and being this close to Market Squares means we need to attract less attention, so it's just as well we leave her behind. Market Square itself is all broad streets and sharp edges, respectable businesses and crisp spats and top hats. There's a faux air of sophistication, but it's all a facade. The cut of the men's suits might be sharper, but the clothes are a lie they tell themselves, as though shiny buttons are an indication of a kind heart.

The cobblestone streets are cleaner than the docks, but the gutters are just as thick with shit. Sparrow and I get the occasional murmur of disapproval from the "gentry," but otherwise we're left to our own devices. There's no law against our presence here yet.

I keep my face pointed toward the ground as much as possible and avoid the more brightly lit storefronts. Bertie's Stupendous Illusions. The Steamworks. Fashionable Fittings. Haberdashers and candlemakers and jewelers. Signs declaring the latest in Meridian technology beckon from the open doorways, but much are refurbished findings of the junkyards, polished up to look new and massively overpriced.

Sparrow lingers beside the sweetshop with a hunger that has very little to do with actual food. I pause beside her, and we both stare at the confections behind the great glass window, all coated with fancy icing and powdered sugar.

The scent is overpowering, and my mouth waters. Sparrow squeezes my hand hard, and I know she's remembering her mother again. I envy her those memories sometimes. Mad Brianna hadn't had time for sweets, and the best I usually managed was found in the trash bins out back. But when Lord Balthazaar's wife, Lady Lydia, was found to be with child, he drove through BrightStone in celebration, tossing pennies and sugared almonds from the windows of his carriage. There'd nearly been a riot in the streets as we fought for a handful of either. Balthazaar hadn't cared, just smiled and waved, heedless of the chaos he left in his wake.

My chest tightens, thinking of the dragon and how much jingle we might get for it. "If we sell...it, I'll buy us one of everything in this whole damn store," I murmur. "Just us."

The fact that such a thing might be possible makes my head swim. Candy is beyond a mere luxury; to buy something so frivolous feels somehow obscene, let alone in the amounts I'm imagining.

"Out of the way, sin-eaters!"

I stumble into Sparrow as a broomstick cracks me in the face. "The hells?"

I blink back a wash of tears, my eyes burning as I squint at the shopkeeper. Flour coats her apron, and her dark hair is pulled back in a severe bun.

"A simple 'move along' would have sufficed, aye?" I say.

"Customers won't come in if your sort is about." She makes a warding-off sign. For all her brave words, this woman is terrified of us.

Another poke, this time in my ribs.

Sparrow gives her a dirty look, helping me to my feet. A quick feel of my scalp tells me the stitches haven't ripped, so there's that at least.

When we don't move fast enough, the broomstick lowers again, but this time I catch it and shove it away. The shopkeeper's face pales, but Sparrow tugs on my sleeve and it's enough to make me back down.

We're drawing a crowd, and the last thing I need is another run-in with an Inquestor. I pull my cap down a little tighter, and the two of us retreat to the far side of the square.

"I'd like to burn that place to the ground," I snarl.

"But then who would make the cookies?" Sparrow gives me a small smile, but she's as hurt as I am. We'd just been looking, after all. "We'll just buy her out, like you said."

I nod, but imagining the place on fire is far more satisfactory. For now we have other business to take care of, though. Keeping a lower profile, we aim for a nondescript door with a rusty cog spinning aimlessly upon it.

The Conundrum.

Part gentlemen's lounge, part tavern, the Conundrum perches on the square like a jewel in a crown made of tin. It's gaudy and loud and winks at everyone who passes by, inviting them to take a gander at the wares inside.

The muffled sound of raucous laughter vibrates from the other side of the door, and merry shadows dance in the dancing lights through the brindled glass windowpanes. There's a scraping sound on the stone steps as the door is thrown open. A man staggers out, his face red with drink, and his hair a mass of greasy decadence streaking over his stained waistcoat. His mouth curves into a sneer when he sees us.

"Sin-eater," he slurs, spittle foaming upon his lips. He makes a halfhearted attempt to squeeze Sparrow's backside before wobbling his way into the street.

"And good eve to you," Sparrow says snidely, kicking the back of his knee so he stumbles. He grunts something and tips his hat before tripping on the sidewalk, his body heaving into the gutter.

I give Sparrow a sharp look, but she shrugs as he rolls onto his side and immediately begins snoring. "He'll be happier there anyway, I suspect."

The sweet scent of tobacco drifts past us, reminding me gently why I'm here. I pat the sack at my hip to reassure myself it's still there. "Come on. Let's see if we can do this quickly."

We cross over the threshold into an intoxicating scene of whispered secrets and furtive glances, a whirlwind of delicate dresses and polite chuckles. There's an odd sense of intimacy in the air that I'd never be welcome to. The sweet smoke lingers in the air, but it only masks the scents of sweat and wine. The lust here is tinged with the same flavor of desperation as on the docks. It's just hidden better.

The parlor is striped with bold patterns of black and white, crisp and stark to show off the beauty that flutters before it. Plush chairs of velvet and brass fittings are placed carefully around the room, strategically placed around a tinkling fountain. Women with flawless skin are clothed in a riot of silks and swirl around us like exotic flowers. They stare at us with luminous curiosity for a moment before moving on to the next object of interest.

A thin ember of envy tugs at my gut that these people should pursue such frivolities when we are starving and living in squalor.

"I'm here to see Molly," I say to the shady man standing guard beside the door, though my words are unnecessary. We're certainly not here to utilize the services of a pleasure house.

He jabs his thumb behind him. "You'll find her at the bar." The words are helpful, but the tone is not; he'd throw us out if he could. He scowls and points out down the alley. "But you go through the side door."

With a sigh, we retreat to the side door leading to the kitchens, and from there we enter into the bar proper. None of the patrons take any notice of us anyway; their focus is elsewhere.

We brush through the crowd of silken beauties with their taut skin on display. A curvaceous automaton winds her way through the tables, passing out drinks with marvelous efficiency, her head tilted in a flirty fashion. She wears a corset and little else, but there's something disturbing about her metallic flesh, even so. There's no indication of awareness in her electric, blue eyes when a curious hand slides over her ass and down her thighs.

On the stage, a naked woman cavorts, her breasts jiggling in rhythm to the beat of a drummer, yellow feathers tied in her hair as she twirls about. Sparrow sucks in her breath as she sees the girl, but it's not the dance or the naked form that concerns her. The dancer's hair is milk white and pale. Not a true Moon Child, but it's enough to convey the intent to the tipsy crowd.

"It's dyed." The envy turns to ashes in my belly, and my jaw tightens in anger.

Sparrow says nothing, but her cheeks burn.

Shame.

I've been around long enough that it shouldn't bother me anymore, but it does. We've been reduced to a passing fetish, but even that is an illusion. I frown as I watch the girl swivel her hips.

"Did you want to try out, m'dear?" Molly's lilting drawl somehow cuts through the din with practiced ease.

"You can't afford me," I retort without thinking. I bite down on my cheek hard enough to draw blood. Insulting the woman gains me nothing. Not when I need her.

"No one would pay to see a broomstick in her smallclothes, you mean." Whatever she sees in my expression sparks an answering smirk. It's hardly reassuring, but reassurance has nothing to do with Molly Bell's business.

Cheers and claps fill my ears as the girl finishes her performance, pulling her lithe form through a series of tiny silver hoops before stooping to collect the coins tossed at her feet. She tosses her white hair so it flutters like a waterfall, her face all smiles and soft blushes. The men eat it up, and another rush of fury vibrates down my spine.

"Something I can help you with, then?" Molly taps her fan upon her palm.

"Rory sent us," I say. "The usual."

"Indeed." Molly crooks a perfectly manicured finger at me. "Come."

Sparrow and I exchange a quick glance before dutifully trailing behind her. The crowd splits like the sea before her, and we have to hurry to keep from being swallowed up as she maneuvers her way through the maze of tables and dancers.

A thick curtain hangs past the bar where a barmaid tiredly hands out flagons of foaming ale. A tall woman, with a jaw too square to be considered anything other than handsome, perches on a stool beside the alcove. Her gimlet gaze rakes us from head to toe, but I stare at her until the corner of her rouged mouth twitches at my boldness. Molly's lady-in-waiting is a formidable creature, austere and prickly, with a high-necked gray gown and a black shawl over her shoulders.

"Martika." I nod politely as she sweeps the curtain aside to let us pass. Molly's bustle sways seductively in festooning pink ruffles, disappearing in the shadows of a long hallway. We emerge into one of the back rooms where she does her more wayward business. It's a narrow space, cluttered with an assortment of books and scrolls. Steam-powered bulbs flicker from the ceiling.

Sparrow and I lean against the wall as the madam shuffles papers on her desk. It's all for show to make us fidgety and off-balance, but it's an old trick and I study my fingers until she's done. My nails are worn down to the quick, dirt crusted beneath them thick enough to grow flowers.

Finally, she takes her seat, one booted heel propped up on the desk. Her striped hose scales her thigh in thick coils, disappearing in a nest of lacy petticoats in a fashion I can't quite comprehend. She stares at us a moment longer, and then her lips split into a toothy smile. The edges of her front teeth have all been filed into fine points, giving her a monstrous appearance. A predator of flesh, perhaps. The shark of the underworld is no less terrifying for the luscious red curls framing her face.

"You don't approve of my dancers." She's still smiling, but there's a hardness to her voice. "There are plenty of folk who take great pleasure in the concept of forcing a Moon Child into carnal submission. Even if it's not the real thing." Her eyes bore into mine. "Forbidden fruit and all that. Sin-eaters are the most forbidden of all, seeing as no one in their right mind would touch one willingly. I simply sell illusions. Makes them feel better, I suppose."

"My approval doesn't matter for shit," I mutter, not wanting a confrontation. "I'm only here to see if you've an interest in something I found."

One brow arches. "Ah, yes. There does seem to be a bit of a dustup involving you and the Inquestors. I'm taking quite the risk meeting with you, you realize."

Sparrow shifts beside me. The flight response runs deep within us, and for good reason. My own gaze warily slides around the room, already half-resigned to seeing the guards break down the door behind us.

"Then why have us here at all?" I cross my arms. "Why not refuse to see us?"

Molly's laughter tinkles merrily at our expressions, and she sits up straight. "Nothing gets by you, does it? Maybe I've my own reasons. Shall we see what you have?" Her teeth clack shut on the last of those words, an echo of finality in those pearly whites.

I pull out the credit chit and toss it on the desk.

She twiddles it between her fingers thoughtfully and holds it up to the light, studying the raised impressions upon the rim. Her mouth purses as she looks at me again. "You can't read, can you? Do you know who this belongs to?"

"No."

"Indeed." She flips the chit up into the air, the light catching the crystal edges so it refracts brightly. "This, my dear, is the credit chit of one Jonathan Jacobs, currently the head architect of Meridion. Or former, I suppose." Her face snaps toward me, her voice cold. "The one found dead tonight, in fact."

I narrow my eyes at her. "I know rumors drop faster than flies on a corpse in this town, but this seems awfully quick, even for you."

"It's my job to know things. The point is, ladies, you're in a lot of trouble right now. Even if I can off-load this, there will be questions." She cocks her head. "And I'm not sure I want that sort of scrutiny."

The side door bursts open, and I push Sparrow behind me, my drive to protect the younger girl almost instinctual. Molly smoothly pops the chit into her corset, as though she's merely attempting to tuck her ample cleavage for better viewing, and her face slides into her familiar business smile.

Martika strides in with a heavy footfall, followed by Inquestor Caskers...and Rory.

"Fuck," I breathe, struggling to stand on my suddenly shaky legs. I know a trap when I see one, and this one has just closed on our necks. My gaze darts wildly about the room, searching for an escape and finding none.

The large woman gives me a sour look. "You have guests, Molly."

Molly straightens up, her mouth quirking. "So I see. Important ones, I'd wager, to not even wait for an appointment."

Rory's eyes are bleeding death at me as the Inquestor bows to Molly. "Well, when it comes to capturing a murderer, one can never be too careful, madam," the lieutenant says, twisting the tip of his mustache, like one of those villains from the penny dreadfuls Sparrow would flip through at the newsstands.

Molly leans back in her seat, snapping her fan out from her sleeve with a thick crack. She pretends not to notice when Sparrow jumps at the sound and flutters it about her neck like a wounded bird.

"Murder?" she drawls. "Oh, come now. Surely you must be mistaken." The fan swirls daintily, drawing attention to her décolletage, which is not inconsiderable. The Inquestor barely glances downward, but his nostrils flare ever so slightly.

"I assure you, good lady, I am not." His voice drops lower, though his words remain pleasant. "I would hate to see a woman of such high caliber be caught up in such a thing."

She cocks a brow and then sighs, her attention falling on Rory. Ghost's warning about the dragon ripples in my mind, echoed in the *tick-thump* of my heart.

If you're caught with it...

Too late, too late.

The lieutenant sneers and jabs his hand at me. "This one assaulted one of my Inquestors when we attempted to question her. It is a matter of delicacy that I cannot openly speak of." I see the glint of his earlier promise lighting up like sparks when our gazes meet. He wants me dead, Tithed or not.

Sparrow pipes up from behind me. "But that's not what happened—"

I stomp on her foot before she can implicate herself any further, but it's already too late as Caskers focuses on her. She hesitates but then thrusts out her chin, stepping forward. "Aye. I was there."

"How convenient to have a witness," he notes and pulls out a small pad of parchment. "And what did you say your name was?"

Sparrow remains silent until Rory raises a hand to slap her. I thrust myself between them, ready to take the blow. Martika watches us all from the doorway with an odd detachment.

For a moment the tension hangs like the scent of gunpowder; the merest movement will set it off. Instead of confronting them, I take a seat in the chair beside the desk and boldly stretch my legs high so my boots rest on the credenza, my mind gibbering madly as I try to organize my thoughts.

A mouse can only bluff in front of the alley cat so long. Wits and claws, Mags. Wits and claws. Watch me, watch me, that the Sparrow might fly free.

Molly raises a brow at me in warning, but I don't move my feet. I pat down my coat to pull out the tobacco I nipped from the architect's body. Rory's eyes nearly bug out of his head at my rudeness, but I busy myself rolling up a hit, scratching my last lucifer on the bottom of my boot. It ignites with a foul odor as I light the tip of the paper.

A moment later, the rich scent of the tobacco fills the room. I take a deep puff and blow out a perfect smoke ring with a sigh. Martika stares at me with hungry appraisal, and I can't quite help returning it with a wink.

"Aye, Sparrow was there, but she did naught to help nor hinder my...adventures." I glance up at the lieutenant and hesitate. Neither he nor Rory had mentioned the architect, but Molly already knew. Whatever game they are playing, I want no part of it. "And why dance around the subject? The only reason you were chasing me was because of the dead Meridian. Who was already dead when I found him, incidentally. This grand bit of stuff—" I wave the cigarillo at him "—is the only thing of value I took from him."

The Inquestor's face darkens as the smoke wafts past him. "Architect Jacobs was stabbed multiple times in the chest. Surely you would have noticed this when you looted his body?"

"Dead is dead. Whether he died from a knife in his gut or not, he clearly fell from a great height." I splay my fingers wide. "Splat."

"And yet you didn't think to report it to me when we ran into you?" he asks.

I can hear the underlying trap beneath the question. Behind me, Sparrow makes a soft sound and I shut my eyes against it before giving the lieutenant a hard stare. "Why answer your questions when you've already decided my guilt?"

His cheeks flush red, raging with the inferno of his anger even as Martika stifles a snort. Molly's eyes dance with stony amusement. She's no happier at this turn of events than I am, but I don't dare mention the credit chit in her corset. She glances at me from over her fan, and I see the warning written there, but there's no time to heed it.

Spittle gums up at the corners of the lieutenant's lips. "You're lying."

"Prove it." I regret the words the moment I say them, but there's no taking them back now.

Suddenly he shoves me out of the chair, my bag tumbling to the ground. The cigarillo flies from my hand, embers smoking upon the blue silk carpet. "Hey!" I move to kick him but Rory is already there, his hands like iron around my wrists as he yanks my arm up behind my back.

Pain twists through my elbow and I squirm, but he leans down to my ear. "Move again and I'll break it so it doesn't heal. Ever."

I freeze.

Molly tsks at the cigarillo smoldering on the carpet, and Martika dutifully stomps it out. "I'll be charging you for that if it leaves a mark," Molly says lightly, her fan fluttering again, this time pointing in my direction.

There's an odd silence where the whole of my breath seems to fill the room with its ragged echo. My bag has begun to move, a sound like a deranged teakettle piercing my ears.

All heads swivel toward it, and Caskers gingerly picks it up, slicing into the burlap with a quick flick of the dagger at his belt. The dragon tumbles onto the carpet with a mechanical snarl, the sound swallowed by a collective gasp. It bares its shiny teeth, the tiny ember in its chest burning bright. The Inquestor reaches for it with a cry of surprise, but it scurries under Molly's chair and launches itself up the chimney, narrowly escaping the lieutenant's white-gloved fingers. A metallic clink chimes when its wings hit the heavy stone, and a storm of pebbles scatter onto the hearth.

Rory gapes, loosening his grip on my arm. "The hells is that?"

I let out a laugh at the dragon's escape, but a stinging slap burns across my face.

Caskers's mustache is quivering now, the wax no longer quite so sturdy. He grasps my chin, the pressure upon my jaw causing me to whimper. "You threw something very interesting at one of my men this evening. Something related to that, perhaps?"

Before I can answer, Molly smacks her fan upon the desk. "I'm running a business here. If you want to bully her some more, then I kindly ask you to take it elsewhere."

"She's a murderer and conspirator," he insists, but she smiles at him with her sharp teeth showing.

"And that may be," she says, "but this is a gentlemen's club, not a constabulary."

He nods, noticeably paler after being confronted with her toothy grin. "As you wish. Apologies for this intrusion, Ms. Bell."

"Quite." Her smile grows broader. "In the future, should you wish to make an inquiry about one of my guests, I insist you go through the proper channels." She winks at him long and slow. "I pride myself on discretion, as well you know."

"Indeed. And I would appreciate as much in this particular matter." His hand strokes lightly over the mantel of the fireplace, his voice dropping low and dark. "I'd hate to see this place shut down for certain...*violations.*"

If she's bothered by the threat, it doesn't show, but she nods in acquiescence, not bothering to hide her amusement.

He smiles tightly, bowing once before whirling on me. "And as for Miss Raggy Maggy? We'll see how accommodations in the Pits suit."

A river of blood
Is all that can flow.
I plant flowers made of tin
While ashes fall like snow.

— CHAPTER FOUR —

N o." The word squeaks out of me as Sparrow lets out a cry
of disbelief.

Caskers's eyes narrow at the sound, and he leans close
to Rory. "If you even think about letting either of them escape, I'll
gladly take you as the next Tithe instead."

Rory snarls something beneath his breath, and Molly snaps her
fingers in irritation.

"If you *please*, gentlemen?" Martika's voice is whip sharp and
deep, and startles the others into action.

The lieutenant strides into the hallway, gesturing for us to
follow. Rory places a hand on my neck and steers me out of the
room, Sparrow trailing behind us. Several additional Inquestors
who appear to have been waiting in the hall flank us and fall into
step behind Sparrow, but they don't take us through the main
room of the bar. A dark passage branches off through the kitchens
and into an alley, and it's here that we reassemble.

Thick, greasy rain has started falling, and everything smells like
piss and shit and the ugly stink of sex gone bad. A baby squalls
from one of the upper windows. It's quickly shushed, and for a
moment there's nothing but the pattering of wet drops beating out
a sullen whimper on the drainpipes.

I eye the drain and the brickwork, and beside me I can sense Sparrow doing the same. Even Rory appears to be carefully sizing up the distance to the rooftops, but I can't imagine him doing it. To have our "leader" so blatantly rebel against the Inquestors?

Rory loves his position too much to do that.

But still, I hope he might anyway. The tide has to turn someday, doesn't it?

Caskers and Rory circle each other, but if Rory had a tail it would be firmly tucked between his legs.

"I can't let you Tithe her," Rory finally says in a halfhearted attempt to defend me. "She's one of my best scrappers. We need her to—"

"I don't give a damn what you need," the lieutenant shouts. "She's seen too much. I've got the High Inquestor riding my ass over the dead Meridian and I've got nothing to show for—" He cuts off his words as though suddenly realizing where he is, and gestures at Sparrow. "She knows too much now, as well."

Sparrow slides into the shadow at my side, a tremble about her lips.

"Right," I say bitterly. "So for finding a body in the street and not reporting it, I end up in the Pits?"

I take Sparrow's hand and retreat a step. If I can get her to the nearest window ledge, I'll boost her up and she might have a chance at escaping.

Rory says nothing, and for a moment I think he's going to help us. He squeezes his eyes shut tightly and then opens them again. "Do what you have to. I wash my hands of both of them."

Sparrow lets out a coughing chuff of despair. "You're supposed to protect us!"

"And I am casting you out." He glares at each of us in turn. "You are no longer members of the Banshees. I am required to do nothing."

Anger flares to life within me as he turns away. "It's fitting that you leave us outside a brothel," I call after him. "You're the biggest whore of us all!"

There's a distinct snigger from behind the kitchen door, and it's clear someone's listening. I've got no time for that, though. Caskers is watching Rory depart and I see my chance. I whirl, my hands already boosting Sparrow up. She scrambles over the bricks, her foot scraping the windowsill before the Inquestors even realize what I've done.

A soft slither above us, nearly silent as a…

Ghost.

A flash of his silver hair shows beneath his cap as his hand reaches down to grab Sparrow's wrist and haul her up. Hysterical laughter bubbles up in me as I catch his knowing smirk, and for a moment I dare to hope we'll escape.

And then the report of gunfire roars in my ears. The whiz of the bullet shrieks past me and I duck, but the blood is already spreading over Sparrow's coat, crimson turning black in the dim, yellowed light of the lanterns.

She lets out a soft cry, small, like her namesake, and it catches in her throat with a confused burble of surprise. She slips from the windowsill, hanging from Ghost's straining fingers. I rush forward as the Inquestors take aim again, and her body sinks like a stone into my arms. I glimpse only the merest outline of Ghost's face when he fades into the shadows. I'm too busy staring at the way the life drains from Sparrow to take note of where he's gone.

"Oh," I mumble, unable to form a coherent thought fast enough to say anything of meaning. My vision vibrates, everything fading away except the girl in my arms, myriad memories scattering like sunlight across the water.

I've seen death before. We all have. And it's fitting that we do. We are the chaperones of the dying, after all. But this is different. Sparrow is the sister of my soul, so much more than a mere clanmate. Without her…I'll be alone.

Her mouth moves, and blood trickles from the corner. I stare at her as though I might capture the shape of her face, the sound of her laughter, and the nattering of her questions, but it's leaving her so quickly.

My breath is thunderous, a husky exhalation that slips between the liminal spaces, a heated mist lingering in the chill of the night air. "Don't..." I whisper. "Oh, please don't."

There's a shift of bodies around me, and one part of my mind shouts at me to get up and run or fight or do anything other than kneel there with Sparrow's life in my hands. It's a bubble ready to burst, and if I move I'll lose her.

An argument breaks out. Someone gets shoved into a wall, and an upset trash bin wobbles past me to spill its festering guts upon the cobblestones. Shouts come from out in the street, which are answered by ominous rumbles.

"Mags," Sparrow whimpers. Her pupils so huge and black I nearly expect to see the moon drowning within.

Pop.

Another bullet slams into her flesh, and just like that, she's gone. My eyes fill with tears I rarely shed, my world spinning off its axis.

I'm jerked away from her before I can really react, and her head bounces off the cobblestones. I flinch when she doesn't move, but her glassy stare seems to pierce right through me.

There's nothing reproachful about it, and that hurts more than I can bear. An ugly keening erupts from my throat, echoing through the alley and flooding my veins, giving voice to my furious rage.

But there's no more time to grieve as the Inquestors haul me to my feet. My arms slide out of my coat sleeves, and I ball my hands into fists before launching myself at the lieutenant. My knuckles scrape the underside of his jaw, but I'm pulled away before the blow lands.

"Aye, but you're a spiteful thing," Caskers sneers, rubbing at the stubble on his chin. He holsters his pistol, unsheathing a wicked dagger from his hip.

"Why?" I choke out. "Why would you do this?"

"Tit for tat," he growls. "You took one of mine. It only seemed fair."

"She had nothing to do with it." My words feel numb, and my throat closes over against a thick sob.

"Sometimes that's the way it is." He rips the cap from my head so that my silver hair hangs down. It's dirty and stringy, but it shimmers in the lantern light. His expression goes oddly gentle. "I've heard they take your eyes. You know, down in the Pits. Lets you use your other senses in those deep, dark caverns so your vision doesn't distract you from the task at hand."

I spit at his feet. "How would *you* know?"

"I don't," he says mildly. "And I never will."

The words dangle there, mocking me in their confidence, that smug assurance that indicates how well he knows his place—and mine. A rolling chuckle escapes him, and the sound ripples into my ears, branding itself upon my memory.

"And neither will you," he adds.

Before I can even comprehend what he means, a fiery sensation scrapes down my rib cage. I struggle, but the burning skitters over my skin before it finds the soft spot and slides in deep.

My mouth drops open, and I try to find the words to curse or to question or to…anything. Just so I don't go silently the way Sparrow did.

"You should thank me," he says. "Look at it this way: I take care of this issue between us so I no longer have to deal with you, and I save you from your fate. We both win, no?"

"The bones of your arrogance will crush you," I cough. "And I'm going to dance them into dust." I spit again, but it's a feeble attempt with the blade still lodged in my side. Copper swirls in my mouth; my blood tastes sour, bile and death all mixed up to dribble down my chin.

He shakes his head, or I think he does. His face is only a blur of dark shapes now. His eyes loom from those shadows, but I can't seem to focus on anything but the curve of his mouth, the way those tight lines stretch and fold to make up his lips and the stained yellow of his teeth.

He twists the knife smoothly, ignoring the wet gasping sounds the pain is pulling from my throat. He drops me, and I move to catch myself, but my arms no longer work. My vision explodes into stars, agony washing over my brow as my face hits the cobblestones. But a broken nose is nothing compared to the fire numbing my side. Everything is wet and warm below me, and I can't tell if it's all blood or if I've pissed myself, but it doesn't matter.

Someone pulls the hair away from the back of my neck and presses their fingers over my clan mark. A mumbled number and a shadow is doing the same to Sparrow.

Taking us off the Tithe rosters, I think absently.

My mind is distant yet there's an odd, calming clarity to it all, as though I'm merely observing myself dying from a distance instead of lying here in the gutter.

Thudding everywhere. My heartbeat? The *tick-thump* of my heart skips and shakes, but everything seems to be fading away into darkness. Footsteps echo beside me, but it's only the Inquestors marching past. Not one looks back. And why should they?

I'm dead.

"Mags?"

I hear my name, followed by whispers in the dark that I can't make sense of. I'm floating, floating, floating, and there's no pain at all.

Someone puts a finger to my temple, and I try to open my eyes. As I do, I squint in the harshness of what might be candlelight.

Pale hair. Moon Child hair. Dusky skin...

"Ghost?" The words slur out of me. I should be happy. Maybe? I can't remember. My eyes close again. "Are you dead like me and Sparrow?"

"No, Mags. I'm…"

His voice whisks into the void, and I follow it, each syllable a twisting butterfly made of light.

Strands of starlight swirl around me as I perch on the highest point of Meridion. Sparrow sits next to me, her legs drumming the walls lazily.

"We made it, Mags, don't you see?"

I strain to focus, but there's nothing but darkness in the distance. My stomach swells because I've eaten the moon.

Moon Child.

"I don't see anything," I say.

"Oh, but the sea! Don't you see the sea? The shining of the sea? I see the sea. I see…"

"—don't you see? This may be our only real ch—" It's a deeper voice this time. I almost recognize the inflection, but the tone is all wrong. It cuts through my muddled dreams, and I stir.

Pain threatens to chase me back into the darkness. I'm cooking in my own flesh, melting into my bones.

"But the risk?" Softer now. Feminine. My mind sluggishly attempts to place the voice.

Molly Bell?

"What better opportunity will we have?" Persistent bugger, whoever he is. Not Ghost. Someone different.

Something weighs on my eyelids. A damp cloth, I think. But removing it seems like too much trouble; moving is no longer my thing.

"If she survives…perhaps." A swish of skirts. "Not much to look at, is she?"

"What difference does that make? We need a Moon Child, and here she is."

"You'd better be right about this." Molly's voice irritates me, itching beneath my skin. I mumble at her, telling her to be quiet, but the only thing that comes from me is little more than a raspy cough.

"She's waking," Molly says. I can't tell if she's disappointed.

"Her fever's breaking." Someone lays a hand upon my brow, and I struggle against it. "Not yet, sweetheart. Not yet."

Wetness drops upon my lips. My parched tongue strains like a salted slug in search of moisture. A ceramic vessel is placed against my mouth, and I sip it. A soft whimper escapes me, it tastes so good. Water, yes, but cleaner than I've ever had, flavored with a hint of something else.

"Slow," the male voice warns. Something splashes nearby, and a new cloth is placed upon my forehead, its coolness sparking a cascade of shivers through my limbs.

"Will she manage?" Impatience runs river swift in Molly's words, but there's a note of genuine curiosity there.

I'm not sure I care as cramps seize my stomach at the sudden intrusion of liquid, and I grimace.

"She needs to sleep some more. If she's strong enough later, we'll see about changing those bandages."

Bandages?

A haze of memories strikes me, and I see Sparrow again, see her falling, and I realize she's dead. Heaviness presses against my heart as more images assault me. Rory. Ghost. The Conundrum. Dying in a shit-covered alley, bleeding out from a knife wound in my side.

I twist, gasping at the implication and the fact that I have no idea where I am or who this man is. I pull the cloth off my forehead, but the room's already started spinning. I catch a glimpse of Molly Bell and a man who looks vaguely familiar, concern written on his face, and then I spiral away again, the drugged water sweeping me into oblivion.

Hidden hearts and empty words
Copper bones and silver scales
Bloody flesh and broken eyes
Dead men tell all sorts of tales.

— CHAPTER FIVE —

When I come to, it's morning. What morning, I have no idea, but it is *a* morning. What little sunlight there is shafts through a window high above, and if it doesn't quite illuminate the room, it's more than adequate to take in my surroundings.

I'm in a small room with well-worn wood floors, and the hearth is banked with thick stone. A kettle hangs over a cheery fire, a fine steam misting from it. There's an acrid scent in the air—something herbal. It's thick and cloying and seems to coat my mouth. It's as though I've been breathing it in for a long time.

The weight of it compresses my lungs, and my limbs twitch with the need to propel me out that little window, but they remain where they are. I wriggle an arm free of the cocooning sheet, amazed at how much it trembles. A small web of fear trickles down my spine at my helplessness. I wiggle my toes as if to take stock of all my limbs, relieved when everything seems to still be here. An attempt to roll over on my side results in something pinching tightly. A hiss escapes me, and I immediately relax onto my back.

Wait...I'm in a real bed. With sheets. And pillows. And a mattress that smells of old feathers but gives beneath my body without protest. It's a marvel, but I don't trust marvels. There's always a price involved.

A wave of despair rolls over me at why I am here, at the unfairness of it. That I should be alive and clean and warm while Sparrow is...not. I push the thoughts away, some part of me unwilling to believe she's really gone, and I fight the urge to hide beneath the blankets.

"Finally awake, are we? Good." A man glances up from a large sitting chair beside the fireplace, lowering a leather-bound book to his lap. His clothing is sharp and pressed but not of particularly fine quality. Someone who used to be gentry, maybe. Hard to drop those airs sometimes, even if your pockets are empty.

His sleeves are rolled up to the elbows, displaying a set of well-manicured hands, but they're stained with ink or something resembling it. He pushes his dark-rimmed glasses farther up his nose to take a closer look at me, and I use the opportunity to do the same.

He's older than I am—maybe midthirties, but it's hard to tell. There's a kindness to his face, and his red-gold hair is pulled into a neat queue, but his gaze burns with a hidden exhaustion and a tinge of sadness.

Secrets make us old, and whatever he's hiding has taken root in the faint wrinkles about his eyes.

I flatten against the bed, ignoring his question. When he approaches, I attempt to sit, wincing at the sharpness in my lungs.

"Admirable of you, but it's better if you stay where you are," he says. "I don't want you ripping open your stitches."

The pain bites into my side again, but I ignore it, my will suddenly focused on the pitcher of water perched on the table beside the bed. My tongue darts out to wet my parched lips, and I stare at it expectantly, as though I might somehow levitate it to my mouth. When this doesn't happen, I reach for it, my fingers sliding over the silver handle and smearing the drops of condensation.

He tsks at me, his boots rapping sharply upon the floor as he beats me to the pitcher and pours me a small cupful. "Slow sips," he cautions, but I'm already guzzling it, each drop of liquid soothing the dry regions of my throat. But it's not enough, and a moment later, I snatch the pitcher from him. His eyes widen in surprise at my quickness, but his face falls as I polish it off, lips pursed when I begin to wretch.

A resigned sigh escapes him. "Well done." He hands me a copper basin, watching impassively as I bring everything back up in a noisy splash. "I told you to sip it slowly." My stomach gurgles in protest, my wounded side burning with each heave until my eyes water against it.

I droop onto the mattress, wiping my wrist across my mouth. My arms tremble with the effort, and he swiftly removes the basin from me. There's no hint of disgust about him as he takes it. He pops his head out of the heavy door on the other side of the room and hands it to someone, his voice a low murmur.

Sour acid stings my lips, and I swallow. I must be making a dreadful face because he laughs when he turns. "Going to listen to me next time?"

I scowl at him and nod sullenly.

"Good. I don't fancy wiping up the floor." He dampens a rag with the remainder of the water from the pitcher and gently blots at my mouth. "I'll have the cook send us up something light. Some broth, maybe."

Confusion washes over me. "I don't understand. Why are you doing this?"

He blinks mildly. "I'm a doctor. Why wouldn't I?"

"Don't lie to me," I snap, suspicion making me lash out. "No one helps Moon Children out of charity."

"Who said it was out of charity?" Molly's soft drawl slurs as she steps neatly across the threshold. She's wearing a silk robe that suggests she's only recently arisen from bed, but her gaze is as a sharp as ever. As are her teeth. They click into a tight smile. "And you might want to consider thanking the good Dr. Barrows, here. Without his insistence and care, you would have bled to death in the gutter like Sparrow."

"Why didn't you try to help us before?" I cannot stop the hurt from welling deep within my chest, but I hastily blink back a sudden rush of tears. "You could have stopped them from taking us."

Molly shrugs, her curls falling loose over her shoulders. "That was Inquestor business. Bold I may be, but I refuse to directly attack one half of my bread and butter."

"So why help me at all?" I glance at the doctor, who's watching our conversation with an air of caution. "Not that I'm not grateful," I add a moment later.

He inclines his head at me. "Of course."

"Dying on my doorstep made you my business," Molly says after a pause.

"If you say so." Defeated by whatever odd logic she's using, I slump against the pillows, another pinching cramp tearing into my side. I ignore it, shuffling through the sheets to pull the blanket tighter around my shoulders. "What happened? I remember Sparrow—" I choke on the words but force myself to go on "—dying. And then I was stabbed?" I don't mention Ghost. There's no sense in pulling him into this.

Whatever *this* is.

"Yes," the doctor says. "It should have been fatal, but somehow he only nicked your lung. As long as you avoid infection, you should be fine, though your recovery may be slower than you want."

The words take a moment to sink in, but my emotions roll over me in an odd combination of mourning and exhilaration. I won't break down over Sparrow here, not with them standing over me.

"Then I'm free?" I ask. With both Rory and Caskers assuming my demise, I would be taken off the roster for the Pits. I would no longer be hunted for murder.

I glance out the window. I can't see Meridion's shadow, but its presence beats through my bones. That much closer to freedom, though the price has already been too high.

"Perhaps." Molly glides closer to me. "But you owe me a debt, Raggy Maggy."

The doctor shakes his head. "One thing at a time, Molly. She has to get better first."

My upper lip curls at Molly's words. "Debts are dangerous things. What is it you want from me? It's not like I have anything of value."

Molly's grin grows wider, her delicate pink tongue rolling over the points of her teeth. "What do you know of dragons?"

"Dragons?"

"Don't play daft with me, girl. We all saw what you had in the bag." She fixes me with a sharp stare, and I scowl.

"That's the extent of it," I say finally, twisting the sheets between anxious fingers. My lungs feel full of ash as I stare at the chimney. "I found it. I was going to sell it, but now it's gone. The end."

"Hmpf," Molly says somewhat beneath her breath.

The doctor lays a hand upon her wrist, and she goes silent. He gives me a strained smile, and again I can't help but think I know him somehow. Some twitch of his lips or the smooth curve of his jaw, but then he moves and the moment is gone. I rub my temples against the rapid onset of an aching head.

"We should let her rest," the doctor says firmly. "Tomorrow will be for explanations and scheming. She's got a long road ahead of her."

I don't remotely like the sound of that. Even less the way she whispers in his ear as he ushers her out. She doesn't touch him, but the jut of her chin indicates her frustration.

The door clicks shut behind her. The doctor stares at it for a moment, his face devoid of expression. "She's impatient." He lets out a low chuckle, but there's no humor in it. "She's waited quite some time for certain opportunities to present themselves. Things are lining up, and Molly's eager to see her plots bear fruit."

"So happy to oblige," I grouse.

He raises a brow. "We'll get along that much better without false-hoods between us...Mags, is it?"

"Call me whatever you like," I say, wincing when I attempt to turn onto my side again.

"As you will, Mags. Rest now. I'll have Copper Betty bring up some hot water later. Give you a chance to clean up."

Hot water. Clean up. Broth. The words seem foreign to me, pattering in my mind like rain, and I let them roll off just as easily. I don't respond, and a moment later he's gone, his footsteps creaking in the hallway.

Finally alone, I let the tears fall. The awful hurt of Sparrow's death rises up to the surface, leaking out of me in a wave of rage and sorrow. Inside me, a worm of self-loathing writhes.

My fault. It's all my fault...

The doctor could offer me a thousand baths, and I'd never be able to wash this stain clean.

"Death flower, death flower, how will you bloom? Will you be red, or will you be white, or will you be my doom?" I whisper the familiar nursery rhyme, one of Sparrow's favorites. The words tremble as my memories slide over her face in those last moments. I might be alive, but nothing good will come of where I am—certainly not if I owe Molly Bell favors.

And then there is Ghost. A loose string in the weaving with his offer of finding a buyer for the dragon. Not that it makes any difference now. But he would have seen what happened in the alley... Does he even know I'm still alive?

I glance up at the window with its shining shaft of light. It's crept up the floorboards, its golden corona flaring to life over the end of the mattress. In a short while it will bathe my feet in a yellow haze. I debate the wisdom of attempting to escape through the window, but it's a futile idea. Even if I can fit through the pane, I've no clothes, no Warrens to return to, no jingle.

No Sparrow.

I give it up for now. The only glimmer of hope in this entire sordid mess is my supposed death. Freedom from Inquestor rule will undoubtedly have its perks, but until I get my bearings and figure out a real plan of survival, anything else will be folly. My side aches something fierce, burning skin along the jagged trail of stitches. I haven't quite managed the strength to pull back the sheets to look at it yet.

Not that it matters how it appears. It's the stiffness that worries me, the sharp pain inside when I breathe. Dr. Barrows may be confident in his abilities, but proof will only come in time.

My stomach rumbles, and I give up my fretting and drift off into another hazy sleep, dreaming of dancing over the rooftops, the wind in my hair, and Sparrow at my side.

I wake up with my belly on fire.

No, not my belly…

I wriggle off the bed, ignoring the twinge in my side. Half-blind with the need to take a piss, I stagger to the door to try to find a water closet, a chamber pot, anything. Someone must be standing guard outside my door because the knob rattles beneath my hand, twisting against my fingers.

I let go as Martika presses her way into the room, her face a study in severity. "Why are you out of bed?"

"If you don't fancy cleaning up a puddle of privy water, you best find me a pot to piss in, aye?" I gasp.

"Come with me."

She briskly disappears into the hallway. I grit my teeth as my bladder spasms, hardly taking heed of where I'm going. A small door at the far end of the corridor opens to reveal the privy. I slam it shut in Martika's face and bite my lip against a yelp as I relieve myself in the porcelain bowl.

A moment later I realize I'm naked. The thought brings a half smile to my lips. It's somehow fitting that I limp up the hallway to where Martika stands without a stitch on me. Her arms are crossed and there's nothing humorous about her expression, which clearly takes my measure with every step.

"What is that?" Martika points to the heart-shaped panel at the center of my breastbone as I shove my way past her. I don't have to look down to see the metallic curve and the intricate filigree of silver and brass to know what she's asking.

"Nothing," I say bluntly, laying my palm over it. Beneath my fingers, the vibration of the *tick-thump* beat is calm and quiet, reassuring me with its continued presence. I can almost hear Mad Brianna scolding me for revealing it, and I wince.

Martika's mouth purses, but she doesn't press, waiting for me to wrap a blanket around my shoulders. "If the others have neglected to mention it, you are on this upper floor alone. No one else save Molly and myself know you are here, and it must remain that way."

"And Dr. Barrows, of course?"

She scowls, impatient with my teasing. "And yes, the good doctor. But look here—I need you to be quiet. No trotting about, understood?"

The Mother Clock rings out the hour in the distance, and the normalcy of the sound brings me back to myself. It's late afternoon. My stomach rumbles again.

"He said somewhat about broth and a bath. Who's Copper Betty?" I intentionally ignore the last of her words, making it fairly plain her request will only go heeded if my demands are met. Even that is debatable, though, once I'm feeling better. But it's a start. I've nowhere else to go anyway.

"An automaton. She's mute." Martika's head cocks as though she's hearing something. "And here." She steps aside as a female automaton clinks her way into the room.

It's the same automaton I'd seen serving drinks in front of the stage, in fact, but with clothes this time, including a much more sedate set of long skirts and petticoats, and high-heeled boots to go with her corset. The lights of her eyes blink in a friendly manner, and she gestures at me with the wooden tray in her hands. I smell it before she uncovers the dish—thick brown bread and a trencher of broth. A momentary glance below reveals what appears to be actual meat floating in the brine.

My fingers twitch, and I fight to snatch it from her, the instinct to find some high, safe place in which to eat at war with the limitations of my body.

In the end, I merely sag upon the bed, smiling weakly when she places the tray on the bedside table.

Something about Martika softens. "I'll talk to Molly about finding you some clothes."

"None of those fancy dresses, aye?" I call after her as she turns to go. I think she chuckles as she shuts the door, but it could have been the squeak of the hinges.

The instant she's gone, I scoop up the bread and tear into it with shaky hands. Copper Betty stares at me with the dull intelligence all automatons have.

I pay her no mind when she leaves, nor when she returns with a ewer of steaming water and several towels, instead focusing on gulping down huge bites without chewing and chasing them down with sips of broth straight from the bowl. The blanket slips from my shoulders, but I don't care because I've never tasted anything so good and its warmth floods my belly. My limbs tremble from holding up the bowl, but I drink the broth down until there's nothing left.

My stomach protests noisily, burbling, but the fullness is pleasant and I sigh, waving Copper Betty off when she attempts to dip one of the towels in the water for me.

I stand, letting the blanket fall to the floor. A mirror on the far wall captures my movements as I approach the table with the ewer. Copper Betty shifts, her bronzed face expressionless. I wonder what she sees.

I don't have to look at my reflection to know what I look like. Tall and thin, with sinewy arms and legs made for dancing on the rooftops, sliding through tunnels, and slipping into the fog with all the grace of a creature made of moonlight.

Molly called me a broomstick in smallclothes, and she's right. I've nearly no breasts, and my hips jut from my skin like bony tent pegs in a circus made of flesh.

The water in the bowl turns rusty as I bathe, the filth of the alley and Sparrow's death rinsing away. I don't linger on the jagged stitches sticking out of my rib cage like the legs of a black beetle.

My hair hangs in loose tangles, but it shines in the mirror, picking up the light from the window so that it almost glows with a silver luster. It's odd to have it hanging free like this, and I struggle with the urge to bind it up and conceal it beneath my old cap.

A swift knock announces Molly Bell's presence, and she sweeps into the room as I finish toweling off. She lays whatever clothing she's brought on the bed.

"We don't have much in the way of trousers. At least none that you'd want to be wearing, I'm sure."

I shrug at her and give a wan smile. "I stole my boots from a dead whore. So long as it's not a dress, I'll manage."

A derisive bark of laughter escapes her, and I hide my agitation by pulling on the trousers. They hang off me something awful, nearly sliding off my hips and tenting over my feet. I'll need a rope to belt them up if I actually want to walk anywhere. I wriggle into the shirt, unsurprised at the way it drapes over my shoulders, the neckline threatening to swallow me.

The mirror isn't any kinder when I look into it, the bruising of my broken nose shining like a mottled beacon. "Broomstick, aye," I mutter, my legs beginning to quake with weakness.

Molly's eyes narrow at Copper Betty. "Why don't you go and fetch our good doctor?"

The automaton nods stiffly and disappears. I stare at Molly for a moment longer and then take a seat on the stool in front of the vanity. She paces around the room slowly, circling me like a shark. Her fingers flex almost as though she's mentally counting.

"What did you do with it? The architect's credit chit?" I mean for it to be a distraction. Her gaze makes me nervous.

She snorts. "Looking for a cut, are you?"

"Well, I *did* bring it to you, aye? It would go a long way to not being so dependent on...on you." Or a clan... But still. I thrust my chin toward the door. "Maybe you should use it to get your broken automaton fixed?"

Molly's stare grows chilly. "Copper Betty was a gift from a rather special patron, one most dearly earned. And I've no wish to have her repaired. I deal in secrets; what use is she if she can be questioned? It's not like she can feel anything, now is it?"

I can only shake my head at this, no answer on my tongue. And yet my thoughts travel back to that little dragon who so clearly did feel, or at least grasp enough of its own situation that it chose to flee from the Inquestors.

"At any rate, the chit went to Inquestor Caskers," Molly says and purses her mouth. "Part bribe, part returning something owed to him. As long as he continues looking the other way from this establishment, we'll be all set."

A beesting of anger pricks me. The money would have gone to the Banshees if I'd been faster or more clever.

"I give up," I say. "What is it you want from me?"

Molly smiles her toothy smile at me. "Why, for you to get better, of course. And then you'll be heading into the Pits."

I blink, confusion washing over me. "The hells I am. What makes you think I'd agree to something like that?"

Molly frowns, clearly not expecting my refusal. "You owe me your life."

"It's not like I asked you save me. I'm *not* going." My eyes dart toward the hallway behind Molly. Injury or not, there are other bonewitches out there.

Molly slams the door. "Oh, no you don't. You *owe* me." Her teeth click shut on her last words, as though the matter is settled.

"If you think a locked door is enough to stop me, you're daft." I glance at the window and up to the vaulted ceiling where a rusted skylight lets in a scant shaft of afternoon sun. "I can be out of here in two shakes of a lamb's tail, and you can't do a thing to stop me."

It's not quite a bluff. Without my wound, it would be an easy task, but if I'm desperate enough, I'll try it. I bare my teeth in a snarl. "You want something stolen or vandalized, or someone to tap-dance on the roof of the Mother Clock, I'm your girl, but the Pits are off-limits. I'm not a bird to sing for your pleasure, nor to die for it."

The door knob jiggles, interrupting what is probably going to be a horrific row between me and Molly. Dr. Barrows pauses when he sees us, a brow cocked in my direction. "Something I should know?"

"There's no reasoning with her," Molly snaps. "I did not put my reputation and business on the line so this…this Moon Child could throw my charity back in my face."

"And I'm not going into the Pits for the sake of the rags I'm wearing," I retort.

Dr. Barrows sighs. "It's not what you think, Mags. Did you even give her a chance to explain?"

"Waste of time, all of it." Molly throws her arms up in the air and wheels out of the room. Dr. Barrows follows suit, shutting the door behind him, but there's enough of a gap for me to hear their hushed tones in the hallway. I tiptoe across the floor so I can hear better.

"What did you expect, Molly? You can't treat her like a prisoner, dropping mysterious hints here and there, and not expect her to be spooked. These Moon Children have spent their entire lives knowing they'll be Tithed at some point. Surely it would be better to offer up our reasons first?"

"Then you do it, if you're so keen on keeping her around," Molly mutters at him. "Might be easier to just start over and find someone else."

His voice drops lower. "Oh no. There's more to this than just our plans. Explain to me how that girl has a piece of Meridian technology welded to her flesh? That heart on her chest? That's d'Arc's work—I'd stake my life on it."

Fear strikes me at his words, even as I resign myself to their ulterior motives, whatever they are. I press my hand against the panel in my chest. Whatever did he mean, Meridian tech? Even Mad Brianna had never told me where the thing had come from.

"Wishful thinking," Molly says, but there's a hint of doubt there that makes me wonder.

Gods, I want no part of this, and I'm not sticking around a moment longer. With my luck, Molly will call the Inquestors on me and I'll be right back where I was.

I head toward the window next to the fireplace, cursing under my breath when I realize it's locked. Nailed shut, in fact. My thoughts scatter in a sudden panic. Break the glass? Or... My eyes roll up to the rusty skylight.

My fine words to Molly aside, it's pretty high up and my ways of getting there are limited. But the door is still mostly shut, and it looks sturdy enough...

Launching myself at the door, the ball of my foot finds purchase on the knob, thrusting me upward to the lintel. I cling for a second, using my momentum to propel me toward the rafters. My tattered fingernails dig into the wood, and I swing my weight forward.

Pain floods my side as I twist and nearly fall, and somehow, I find myself wedged on top of a beam. I suck in a sharp breath when I feel the dampness upon my fingers, pulling at the shirt to reveal fresh blood. "Dammit."

Just one more hop to reach the skylight. The pain cramps tighter, the shirt sticking to my wound. If I time it right, I'll be able to balance on the side of the chimney, my feet against the wall. I swallow down the aching wretch of pain.

Something rips open when I jump this time, and my right arm is nearly numb with agony. My fingers slide down the brick even as my naked toes scratch into the grit. The skylight is closed and heavy with rust, but the latch turns beneath the pressure of my fingers until it gives way and the window flips open with a bang. The cool air rushes past me, sending goose bumps skittering down my spine.

Free, free, free...

"Mags!" Dr. Barrows bursts though the door, shouting after me, but I'm already wriggling through the opening and onto the roof.

A snicker escapes me at Molly's squeak of fury, but I can't bring myself to care. Of course that's partially because I'm bleeding something fierce and shaking like a squalling newborn. But at least I'm free.

I stumble around the chimney, my hand clenching at my rib cage as I attempt to bind my shirt more tightly over the wound. Slumping, I lean against the brickwork, my muscles shivering. I can't seem to make them stop.

I shift and lurch to my feet. My toes scrape on the shingles, the cold lancing through them. I linger on the roof and take in my surroundings. Below me is the alley where Sparrow died. It was only a few nights ago now, but it feels like years. I shake away the memory of the blood blossoming beneath her shirt.

Ghost materializes out of the shadows, and I startle. He reaches out to steady me, careful of my injury. "They don't mean you harm."

"And how would you know anything about it?" Neither Dr. Barrows nor Molly had mentioned Ghost in any of this. But the ease with which he speaks of them could only mean they are somehow working together. I push his hand away. "They mean to send me down to the Pits."

"I know," he says. "It was my idea."

"What?" I step back, a sick lump tight in my gut. I can't outrun him, wounded as I am. I'm standing on a wire over some great hole, the hollow ache of betrayal deep within my bones. One wrong step and I'll tumble into the dark, swallowed into the belly of some great beast.

Realization snaps through me. My fist connects with his jaw, drawing a surprised grunt from him as my knuckles crack with the impact and he staggers away. "Your idea? Your *idea*? What, lure Sparrow and me here on the premise that you'd found a buyer? All this was, what? Some sort of setup?"

Somewhere in the tangled thread of my thoughts I know what I'm saying isn't quite right. I would have been at the Conundrum regardless to trade in the chit, but staring at the alley fills me with nothing but images of Sparrow, and my grief attaches to the nearest target.

"You knew!" My voice is a whisper, but I'm screaming in my mind. "You knew they were coming for me. For Sparrow."

"I *didn't* know." He rubs his chin with a grimace. "My offer of a buyer was genuine. And even if I *had* known they were coming, you wouldn't have listened. You didn't exactly welcome my company," he points out dryly.

I still can't seem to stop shaking, and I sink to my knees, bile filling my belly.

He squats beside me, and I stare blankly at him. "You need to rest," he says.

I blink rapidly as I try to focus, though my head spins like a lopsided top. "What about Sparrow? What happened...to her?"

"When it became apparent that Rory wasn't going to collect her, I did. I burned her bones at the Salt Temple and scattered her ashes upon the sea. I think she would have liked that." He pauses and I catch the sorrow in his eyes, but as apologies go, it's empty.

I swallow my bitterness. "Aye." For a moment I wonder where he would have spread my ashes, had it come to that. But what did it matter? I wouldn't care at that point anyway. I press my face into my hands, whimpering as my stitches catch on the cloth of my shirt.

"Come on, Mags. Let the doctor fix you up at least. Before you make a decision." He exhales sharply. "I'll make sure they tell you everything. And if they don't, I will." His mouth curves into a sad smile.

I lift my eyes to meet his. "Why should I?"

His gaze rolls skyward, away from me. "Because if you do this, I'll take you to Meridion."

Trip Trap, Trip Trap
Cloven hooves clatter to reveal.
Beneath the bridge, the goats attend
Impale the troll on horns of steel.

— CHAPTER SIX —

I'm partially wrapped in the blanket, standing beside the fire. The doctor inspects my wound with precise fingers. He doesn't say anything, but he doesn't have to. His anger hisses through every exhalation.

The scrapped remains of the bloody shirt lie at my feet. My toes wriggle on the hardwood, cramping beneath the rush of heat from the flames. A bowl of warm water sits on a table beside us, bandages and a spool of fine catgut beside it.

And then there's the doctor, threading his curved needle through the parchment-thin layers of my skin. Each prick jolts me back to the moment, though the sensation is distant compared to the chaos of questions in my head. But I'm not getting any answers until Dr. Barrows is satisfied I haven't done any lasting harm to myself.

Ghost has taken up guard beside the doorway. I still don't know what to think. His previous words have left me reeling.

Finally, the doctor eases back in his chair. "I'll tattoo it once it's healed a bit more. Assuming you rest this time," he adds, getting to his feet. I poke at one of the stitches, snarling when he pushes my hand away and then picks up the shirt. "I'd rather been hoping this would have lasted longer than a few hours."

I blink. "It's yours?"

"Well, we weren't exactly going to steal from the customers to clothe you. If you'd prefer a corset next time, I'm sure that could be arranged," Molly says from where she's coiled upon the plush sitting chair. She sips a bronze liquor from a snifter, swirling it with a delicate flick of her wrist.

Ghost snorts, and I shoot him a glare. "That won't be necessary." I swallow. "And I'm sorry."

"It's fine." Dr. Barrows gathers the bowl and the remaining bandages. "Wash day tomorrow. We'll get you something better fitting."

"I want some explanations first."

"We can't tell you all of it. Not yet." Molly stares at me, her eyes hard. "Not until we know you're with us."

"Try." I pull the blanket tighter about my shoulders and press my lips into a thin line.

She inclines her head at Ghost. "If you would?"

He nods and slips out the door. The doctor follows behind Ghost, leaving me alone with Molly and the two of us size each other up like a pair of alley cats.

I keep my thoughts to myself. At least they're attempting to show me *something*. I've no interest in fighting with Ghost's promise of Meridion dangling in front of me. After everything he's said I'm not sure I really believe him, but I'm willing to at least hear what they have to say.

Molly clears her throat. "I'm not sure where to begin. There are years of history here, but the long and short of it is that we need someone down in the Pits to find information." She raises her brow at me. "This is where you come in."

"Maybe you're not aware of it, but *none* of us comes back." I stare at my hands sourly and sigh. "What kind of information?"

"Indeed. And we wouldn't send you down there without an escape plan," Dr. Barrows says as he returns, hands freshly washed up and carrying another shirt over his arm. He quickly shuts the door. "What do you know of the Rot?"

I snort. "Only that I can't get it and somehow that makes me worth less than a gutter rat, according to the Salt Temple." My voice turns singsong as I parrot the Tithe prayer at him. "'Blessed are the sin-eaters, the embodiment of the damned, cradling the sins of the people within as we sacrifice those suffering from the vices leading to the downfall of civilization.' Blah, blah, blahhhh, blah, blah." My upper lips curls. "Not a particularly encouraging religion, mind."

"I imagine it might be difficult to pray to a god that insists upon your demise before most of you reach twenty, yes," he retorts, but not without sympathy. "Well, the Salt Temple aside, there are certain...rumors that indicate Meridion's role in the rise of this plague. That putting those who succumb to it into a forbidden place is perhaps less about protecting others from contracting the disease and more to hide their culpability."

"Their what now?" I frown, trying to make sense of his words. "I don't follow."

"There is evidence to suggest the Meridians actually created the Rot." His lips purse. "And speculation that they unleashed it on purpose."

Confusion twists my face. "But why? All those people, condemned to a living death?"

He shrugs. "That's one of the things we mean to investigate. I have suspicions as to how the plague is currently being spread, and I wonder if the bonewitches may not inadvertently be distributing it."

My brows furrow. The salt priests insisted only the sinful could catch it, but I've never noticed that being pious had any effect one way or the other. "But the bonewitch tattoos...That's why the Inquestors enforced the policy in the first place. So there's a record of patients."

"But the Inquestors don't share their records with us. I'm hoping to find a pattern—perhaps an increase of infected patients who might have visited certain bonewitches recently or bonewitches who might be getting kickbacks from the Inquestors themselves. If we can find proof of their work—perhaps via the bonewitch marks on those sent below—we'd be one step closer to figuring out the mystery."

"Might be simpler just to ask the bonewitches," I point out.

"We tried that," Molly says. "But desperate witnesses make desperate claims, and before long, we realized many of them were just saying what we wanted to hear for the chance to make a few shillings. Not the type of evidence we can rely upon."

"And don't even bother mentioning the salt priests." Dr. Barrows rolls his eyes. "They're too caught up in their own self-righteousness to even question what they're doing. Whatever their silly dogma says about sin, don't you believe it. The Rot is caused by a virus—a highly infectious pathogen that can be spread by multiple means. Blood. Saliva. Most bodily fluids, really, but direct contact is required. By rights, a heavily enforced quarantine should have wiped it out ages ago."

He eyes me shrewdly. "If Moon Children are truly immune, why haven't they studied your blood? Tried to figure out an antidote? The Inquestors must know the Tithes to the Pits are a ludicrous concept if their intent is to prevent the disease from spreading. Hell, aside from the early breakouts when the plague first hit, it seems almost...cyclical in nature now. Therefore, the only conclusion I can come up with is that they actually *intend* for citizens to become infected."

I recoil at the idea. "That's monstrous."

"Yes, of course it is. That's why we want to stop it."

"Not that," I snap at him. "Yes, it's tragic that innocents are dying for nothing more than a religious farce, but why are you trying to discover it only now?"

He blinks at me. "Nearly half my life I've been working to find the answer. If I can figure out a way to at least keep the Rot from spreading, a vaccine, perhaps, *something*..." His eyes meet mine, burning with such intensity I nearly expect it to scald me. "I just hadn't thought about using a Moon Child before."

I scoff. "Why would you? Moon Children are invisible until you need us, right? It's like asking a cow for permission to butcher it." My voice shakes with anger, at the loss of so many of my clan to the Tithes. And for what? A charade? I press my palms against my forehead, unsure if either of them can understand the sudden wave of grief threatening to wash over me.

"Mags," he says gently, "that's not what I meant."

I wave him away, swallowing my fury. "Even if I found proof down there in the Pits, who would ever believe it? You think the Inquestors will give two shakes if a Moon Child comes to them bearing accusations?"

"They might if the BrightStone Chancellor is the one doing the accusing." His mouth quirks into a half smile. "With the right evidence, we might have a chance at changing things. Or at least getting Meridion to pay attention to what's really happening down here."

"Why would the Chancellor care what we say? I thought she was just a figurehead. The gods know she's never helped me or mine."

He tips his head, musing over the question. "Perhaps in the past that was so, but Chancellor Davis is newly elected into her office and she is determined to set things in motion."

A frown creeps over my face. "You seem to know an awful lot about what the leader of BrightStone wants...That's pretty impressive for a bonewitch living in a brothel."

"Indeed," he chaffs. "I am the Chancellor's personal physician to start with, but we go back a little ways further than that, under circumstances you don't need to know just now."

"If you say so," I mutter. "Better start stockpiling weapons, then, because I doubt the Inquestors will listen to anything without a gun pointed at their heads."

"That, too, is an option," the doctor says, staring at me. "Though not ideal, the Chancellor is not above such considerations, should they be needed."

"Now I know you're insane." I cross my arms, rubbing at the sudden rush of goose bumps. It had never mattered to me before who was running BrightStone. After all, my living conditions never changed regardless of who was passing the laws. That the actual Chancellor of the city might be involved gives this entire discussion an air of seriousness I hadn't considered. The idea of a revolution has always seemed laughable. But here, discussing treasonous secrets with the doctor and Molly, the concept suddenly seems all too possible. A nervous flutter takes root in my gut.

The door rattles, and Ghost emerges from the hallway before anyone can say anything else. He's carrying a box and shuts the door with his foot. My ears prick when the sound of metallic hissing echoes from within.

I thrust my chin at him. "Dragons, is it?"

He opens the box to reveal a cage with my dragon pacing inside. My eyes narrow at Ghost, and he nods. "Peace, Mags," he murmurs, unfastening the cage door.

Molly stands in front of the chimney this time, though they seem to have forgotten the skylight is still open. I don't enlighten them of this fact. And it doesn't matter anyway because the dragon shoots from the cage into the room...and straight toward me. I duck, the blanket falling to my waist, but the dragon lands on my wrist and clambers onto my shoulder, its tiny claws digging into my skin. Ghost pointedly ignores my naked chest, but the doctor hands me the shirt he brought without a word.

Molly chews on her lower lip. A crimson drop winks at me from the tip of a pointed tooth. "It seems to have a fondness for you, doesn't it?"

I wince, trying to pull it off my shoulder so I can put on the shirt. The linen smells of lavender, as if it's been locked in a trunk somewhere. The dragon settles itself on my shoulder again when I'm done, its tail coiled partly around my neck. Almost on instinct, I stroke its spine, the beating ember of its glass heart oddly comforting.

"I told you before—I don't know anything about it. Sparrow and I found it in the slag heap outside the Warrens."

Molly shakes her head. "The Inquestors are trying to keep them from being discovered. You did say you found more than one?"

"Part of one. With the body of the architect. Are there more?"

"The one you have is the only one we know of that's whole," Dr. Barrows says. "Considering the architect had one, it's only reasonable to assume Meridion is using them for some purpose. Probably some form of communication, but we haven't discovered much more than that. With any luck, we'll able to study this one."

"So why not tell the Chancellor about the dragon?" I ask bluntly.

"The Chancellor will need more than rumors and fairy tales to bring before the council. The dragon's purpose is still unknown to us; without proof, I run the risk of being called a fraud for my pains. And as for the architect, I made some inquiries at the morgue. They've ruled his death 'accidental.'" He makes a face. "So much for those murder charges. And there's no way to reopen the case at this point as the body was cremated shortly after."

I sag onto the bed, my head spinning with everything that's been thrown at me this evening. Politics, the Rot, secret messages, conspiracies...I'd be overwhelmed about any one of those on a good day, even if it didn't sound like something out of a penny dreadful.

Fool's game, Mags. You cannot even read. What help could you be?

I say as much aloud.

"That was my point exactly," Molly says, irritation radiating off her in waves.

Dr. Barrows nods. "We'll do the best we can to figure something out. We've a bit of time before my next meeting with the Chancellor. I can teach her what she needs to know in the interim while she continues to heal—the basics of bonewitch marks, reading, writing." His face becomes serious as he looks at me. "But I'll need all your attention, all your effort. Your physical skills are quite obviously without question, but if you can't steal the information, we'll need you to memorize it."

"You all must think I'm soft in the brain. Why waste your time on me?" The dragon grinds into my shoulder and nips my ear. I point at Ghost. "Why don't you go instead?"

Ghost steps forward, his hands shoved deep in his trouser pockets. His cap hangs from his belt, showing off his shining and shaggy hair. I've never seen his head uncovered before. It makes his face seem older somehow. He turns around to show me his neck. It's unmarred, with no sign of a brand. "Because I can't."

I frown, a piece of the puzzle falling into place. Of course. The Inquestors record the clan brand of each Moon Child entering the Pits during a Tithe. Without a brand, there is no way the Inquestors would let a Moon Child through the gates. They'd know something is up.

Still.

I lift the hair from the nape of my neck, exposing my own brand. Not that I've ever seen it directly, but I'd seen Sparrow's often enough to know what it looked like. A crescent moon and a number, burned into my skin the day Mad Brianna sold me off to the Banshees. "Well, we might have a problem anyway, seeing as when I 'died' the Inquestors would have taken me off the Tithe roster. Last-minute substitutions sometimes happen, depending on certain circumstances, I suppose, but if they look too closely..."

Molly's mouth opens and then closes again.

"Even if you were to sneak me into a Tithe somehow," I continue, "we'd have to make sure the number matched up with whoever they're expecting. And that would require cooperation with the leader of a Moon Child clan. They're the ones who determine which one of us is given up for the Tithe."

I let my hair drop and shrug. "And since I rather doubt Rory is going to welcome me back into the fold and the other clans will probably try to beat the crap out of me for invading their territories, that's going to be a bit touchy, aye?" I slump, my mind whirling with more important questions. "Forget even trying to get in... How am I supposed to get *out*?"

Dr. Barrows frowns, but there's something thoughtful in the lines crossing his brow. "We've certain contacts in BrightStone with very similar interests in this mission. They are currently working on the logistics of the gates to the Pits—namely a way to unlock them. If we can manage that, then once you are below ground, we would have a set time arranged to force the gates open long enough to let you out. Between the fact that they're heavily guarded and the mechanism can only be accessed by airship, well..." He gives me a wry shrug. "We're still working on the details of that, clearly, but we wouldn't send you down there until we had a workable plan."

"Empty words are like empty pockets," I retort with a frown. "And about as useful."

"Do what you like, then," Molly says. "It makes no difference to me."

It's on the tip of my tongue to ask if doing this will bring Sparrow back, but that's not even worth voicing. How different would our lives have been if the Rot had never existed? If what I agree to today save others from a similar fate, it will be worth it. "Fine. I'll think about it."

"Then it's settled," Molly says with a smile, her teeth glinting in the firelight. She drains the last of her glass. "Now, I have a business to run, so I'll leave you under the doctor's care." Her smile grows tighter. "I look forward to seeing what you can do."

"Oh, aye." I sigh. "Me too."

Ghost and I crouch beside the fire. The doctor and Molly have left us, and the dragon has taken a perch upon the mantel of the fireplace, its golden scales fiery as it lazily puffs small clouds of steam. If a mechanical dragon can appear smug, this one certainly does, staring at us with half-lidded eyes filled with satisfaction.

"How long have you been working with them?" I sip sweet tea from a steaming mug, marveling at the flavor as it fills my belly. Dr. Barrows has infused it with some sort of painkiller, numbing my side and making my thoughts whirl in a pleasant fashion.

Ghost stares at the fireplace, his legs stretched out so his heels bask in the warmth. His feet are clean, but the soles are hard as horn from the looks of it. "Years," he answers.

I want to ask him more, but his face is expressionless as he says it. It's a story for another time, perhaps.

"Not sure I trust them...or you," I add a moment later, giving him a sideways glance.

"I wouldn't expect you to. Not yet. But you can trust that they want to succeed. You and I are merely tools to that end, but I'm willing to be used for the cause." He turns to me, a half smile playing over his lips. "Besides, I don't want us to merely succeed. I want *change*."

"Bold words," I say. He snorts, and I lay my now empty mug on the hearth, wiggling my toes at the fire. "So, tell me something. Just how do you intend to make good on your offer to take me to Meridion? And for that matter, how did you even know I wanted to go?"

His face flushes. "I…overheard you and Sparrow talking about it awhile ago."

"Overheard, aye?"

"I wasn't spying on you," he mutters. "I was sitting up in that little overhang at Blessing Bridge a few months back when you showed up. You, Sparrow, and Penny. You didn't notice I was there, but you seemed pretty busy, what with the red paint and all."

Now I laugh, but it's tinged with memories and pain. "Caught us marking up the bridge, did you?" I push the hair from my eyes. "Poor Sparrow. Dumped that whole damn tub of paint down the side by accident. Penny was so angry, I had to pay her off with half my scrap for a week."

A hot rush of tears fills my eyes, my breath suddenly shaky. "You seem to have overheard a lot for someone who says he wasn't spying on us," I say, when I finally find my voice again.

"Ah. Well, my name's Ghost for a reason," he says dryly. "Not belonging to a clan has its own issues. Having to sneak my way through three different territories requires a fair bit of stealth."

"Do tell," I drawl. "So what was your real intention with finding a buyer for the dragon? Feels a bit too convenient, given everything else that's happened."

"I saw what happened with the Inquestors when you ran from them after finding the architect," he admits. "Though I didn't actually know what was in the bag until you opened it. The offer of the buyer was genuine, though truthfully it was more of an excuse to talk to you."

"Talk?" I raise a brow at him.

"Perhaps *recruit* is a better word." He shrugs. "We knew we were going to need additional help from Moon Children if we were going to set our plans in motion. Initially, I'd hoped an insider like you might be able to look at uniting all the clans as part of a way to overthrow the Inquestors, but Dr. Barrows feels we need the backing of the Chancellor if we are to convince the rest of BrightStone to support us. So here we are."

"I'm not sure any of us could ever get the clans to stop fighting long enough to talk." A snort escapes me. "You might as well try to insist dogs and cats keep house together."

"There is that. It's why the Inquestors separate you all, you know. Keeps you focused on your own issues instead of the larger picture. At least, that's my theory. Divide and conquer, as they say." He turns toward me, his head cocked. "So why *do* you want to go to Meridion so bad?"

"Why do any of us want anything?" I shrug. "I don't know. To find out who I am, I guess. It sounds mad...like a fairy tale. But we're half-breeds, right? Sparrow and I would talk about it all the time. What we'd do once we got to the floating city—find our real families, escape all this...bullshit."

The words are hard to say aloud, but the drugs have made me chatty and they slip out. I give him a pained smile. "Or at least, that's what I would have told you a few hours ago. Now though..."

He nudges me gently with his knee. "No, I get it. I was just curious."

"I don't think you do. If what Dr. Barrows said is true—about the Rot being unleashed by them..." I lock gazes with him, deadly serious. "Well, I might just be inclined to bring the whole thing down."

"And you thought *I* was bold," he mutters, surprise flickering over his face. But in the end whatever he might have said drifts into silence. For a time, the crackling of the fire is the only real sound, and after a little while longer, even that fades.

I yawn, the medicated tea making me sleepy. "Are you staying?" I mumble the question at him, shaking my head to clear it.

It seems to amuse him greatly, his mouth pursing. "With you, here? My, my, what will people think?"

"Not with me, stupid," I say, struggling to keep my eyes open. "I meant here in the brothel."

"Yes." He tucks his hair beneath his cap. "Stay here and get better. We need you, Mags. You have no idea how much."

And then he's gone, the door closing behind him with a click that only sounds like weeping.

Jack Sprat's wife grows fat
For Jack is nimble but not so quick.
He trips and stumbles in the dark
And she eats all but his candlestick.

— CHAPTER SEVEN —

I'm sitting on the floor of what I'm beginning to consider my room. It's a dangerous thought to have because Moon Children don't own anything. If I'm not careful I'll start thinking I'm an actual person. And yet, here I am, hunched over a book and pretending the squiggles make sense.

"Mags?" Dr. Barrows taps me gently on the shoulder to bring me back from my reverie.

Frustrated, I turn the book around so it's upside down, but the words aren't any clearer. "We've been at this for hours."

He turns his mild gaze to his cup of chai. "It's been thirty-five minutes, Mags."

I scowl. "Well it feels like days." My stitches itch, and I slap at them. "It's been nearly a week as it is. When will you take these out, anyway?"

He sips his tea and scratches something out in his moleskin notebook. "When you've made some progress."

"How can I make progress when I'm itching all the time?"

He peers at me from behind his glasses, his golden eyes gleaming with humor or anger. I'm not sure which. I'm not sure it really matters. He doesn't say anything, though. Just stares at me until heat rushes over my face.

I shift my body so my back is to him. Let him stare at my bony shoulders, then.

The dragon coils about my neck. I flick it a piece of coal from the bin, letting it munch until its metal body grows uncomfortably warm and I dump it in front of the fireplace. I shove the sweaty tangle of hair from my face and try again.

Yesterday was spent practicing the alphabet, and my fingers are still cramping from the awkward way I held the pencil. After hours of repetition, I'd finally managed to scrawl a reasonable suggestion of my name, though the piles of wasted scrap parchment threaten to overtake the bin beside the fireplace.

Today it's all symbols—the tattoo calling cards of Meridian medical practitioners. Dr. Barrows still hasn't tattooed me yet, which I find a tad suspect, but maybe he'll do it when he takes the stitches out. The symbols on the pages themselves are brilliant works of art, a riot of fancy colors and intricate line work: trees, leaves, flowers, fantastical beasts. Some of them are so small and fine it seems nearly impossible to imagine them being tattoos at all.

Only a Meridian would flaunt their injuries in such a way. Only they would have the time to etch such memories into their skin. All the BrightStone bonewitches have simple marks. A cluster of dots or wavy lines. Certainly not more than one color. They are meant for patients who cannot read and don't have time to learn. As systems go, it works. Even the bonewitches themselves don't mind it. Circumstances being what they are, maybe going by names like Three-Line Sally or Half-Cross Jimmy makes it easier to hide from whoever they had been.

Once I established with Dr. Barrows that I was already quite familiar with such mundane BrightStone marks, we moved on to the Meridian designs. The one I'm studying now is surprisingly simple: three black dots, so small and close together that they are barely separate shapes. It's out of place among the others with their extravagant flourishes and rich colors.

I frown. "Whose is this? I've seen it before."

He peers over my shoulder. "Ah. I doubt that."

"You think I'm lying?"

"I think you believe you have seen it, but that particular mark hasn't been used on Meridion for nearly twenty years." He picks up the pencil to begin sketching something in the margin of the book. "Undoubtedly, there are those who would have attempted to fool their patients, but the woman who used it actually hid an additional pattern in the ink that can only be seen beneath a special light."

He shows me the page where he's drawn a series of lines around the dots so that it has become a circle, or maybe a cog. "This is the mark of Madeline d'Arc."

My ears prick up, remembering the overheard conversation between him and Molly from the other evening. I shift away from him, fighting the urge to cover my chest with my arms. "The original Meridion architect? But she's—"

"Gone. Yes," he interrupts. "You've heard of her, then?"

Of course I have. Most Moon Children may not be literate, but we know that much of our history, or at least whatever bits and pieces we were able to pick up on the streets. Rumors had a way of changing almost hourly, but some things remained consistent.

"Aye," I say. "She created Meridion."

He nods. "In a manner of speaking. She created many of the mechanisms that allow it to fly, it's true, but she also made many advances in surgical techniques, most of which have never been able to be repeated. But the day Meridion's engines stopped, she disappeared without a trace."

"Stopped, aye?" I flick my gaze out the window. "Seems to float up there well enough to me."

"Floating isn't flying," he points out. "Without the anchors keeping the city in place, Meridion would drift away. I'm not sure there's even a proper way to steer it at this point. At any rate, we have no idea what happened to d'Arc." He glances up at me. "I don't suppose you do?"

I scrunch up my face. "Why would you expect me to? She disappeared before I was born."

"Well, that's the rub, isn't it?" He cups my chin for a moment. "Why do you wear her work upon your chest?"

"The tattoo, you mean? I don't have that."

"Don't play dumb. I took a close look at it when I stitched you up. The panel on your chest? It's a clockwork heart, Mags, and it's one of the main reasons you didn't die the other night. It kept beating far longer than any regular heart would have." He shakes his head at me. "The Meridians create many mechanical wonders, but there is not a one of them able to make working metal organs."

I still. "I've always had it. For as long as I can remember."

"Your mother never told you?" His eyes narrow sharply at me. "I find that a bit hard to believe."

"She died giving birth to me," I grind out. "I already told you I don't know. What else would you have me say?"

The truth of it is that I *don't* know. Mad Brianna half raised me with all the other orphans she'd kept and never enlightened me as to its appearance except to tell me not to show it to anyone. Getting a straight answer from her these days is an impossibility, too. I can get better counsel from a cat.

I pull the collar of my shirt down, inviting him to take a closer look. My fingers trace the outline of the heart-shaped panel. "I tried taking this off once, but it hurt something awful. I think it will stop functioning if it's opened, but I mean, there's curiosity and there's cats, aye?" I shrug. "Tell you what, though... If I expire before this little excursion to the Pits takes place, you've my permission to slice me open and figure out how it works."

Frustration flashes in his eyes at my jest, but he retreats to his chair with a sigh. "Forgive me. It's been so long since we've seen any evidence of her existence. And to find it on a Moon Child doesn't make a bit of sense."

"No doubt. Why waste such technology on someone like me, right?" I stare at the dragon. *My dragon.* A roll of satisfaction thrums through me at the thought, though I can't truly claim ownership. Whatever mechanics drive it to motion, it's become more than clear that it does so on its own power.

Dr. Barrows shakes his head, his face stricken. "That's not what I meant."

"Yes, it is." I give him a hard smile, all too familiar with this sort of bias. I tap on the design on the page in front of me, determined to pull the conversation from the morbid turn it's taken. "I mean, if you need special light for this, what's the use? I've seen three dots like this before on injuries."

"Oh, I'm sure there are many who have attempted to use that mark to bilk people into paying more than they should," he agrees. He sips his chai again, but he's stalling now. I set the book down and stare at him until he's forced to look at me, his mouth compressing.

"D'Arc," he says finally. "She was a brilliant doctor, and I have no doubts she was working on some way to unravel the secrets of this plague. None. Things were very…chaotic, before she disappeared. It is my personal hope that you might find traces of her work in the Pits. Or of any of these doctors, for that matter. Something to give us clues as to how all this came about. I don't know where else they would have disappeared to."

His words linger like a fever dream, nearly tangible in their temptation. And it's all the worse because I want to believe him. That secret sorrow of his seems to deepen the lines on his face, and whatever he thinks he's trying to do, I can tell that somewhere along the way his past is tangled with this disease. Perhaps a family member got it when he was a child. Maybe a wife.

Not that it's any of my concern anyway.

He gives me a wry half smile. "It sounds so simple, doesn't it?"

"Not really, no." I scowl.

He laughs despite his apparent distress. I'm wavering on his words, but I haven't lived this long on the streets to not recognize a shill when I see one. I open my mouth to snarl something rude at him, but the sudden peal of bells from outside stops me cold, my blood freezing in my veins.

A Tithe procession.

Dr. Barrows says nothing as I stand. I don't want to look. Not really. And yet my feet pull me toward the little window beside the fireplace as I bite down on my lower lip. Below is the alley behind the Conundrum, but the street beyond that is the main thoroughfare through Market Square. I can't see the square, but I know it will be empty. The bells herald a warning, and only the very desperate or stupid would remain to watch the Tithe.

I stare at the open spot at the end of the alley. Inquestors flank the procession to ensure no one runs, but even from this distance I can see no one is attempting to escape. A Moon Child leads the way, her head bowed as she rings the bells hanging on a leather strap at her waist.

I clench my jaw against my fury. I can't tell who it is from here, but her pale hair blows freely in the breeze. She's dressed in a simple gown. Behind her trail those unfortunates who recently contracted the Rot, their white masks covering their faces. And yet for all that, it robs them of their dignity. Cowards, all of us, unable to look upon the fates of others, and only because we have some misguided hope that we might avoid the same.

In another moment, the procession is gone, but the bells continue to echo through the streets, and the sound mocks me.

Dr. Barrows closes the book and lays it on the table beside my bed. "I think that's plenty for one day."

I lean against the wall as I face him. "Why?"

"Well, I assumed you might want to—"

"To what? Mourn?" The anger gnaws at my insides, and I point out the window. "What good does pissing and moaning do? How does that help us? How will it help *her*?"

"It doesn't," he admits, handing me the book again. "As to—"

A knock on the door interrupts whatever he's about to say, and he nearly sags with relief as Ghost enters the room.

The other Moon Child glances at the book I'm holding, a smirk twisting his lips when he sees the tattoos, but there's no humor in it. "The Tithe... It's Penny."

I gasp, despite my efforts to contain myself. "Penny? But she's second-in-command among the Banshees. Rory would never have sent her if he had a choice." I swallow hard against a sudden wave of sadness. Or maybe it's guilt. It's certainly realization. Inquestor Caskers must have demanded her as part of his recompense for what I've done.

I drop the book and lurch to my feet, unable to look at it any longer. My fine words to Dr. Barrows mock me, but it had been easier to bear when I didn't know who it was.

The dragon alights on my shoulder, and I pull on my coat. Well, it's one of Dr. Barrows's throwaways, like his shirt, but I've come to think of it as mine.

"You can't possibly be thinking of going out now—in the daylight." Dr. Barrows frowns at me. "And surely not with the dragon."

"I know better than you how to move about without being seen," I snap, pulling the large hood up so it covers both me and the dragon. "Don't fret yourself about it."

"But—"

"I'm not some servant to do all you bid. 'Tis Moon Child business. That's all you need to know." The fact that he's probably right only irritates me further, but I've already lost Sparrow. I may not be a clan member anymore, but Penny was my friend. I owe it to her to bear witness.

And perhaps a bit of solid reconnaissance is in order. I've never watched a Tithe with anything other than fear or sorrow; if I'm truly going to be placing myself in this position, I need to watch it with a fresh set of eyes.

"I'll go with her." Ghost gives me a half smile. I can't tell if he's humoring Dr. Barrows or mocking me, and I don't much care. It's not for me to tell him no. He's a Moon Child, too, after all.

I weigh my chances of fitting through the window without tearing my stitches, but Ghost gestures for me to follow him. "We can take the servants' stairs. No one will bother us there."

Dr. Barrows snorts, but he lets us go and we shut the door behind us. I haven't actually seen much of the brothel, except for the water closet at the end of the hall, my room, and the bar. Far below, I can hear the distant sounds of merrymaking of one type or another as Ghost leads me down to the first landing and through a nondescript door into a narrow set of windowless passages. A few flickering light bulbs illuminate our way.

"This floor belongs to the working girls," he says suddenly, as though to fill the silence with something other than the sigh of our breath. "Their private rooms, I mean. They do their actual...work in specialty rooms on the first floor. Honestly, the only other things worthy of note are the kitchens and the baths below."

My eyes widen. "There's a bathhouse here?"

"It's mostly for customers, but Molly overlooks the times I've used it, as long as I'm discreet. Probably wouldn't do much for business if people knew Moon Children were washing in it."

"Even the baths are full of secrets," I mutter.

He chuckles. "Ah, well. That's her business, isn't it?"

"Never thought about it, I suppose. I've always been too busy looking for my next meal to worry about intrigue." I say it matter-of-factly. There's no shame in being hungry.

He mulls this over for a bit, even as we exit through the kitchens and out the side door into the alley where Sparrow and I were ambushed not so long ago. Daylight does nothing to improve its looks. I sigh when Ghost tugs on my coat, my chest aching with the memory of Sparrow's face.

We cling to the shadows as we emerge from the alley. Market Square is normally bustling with activity, but the streets are mostly empty, leaving us more exposed than I'd like. The dragon squirms restlessly upon my shoulder, and I give it a gentle poke, ignoring the way it gnaws on my knuckle.

We'll have time to make it to the entrance of the Pits without much trouble given the Inquestors insist the Tithes wend their way through much of city, to remind us of what they protect us from.

We take the side streets, cutting through Prospero's Park along the way. It's a small bit of space, crowned by the tattered remains of a garden long since dead. All that's left now are a few stone benches and a headless statue overgrown with vines of a dubious nature.

The silhouette of the town hall lurks over the park, and beyond that, the Mother Clock stands like a skeletal crone in a cape of blackened bricks and skinny windows the color of burnished gold. One of the tallest structures of BrightStone, the Mother Clock shadows some part of the city at all times, like the center of a sundial. The Tithe processions start from her courtyard before spiraling through the city in its offering of flesh and sickness.

Ghost and I head for Blessing Bridge, sneaking through the tent city without issue and into the Warrens proper. I pull my hood closer to my face. Whether Rory thinks I'm dead or not, I was cast out from the Banshees. Without clan protection, I'm trespassing in their territory.

I look to the rooftops, feeling very much a target as I trudge along the greasy cobblestones. Imagined stares make me fidgety, and the dragon nips me again when I shift my shoulders. If there are other Moon Children about, they aren't making themselves known, and that's probably just as well.

The Tithe bells continue to ring on and on; the very bricks are weeping with the echoing sound. Ghost pauses at a street corner to peer into the fog and then waves me forward to settle into a hiding spot behind a stack of broken barrels. The gated entrance to the Pits looms before us, glowing red beneath the guttering torches. For all the rust in the Warrens, these gates are all the more terrifying with their carved beauty and well-oiled hinges.

In the distance, the Tithe marches up the street. I suppress a shudder when I see Penny at the front of the procession. Her head is still bowed, as though she can't bear to look where she's walking, the bells dangling from her crippled hand.

The Tithers flank her on either side, dressed in their crimson Inquestor robes and pale bird masks. The long, curved beaks make them look like ethereal crows ready to pluck the eyes from the damned. At the end of the line are a pair of gray-cloaked salt priests, sprinkling a trail of purified sea salt upon the cobblestones and calling out their prayers to any who might be listening.

I doubt it's any great comfort, though. Certainly not to those in the procession. It's awful enough to know you've contracted an incurable disease, and even more so when the rest of BrightStone thinks you deserve it because you've sinned, maybe gambled too much or took a lover.

The Tithe procession slows here, three Inquestors peeling away from their charges to man the gate. A heavy, ornamental lock rests on the entrance, but it's all for show. The real lock is a series of winches somewhere high above, only accessible via the Inquestor airships. A scout ship is docked there now, drifting softly against the tower.

Penny has stopped ringing the bells and is clenching the strap in her fist. The Inquestor at the lock motions above him, signaling the crew in the airship. The winches creak softly until the gate opens with a whine.

Behind Penny, the Rotters begin to moan; panic and fear and despair fill the voices behind the masks. The Tithers are well prepared, armed with Tithe wands, copper batons that crackle with arcs of silver electricity at the press of a button.

I shift in the coat, steeling myself against what comes next.

It's almost always the same. No matter how cowed the Rotters are, one or two try to run. They never escape, the electric leashes nabbing a limb or a neck, forcing them to their knees or facedown in the street, bodies flailing in uncontrollable shudders.

This time is no different.

Penny remains still among the sudden outburst of movement. No Moon Child has ever attempted to run with the others, but it's hard to flee when the Tithers have drugged you out of your mind to keep you docile.

I've often wondered why they don't do the same for the Rotters, if only to spare them the horror of their own existence. But I suppose that would be a mercy, in its own way, and the last thing the Inquestors ever show is mercy.

The Mother Clock clangs out the midday hour with a finality that cannot be denied. Inside my coat, the dragon lets out an answering rumble, the sound lost in the vibration of the metallic *bong-bong-bang* of the clock.

The Inquestors round up the last of the stragglers, using their electric prods to force the miserable lot past the gates. Penny waits until they're through, staring past them hollowly as the Tither pulls Penny's hair from her neck to observe her clan brand, writing her number down in the Tithe roster. He takes her wrist and undoes the strap, his mask pointing at the entrance.

Her nostrils flare wide, and then she flees into the darkness with the others, a pale, graceful bird set free into the gaping maw of a monster whose belly will never be filled.

With the Tithe complete, the Inquestors linger only to lock the gates before heading to their private quarters on the far side of BrightStone. The rest of the citizens gradually emerge from their doorways and hiding spots. For all their quiet now, the pubs and brothels will be packed tonight, filled with people trying to forget. The salt priests can mumble on about vice all they like, but some nights only a stiff drink and an even stiffer shag will wipe away the horror.

I scowl, restless with anger and sadness. Ghost and I cross over Blessing Bridge toward the Market Square. I've no strong urge to return to Dr. Barrows and my lessons. Jamming my hands deep into my coat pockets, I'm pleasantly surprised to find a sixpence.

Ghost watches bemusedly when I stop by a street vendor for a cigarillo before ducking into an alley. I tweak the dragon's tail, and its mouth opens to let out a surprised puff of flame, lighting the twisted bit of paper. "There's a love."

I take a deep pull and offer it to Ghost, but he waves it away. I shrug. More for me. My feet burrow a trail in the muck as I pace, trying to smoke the cigarillo slowly but failing miserably.

It's nothing but an ashy memory a few minutes later, leaving my fingers empty and twitching. After being cooped up in that little room so long now, I'm nearly trembling with the need to run.

I imagine that for a brief moment, letting the distant promise of Meridion slip away. What loyalty do I truly owe Molly or the doctor? For a few meals and some bonewitchery, the Pits are a rather steep price to pay.

Ghost lets out a quiet sigh. "Trouble coming our way. Don't look up."

A pair of Inquestors glide up the street, red robes contrasting brightly against the backdrop of the crowd. No Tithe masks, so they're regular patrols. I try not to tense, and they pass us by without incident.

I watch them go with relief, my thoughts continuing to patter between running away and making a stand. I glance sideways at Ghost and shake my head. "It occurs to me that the Pits used to be a mine, aye? I suppose it's too much to hope any of you might have a map of the underground? Might make escaping a bit easier if I have the lay of the land, so to speak."

He frowns thoughtfully. "Not that I know of. Most of the records from that time seem to have disappeared."

"Be a damn sight more useful than memorizing bonewitch marks," I mutter. "Come on. I've an idea of someone who might know something."

"Where are we going?"

"The museum. Sparrow and I used to go there when we needed to lie low." A raw sadness flushes through me. *Used to.* Only a few weeks ago we'd crashed there one rainy evening, looking through picture books stored away in the attic.

"I never really took you for being scholarly, Mags."

"Just because I can't read doesn't mean I'm stupid," I snap. "Besides no one ever thinks to look for us there."

His cheeks redden. "I'm sorry. That was wrong of me."

"Aye." I turn away, storming my way into a crowd of people on the street.

"Hey, watch where you're going!" Something large slams into my shoulder, shoving me back into the alley and knocking me down hard enough that my hood slips off. The dragon tumbles down the inside of my cloak, its claws catching on the back of my shirt. The stitches in my side burn sharply, leaving me gasping as I struggle to my feet.

"You're supposed to be dead," a familiar voice hisses in my ear. Rory.

"Well, fuck," I mutter, pulling the hood partially over my head as quick as I can.

"Fuck, indeed," he snarls. "They made me give up Penny to the Tithe. *Because of you.* You couldn't keep from sticking your nose where it didn't belong, and now she's gone." His voice shakes as he says it, from anger or sadness or some mix of the two.

An answering twinge of guilt punches me hard in the gut, but I raise my chin all the same, refusing to look away. "Yes, she is. Just like Sparrow." My lower lip trembles, and it's hard to get the words out because Penny didn't deserve this, either. "And whose fault is that?"

A soft scuff above me indicates Ghost's presence. He must have climbed the walls as soon as he saw Rory. To an outsider it might seem like cowardice, but I suspect it's more about practicality. It's for the best anyway. This is between Rory and me; Ghost doesn't need to be part of it.

His eyes narrow. "And yet here you are."

I let out a bitter laugh. "And where else would I be? You think that just because I somehow managed to survive a knife between my ribs, I should come crawling back to the clan that cast me out? You really think you command that level of loyalty anymore?"

I advance on him until he's pressed up against the wall, anger boiling white-hot beneath my skin. "You made your position perfectly clear that night when you let the Inquestors take me and Sparrow. Now let me make mine clear to you: I lost the only person I've ever truly loved because you were too chickenshit to do your duty to your clan. You abandoned us, and therefore, we're no longer your concern."

I flick him in the nose with my fingers, and his head snaps back as though he's been slapped. I watch him, nearly dizzy with all this sadness and fury and frustration at the unfairness of Sparrow's death, not to mention the unknown situation I'm now in. It's so much easier to take it out on the man before me, to focus my wrath upon him.

But Rory is a coward, and we both know it. Unused to having his clan talk back to him, it takes him a moment to regain his composure. His hands have tightened into fists, but he makes no move to strike. Something unreadable washes over his face, as though he's weighing his options.

I brace myself for an attack, but he merely nods. When he speaks, his voice has a quiet darkness to it, a bit of fear threading its way through his words, undermining any threat he attempts to make. "Fair enough. We're finished here. But if I catch you in the Warrens again, Raggy Maggy, I'll kill you. Permanently, this time."

Before I can respond, he's gone, briskly heading toward the street only to be swept up into the remainder of the crowd.

"Charming. Slugs never stop leaving slime behind them," I murmur at his retreating back.

"Remind me never to get on your bad side." Ghost slides out from around a dormer window, easily landing beside me. "He nearly pissed himself. Do you think we can trust him to keep his mouth shut?"

"Maybe. He's hurting a lot over Penny. Not sure he wants any more scrutiny from the Inquestors at the moment, but I wouldn't be placing any wagers on it. I'll have to be more careful about where I go."

I say this with more confidence than I actually feel. Rory being aware of my circumstances is bad news. But short of killing him outright, there wasn't anything I could really do about it, and murder isn't exactly on my repertoire of skills. I say as much to Ghost, and he shrugs.

"You seem like you can handle yourself. Besides, I doubt the Inquestors will be too keen on having their shortcomings pointed out—if they even believe him. Admitting that they failed to kill an injured Moon Child isn't exactly something to be proud of. The High Inquestor isn't known for being a patient man."

I shift in the cloak until the dragon is back on my shoulder. "Point taken. Just don't tell Dr. Barrows. If I have to listen to another of his lectures I'm going to brain him."

He smirks, falling into line beside me as we join the rest of the crowd trailing out of the Warrens. "Deal."

The BrightStone Museum is a pillared monstrosity, perched on a series of thick marble steps leading to a set of metal doors flaked with rust. Being this close to the river means the brine and stink of the water tends to eat through anything that isn't sealed properly.

Not that it matters. Most of the artifacts are imprisoned behind thick glass, untouchable.

Ghost starts for the steps, but I tug on his sleeve. "Not that way."

"We don't have to sneak in. There's no admission fee." He frowns. "Are they even open?"

"They close during the Tithes. But it's the principle of thing. Besides, Sparrow and I had a private entrance." I lead him to the rear of the place, eyeing the rooftop dubiously. "Of course, we have to be up there to get in."

He rolls his eyes at the broken fire escape ladder and cups his hands. "I'll boost you up."

It rankles my pride, but I lean on his shoulders to step onto his palms. My stitches pull when I raise my arms to hoist myself to the lowest level of the fire escape. He braces my feet on his shoulders and lifts me higher until I'm able to wriggle over the railing.

He follows suit, scaling the wall with an easy grace.

I pull back my hood when we reach the top landing, shaking my hair free. The dragon shifts, its wings unfolding with a soft whir. I creep sideways onto the window ledge next to the fire escape, and then the one after that. I stop at the third window and give the lower sash an experimental push. It slides open easily, and I gesture to Ghost before scrambling inside.

The museum's attic is as Sparrow and I left it, full of broken artifacts and worn-out furniture. The air is thick with a musty dampness that clings to the skin and coats the pages of the few picture books I've tucked in the moldy cushions of a sagging couch.

I study a crumbling map spread over the largest table with a bittersweet smile. It's an aerial view of BrightStone and one that I'm most familiar with. I trace my finger over the Everdark River, winding through the city and out to the sea.

"So that's your secret for moving across the rooftops so quickly," Ghost muses. "I don't think I've seen a map quite this detailed anywhere else."

"I like it because it shows BrightStone before the Rot. Before the fire that took out the Warrens. I always try to line up the ruins with this, imagining what it must have been like. How things might be different today." I snort ruefully. "Of course, it's a wee bit out-of-date. Took a few close calls in dead-end alleys to get me to be more careful about trusting all of it."

Ghost grimaces at the bedraggled feathers of a stuffed bird, its moth-eaten body nearly tipping off its rusted brass perch. He touches it bemusedly, watching as a pinion disintegrates beneath his fingers. "I'm not sure this species even exists anymore."

"It's a museum. Lots of stuff here doesn't exist anymore." I pause for a moment. "Sparrow named that thing Hideous Lydia. Said it reminded her of those wretched feather hats Lady Lydia wears when she sets up those donation tables in the square." As Lord Balthazaar's wife, she always had her pet projects, but it's easy to pretend to be a philanthropist when your family controls nearly the entire food supply in and out of the city.

"She wasn't wrong," Ghost says. "At least the feathers of this bird look like they belong there." He brushes the dust off a pile of books, peering at their titles. "Molly says Lydia's caught the Rot." He sneezes. "And that's why Lord Balthazaar said she lost her child."

I glance up at him, frowning. "I don't understand."

"He told the masses she was pregnant, and then she conveniently started an extended mourning period after giving birth to a stillborn baby. Dr. Barrows argues the point with Molly all the time, but the running theory is that she really has the Rot and instead of Tithing her, Balthazaar's hidden her away somewhere."

The dragon leaps from my shoulders to glide across the room to the top of a large bookshelf filled with jars of preserved rat fetuses. "What difference does it make?" I ask. "It's got naught to do with us."

"Perhaps. Perhaps not. If such a thing were true, undoubtedly Lord Balthazaar would go to great pains to hide it from the general populace," he points out. "He may be the main food importer in BrightStone, but no one will buy his stock if it's suspected there's plague in his household."

I pace by the window and freeze when I see a flash of red below. I gesture at Ghost, and he swears softly, watching as an Inquestor takes a position beneath the fire escape.

"Pretty pickle." I sigh. "Where's there one, there are at least two. If they saw us climb the escape, they'll be up here quick. Come on."

The door handle rattles, and I duck beneath a dusty table. Ghost twists to the far window, taking refuge behind a curtain.

"—and I assure you, we have no such riff-raff in here," a female voice says loudly.

A smile creeps over my face. Archivist Chaunders isn't one for putting up with nonsense from anyone, least of all the Inquestors. She bustles into the room, her long amber skirts swirling. An Inquestor shoves past her, ignoring the way her lips press into a narrow line.

"Don't touch anything," she snaps. "Most of these items are priceless and deserve to be treated with respect."An incredulous snort from the Inquestor is the only response, and she reddens. "Just because you hold yourselves as our betters doesn't mean BrightStone's history isn't important."

"A treasury of knowledge, to be sure." His gaze rakes the shadows, and I hold my breath. "And you might show a little respect of your own, mistress. A concerned citizen indicated a pair of miscreants was seen entering this establishment from the upper window. I'd be remiss in my duty if I failed to investigate the possible presence of thieves."

Her jaw tightens. "As you will, then."

I ease back to rest on the balls of my feet, every muscle freezing as the Inquestor slows when he reaches the bookshelf.

Oh shit. The dragon. I've left it out in the open.

"What's this?" The Inquestor raises a finger to poke at it. It doesn't move, but the barest trace of smoke feathers up from its nostrils.

Archivist Chaunders cocks her head around his shoulder, her brows drawn and heavy. "We haven't had time to catalog that one yet, so I can't give you any details on it."

He raises a brow, clearly not convinced. She lurches forward suddenly, clutching at his arm so they're both slightly off-balance.

"Clumsy me," she says, patting his arm. "Here now. Since you're so interested in this piece, let me clean it up for you and find out what I can about it. Next time you return I'll tell you what I've discovered."

He looks over at the shelf, but the dragon is gone, and he shakes his head. "But…"

"No 'buts' about it, young man. I'd be remiss from *my* duty if I didn't give you a full report on its historical significance. Undoubtedly an allegorical reference to IronHeart, taken form in bronze sculpture."

"There was smoke coming from its nose."

"Aye, well. It's not that hard to create the effect if you have the right tools." She pulls her goggles over her eyes. The right one twists as though it's focusing on something only she can see and scans the room.

She hesitates only briefly when her field of vision crosses my table and Ghost's curtain, but she passes us by. "There. I've scoped the place out and can tell you whatever you've heard, no one is in here now. Perhaps they've already left again?"

He backs up a step to peer out the window, signaling to his compatriot below with a salute. "Not likely."

"I know a lot, boy. I've been around far longer than your city's arrival, and I expect to be here when you're finally gone." She taps her goggles. "These can read nearby body heat, and I assure you, it's not picking up anything but the two of us."

My thighs are beginning to cramp, and I shift in my coat so that I'm leaning against the table leg.

But the archivist is already ushering the Inquestor out. "Believe me, I'm very grateful you're looking out for our artifacts. Can you imagine if some of these got into the wrong hands? Just think…"

The door shuts behind them, her nattering voice fading. I ease onto my knees, ears pricked in case the Inquestor decides to reappear. The curtain twitches a moment later, and Ghost's face peeks out.

"That was close," he whispers. "Dr. Barrows was right about that dragon, Mags. You have to keep it under wraps or you risk bringing everything down."

"It's not like I knew they would come up here." I crawl out from beneath the table. "Concerned citizen, my ass. I suspect this was Rory's parting shot." I let out a quick whistle, my heart sinking when there's no response. "Where the hells did it go?"

"She must have taken it." Ghost rubs his face. "We're going to have to get it back somehow."

"I'll manage it. There's a room downstairs where they catalog artifacts for research. She'll have taken it down there. We can steal it back." His brows raise at me and I shrug. "Used to sneak in and look at the exhibits in the middle of night. Besides, rooting around in the slag heaps means trying to figure out how much our finds were worth. If I could prove what it was, then Rory would have more justification in setting the price."

A smile crosses over his face. "You're a surprising person, Mags."

"Why? It's not like anyone else will teach us anything of their own accord. You think I'd let a locked door stop me from taking a peek?"

"Indeed I did." I whirl as Archivist Chaunders opens the door to fix me with an exasperated stare. "And by all rights I should have let him find you."

"We were sloppy," I admit. "And I don't move as fast as I used to at the moment." I pull up my shirt to show her my stitches.

Her face softens, the gray hair frizzy beneath the goggles now pushed onto her forehead. "That was bad business there, Maggy. I'm sorry about Sparrow."

Ghost does a double take. "You know each other, I gather?"

I give him a sour grin, and the archivist laughs. "Yes. Maggy and Sparrow would bring me interesting things they'd find, and in return I let them hide out here from time to time." She gives the bookshelves a fond look. "It made for fine entertainment on rainy days, I imagine."

I flush. "Where's the dragon?"

She pats her shawl with a gloved hand. "Hiding in here apparently. It's a rather tenacious little thing, isn't it?"

Reaching behind her shoulders, she gives an odd wriggle and pulls the dragon from beneath the shawl. It leaps to the bookshelf for a moment before taking to the air to find my shoulder again.

"Isn't that interesting?" The archivist's steely eyes find mine and she pins me beneath a gimlet stare. "I'm not even sure I really want to know where you found it, but I'd be especially careful, Maggy. The Inquestors may only be attempting to protect the secrets of Meridian inventions, but I wouldn't risk being seen with one."

"You know what it is?" Ghost stares at the archivist. "What it's used for?"

She shrugs. "It's one of d'Arc's inventions. Or Meridian spies, or ways of communication between the Inquestors and those on Meridion. Or they are IronHeart's children, looking for their lost creator." A wry smile crosses her face. "Any theory might be right, so take your pick."

IronHeart.

The words chill me, and I fight the urge to touch my clockwork heart. What if Dr. Barrows is right? I have no memory of where the heart came from. And if d'Arc built it, why do I have it?

"'Ware IronHeart's breath and IronHeart's claws, for when IronHeart roars, Meridion falls," I mutter, almost like a warding prayer. I'm not superstitious, but the familiar words feel somehow darker, all the same.

Ghost rolls his eyes at me. "IronHeart is a metaphor."

"Is it?" The archivist points at my dragon. "Be careful about dismissing metaphors, my lad. Sometimes they have a way of sneaking up on you and biting you in the ass." She stills. "I take it this isn't a social visit?"

"I need to find out about the Pits," I say, ignoring the warning look Ghost shoots me. "Are there any old maps? Maybe in the archives?"

"Well there's certainly nothing available on public display," she says, but she opens the door to the main hallway and ushers us through. I already know my way around, so I take the lead down the first set of stairs, Ghost trailing behind.

The museum is made up of three floors, but only the first two are actually used for the display of artifacts available to the public. A central, shared space pillars each floor, so that you can peer over the railing at the visitors below. The skull of some enormous ocean beast hangs from thick wires, its mouth wide enough to swallow us whole as we pass by. It looms over the entirety of the museum proper, the blackness of its eye sockets seeming to swallow the shadows.

I glance behind me to see Ghost standing before a bit of parchment enclosed in glass. His mouth is drawn into a tight line, and I retreat to stand beside him, peering over his shoulder. "What is it?"

"A time line," Archivist Chaunders notes, her wrinkled face growing dreamy, the way it always does when she's warming to a subject. "This one shows us the details of when BrightStone converged with Meridion."

"Ancient history," Ghost scoffs. "The floating city showed up here twenty-five years ago and never left, slowly placing BrightStone beneath its rule and using the plague as an excuse to close it off from the outside world." He says it matter-of-factly, reciting it in a singsong voice.

Archivist Chaunders smirks. "Someone's been studying *D'Arc's Manifesto*, have they?"

He ducks, flushing. "My...mother used to read it to me," he says smoothly, as though realizing he's said too much.

I crane my head over the archivist's shoulder, straining to figure out the numbers. The time line stretches across both pages, and the upper left corner has an etching of a winged dragon.

Year 1032. MF.

I see it but can't figure out what it means. Frustration grinds my belly. "What does it say?"

"MF is 'Meridion Founding.'" Ghost points to the tick mark. "Everything before that is BrightStone history only. Everything after is indicated by an MR for 'Meridion Rule.'"

"Very good." Archivist Chaunders is impressed. "And here at 1034 MR is when the Rot first appeared." Her face grows grim. "Didn't take them long to crack down on us after that. The Salt Diaspora occurred as a desperate measure to control the plague... and in 1036 MR, the Pits were founded."

I shudder, and the archivist smiles soothingly at me. "The Pits as they are now are not well-documented, I'm afraid, but we do have some basic maps of the original salt mines." She gestures for us to follow, continuing to chatter at us as we go.

"Of course, these drawings are at least twenty years old," she says, "and mines have a way of changing shape. Tunnels collapse, new caves are discovered. It's hard to say if the Pits bear any resemblance to them at all anymore."

"Someone must know," I insist as we come to a door.

Archivist Chaunders pulls a key from a ring hanging at her waist and fumbles with the lock. "You're right. Someone must," she agrees, fussing at a cabinet to retrieve a set of parchment scrolls. "The Meridians hired the same men who used to work the mines to build the Pits, digging through the rock to make whatever facilities the Meridians wanted."

"And we can't ask one of them?" I wonder aloud.

There's an odd tremble in the archivist's voice as she turns away. "No, dear. They're all dead."

I sip from the mug of steaming tea before me, nodding when Ghost holds out a few lumps of sugar. We're crouched at a cluttered table at the back of the records room, a struggling light bulb overhead bathing us in shadows every few seconds.

"There was an accident, you see," Archivist Chaunders says, her eyes distant. "Or that's what they called it. I never believed it, and neither did my mother. Or any of us with miners in the family, for that matter..."

"What happened?" Ghost prompts her after sharing a quiet look with me.

Archivist Chaunders sets down her mug. "Part of the mines collapsed. My father had said they were to be working on the last of it—a chamber that needed reinforcing." She shivers. "I was waiting for him by the entrance with some supper, as I always did. The explosion shook me off my feet, the ground rumbling like an earthquake. Smoke and dust were everywhere, coating the ground, my hair, the very air itself. I waited and waited, but he never came out. None of them did. The Meridians made a big show of rushing about, but it didn't matter by then."

A slow horror creeps over my skin, watching the expressionless bent of her face as she speaks. "I'm sorry. I didn't know."

"Why would you? There's nothing about it in the museum." She eyes the dragon on my shoulder sadly. "Just like there's nothing about clockwork dragons. I'm not allowed to talk about it or put anything about the Pits on display. I'm not even supposed to have the things in here that I do—those mine blueprints, the samples of Rot collected by the Salt Temple, the early interviews with the sick—but it's what I am." Her voice grows hard. "History is written by those in power, but there is always another perspective, even if it cannot be told. Never forget that."

Her eyes gleam as bright as an owl's, and she turns to Ghost. "And I think it's about time you both stopped playing games."

Ghost sets his cup down a little too quickly. "Your pardon?"

"I wasn't born yesterday," she says dryly. *"D'Arc's Manifesto* is forbidden reading material, and yet a Moon Child recites it to me as though it's nothing. Between that and the dragon and asking for blueprints of the mines..."

Ghost nudges me with his foot beneath the table, but I don't need the subtle reminder to tread carefully here. On the other hand, I've known the woman for far longer than I have Ghost or Dr. Barrows.

The dragon nips at my ear, and I reach up to stroke it, its thumping ember heart soothing against my fingers. "It's complicated."

"I'm sure." Her gaze darts between me and Ghost. "You're not doing what I think you're doing, are you?"

A cough escapes me. "Maybe. Probably. If you're thinking we're planning on sneaking me into the Pits to find evidence of a

Meridian conspiracy in the creation of the Rot, that is." I give her a forced half smile as something unreadable crosses over her face.

"I...see. Give me a moment." She whisks out the door then, leaving Ghost and me standing there holding the maps. I frown, unsure what she's about, but a minute later she reappears holding several battered notebooks.

"What's all this?" Ghost reaches for them, flipping through the pages with a bemused smile.

"If you're going to be trotting about the Pits for any length of time, you might want to give those a read," Archivist Chaunders says firmly. "These are my father's notes; there's a bit more to living underground than simply sneaking your way in." She presses her lips together for a moment. "I don't know what you'll find down there, but if you at least understand the basics of surviving in the dark..." Her voice trails away, and she swallows hard. "Might help your chances, anyway."

I glance over at the pages Ghost has open, spotting diagrams and charts and other assorted information that I will undoubtedly need help understanding. But still. I give her a lopsided smile, but she leans forward in an uncharacteristic rush of maternal concern, her hand brushing the hair back from my face.

"If you need help...anything at all," she says fiercely. "Please, please come to me. We'll figure something out."

I swallow the aching lump in my throat, scanning the shelves with their myriad artifacts. There's far more information here that might help our cause than I will ever be able to look through. But..."I will. And perhaps if a Dr. Barrows should come here, you might let him have a bit of a look around?"

Her gaze darts between me and Ghost and then comes to rest on the dragon, who preens upon my shoulder, ruffling its tiny claws in my pale hair. "Yes. If it means finding answers...? Yes, of course." The words slide out of her with a careful politeness, but beneath it all, I can sense anger at her past, a desperate need to know what happened. It slices through me, kindling an answering fire in kind, and for that brief span I can see her as the woman she had been, the lost look of terror upon her face.

I can hardly bear it.

"We should probably go." Ghost echoes the sentiment, clearly recognizing my restlessness.

"Aye," I say softly, pulling my hood up and tucking the dragon well into the cloth shadows. I cradle the scrolls against my chest, careful not to ruin the fragile parchment. "We'll be in touch soon."

Archivist Chaunders leads us to the exit at the back of the building and gives my hand a squeeze as Ghost and I slip out the door. "I look forward to it."

Blackbird, linnet bird, swallow, and swan
Where do you fly to, where have you gone?
My feathers have fallen, and my mate is long dead
The trees are all bare, and I have no bed.

— CHAPTER EIGHT —

O uch! Not so hard!"

"Then stop squirming, Mags. The more you move, the longer this is going to take," Dr. Barrows says with a long-suffering sigh.

I'm stretched out on the mattress, trying to ignore the tiny pricks from the tattoo gun. My freshly removed stitches sit on a tray resting on the nightstand, fraying bits of catgut looking like so many desiccated worms.

His tattooing is fast, as it should be. His glasses are pushed onto his brow, and his hands are steady as he manipulates the twin-coil tattoo gun with practiced ease. As tattoo equipment goes, it's a rather expensive piece of hardware, but it doesn't surprise me that he has one. Whatever his past, Dr. Barrows isn't some common bonewitch. He's been taught in a proper hospital, I'm sure of it.

"Nearly done," he murmurs.

On the other side of the room, Molly's face grows grim as Ghost relates what happened with the Inquestors at the museum. Her fan snaps out, and she taps her palm with it as she begins to pace. She pauses before the fireplace, baring her pointed teeth at the dragon lounging on the mantel. It puffs a smoke ring at her, and she snorts before turning to inspect the doctor's work on my rib cage.

"Gods, but you're a bony thing. Forget sneaking about in the shadows. Get any thinner and you'll be nothing more but a shadow yourself."

I shrug. "Think of all the money you're saving when you feed me."

"I'd save that much more if you weren't here at all," she grumbles. "And if you've led the Inquestors back to my door with today's foolishness..."

I let her words roll over me, familiar enough with her now to know most of this is bluster. The sooner she yells at me, the quicker she gets over it and the quicker we can move on.

Dr. Barrows wipes at the tattoo with an alcohol-soaked cloth, ignoring me when I mutter something rude at him. "You're all set. I'll give you a bandage to keep it covered for the next day or so. Try not to tear anything open in the meantime, yes?"

"Aye." I roll off my bed to inspect the tattoo in the standing mirror. His mark is a salmon, a tiny thing with scales of exquisite detail. Of all the tattoos I've received, this one stands out with a level of artistry none of my other marks remotely possess. I trace my fingers over it, remembering my studies of the Meridion doctor marks, and the realization hits me instantly.

He's a Meridian.

I nearly say it aloud, my tongue burning with the urge to set the words free. But what if I'm wrong? It's not the first time I've jumped to conclusions. His skin doesn't shine or shimmer like that of Architect Jacobs.

But still. All his seemingly innate knowledge of the Rot, his suspicions of the Meridians. Perhaps there truly is more to his intentions than simple rebellion. And more importantly, why is he here instead of on Meridion?

I tear myself away from the mirror to find Ghost leaning against the fireplace, his arms crossed. Molly shakes her head at him, and he open his mouth as though to snap at her. I wave my fingers at them to catch their attention.

"Listen, if you're that worried about the Inquestors finding us here, why not let Ghost and I leave altogether? Just to lie low for a day or so—I'm sure we can manage that much." My gaze flicks to Molly, but her mouth creases. Annoyance grinds in my guts, and I let my shirt drop, scowling at her. "I'm healed up now, and if we don't return here, well there's nothing to trace back to you, aye?"

Molly points her fan at me. "How do we know you won't run off and leave us in a lurch?"

"You don't," I state. "You just have to trust I have *some* honor, even being what I am."

Her lips stretch over her pointed teeth, leaving a smear of crimson across them. Lipstick surely, but the effect is as disturbing as if it were actual blood.

"Do you want me to find a way into the Pits or not?" I finally ask, frustration making my voice prickly. "Inquestors or no, Ghost and I turned up just fine. And I found us some maps."

The doctor glances sharply at Ghost. "Maps?"

I point to the mantel where I laid the scrolls earlier, my dragon watching over them with a guarded expression. "And notebooks written by one of the original miners. Forgot to mention that part of today's adventures." I nudge the dragon away from the mantel to retrieve them.

Ghost ducks his head beneath the doctor's sudden scrutiny, and I wonder at the annoyance in Dr. Barrows's eyes. Is it simple irritation at my words or something more?

"Mags had the idea of asking the archivist of the museum for maps of the Pits, or the mines beforehand as it turned out." Ghost takes the scrolls from me and hands them to Dr. Barrows.

"You discussed our plans with someone else?" Molly's worry lines deepen. "I knew this was a bad idea," she barks at the doctor. "You and your lofty ideals will bring this down upon our heads!"

I wave her off. "Archivist Chaunders knows me from long before this. I'd trust her with my life."

"Bully for you." Molly shakes her head. "I've no intention of trusting her with mine."

"She doesn't *really* know the details," Ghost says, as though to draw Molly's wrath away from me. It even works for a short moment as her fan flits out at him like the irritated twitch of a cat's tail.

"Except the bit about seeing the dragon," I say, unable to leave it alone.

Color flares in Molly's cheeks, and she storms from the room, the tension rolling about her in a thunderous miasma.

"Now you've done it." Dr. Barrows sighs, but he doesn't seem too put out by it. Instead, he unrolls the maps on the floor and kneels for a better look, making enthusiastic sounds in the back of his throat as he studies them. "The archivist, you say? I've never been able to get anything of real value from her—nothing she was willing to discuss with me, at any rate."

"Yes. I had an…an understanding of sorts with her. But she's willing to help you out some now, if you want to see what other information she has. She said something about a sample of the Rot, too."

His head jerks up, eyes burning with sudden interest. "Truly?"

"I told her you'd most likely stop by," I explain when his expression grows thoughtful. "Should be worth a few days on our own, right?"

He pauses. "Given what you've already managed to do, I'll admit it's tempting. But we can't just have you out there running wild. If you'd been caught today, we would have had no idea. And we've still a few additional lessons to cover."

A sigh escapes me, and I decide it's not worth fighting the point. It's not like he can really keep me here, anyway. If he wants to pretend otherwise, I'll let him for now.

"Fine. I'll spend some time looking over the maps, at least. But give me something else to read other than alphabet primers. Something with meaning... Something like *D'Arc's Manifesto*." I'm not even sure why I say it, except that Ghost has apparently read it and the fact that it's forbidden intrigues me. I'm tired of being fed answers without context.

Something odd flashes across his face, and he stiffens. "Out of the question. It will be too difficult for you, for one thing...and you're assuming I even possess a copy. Which I do not."

I suspect he's lying, but he rolls the maps back into tight scrolls and hands them to me before I can say anything else. "This was a brilliant idea, Mags. I truly mean that. Perhaps it is time to widen our nets as we search for answers. A pity there's so much risk involved."

"Information isn't worth anything if there's no risk to get it." I bristle, irritation making my temper prickle.

Ghost steps on my foot, interrupting me before I can say anything else. "If you really won't allow us to leave, at least give us the means to disguise ourselves." He runs a finger through his pale hair for emphasis and winks sideways at me. "Just in case."

Dr. Barrows gives Ghost a sour look but finally nods. "You're probably right. Haircuts and dye jobs, if nothing else. I'll have Martika see to it shortly."

Pale locks of hair shine in the basin where they fall, fluttering in time to the *snip, snip* of Martika's scissors behind me. My heart gives an awkward lurch when I see it, simply because it seems so wrong that it should be there. I shut my eyes against it, and Martika snorts.

"I didn't intend for you to shear me like a sheep," I grouse.

"Ah, well, there isn't enough of the dye to do all of it if we leave it the way it is."

I grow nervous as the pile grows thicker. "Stop. You're cutting it all." I glance in the mirror, not quite recognizing the face reflected there. My hair had reached my waist when it was loose, and now …

"I look like a lion dandy."

"Dandelion," Molly corrects me from the doorway, clearly amused at my discomfort. "I'm sure it will be fine once we darken it up some. And it's still long enough to cover that brand on your neck."

"If you say so." Martika stirs a paintbrush in a little pot of an oily liquid, and it oozes with a foul stench. My nose wrinkles. "Forget hiding. They'll smell us coming a mile away."

"They already could," Martika mutters under her breath, earning a dirty look from me. But she's started brushing the dye onto my hair, carefully working around the still healing wound where the bullet grazed my scalp.

"What's in that stuff?" I ask.

"It's ink," Martika says. "Now hold still, and keep your eyes closed. It will burn like the hells if any drips. Think we'll do your brows, too." The brush traces my eyebrows, pulling slightly. The acrid sting of the ink's odor makes my eyes water, and I blink against tears.

Sparrow and I tried dying our hair a few times, but boot black only lasts for a short while. Something about the texture doesn't want to hold color. Not to mention the Inquestors tend to frown on Moon Children hiding what we are; it usually meant a beating from Rory, at the very least.

"There now," Martika says. "Let's leave it wrapped up in that towel for a bit to give the ink time to set. You can open your eyes, Mags."

I do so, fighting the urge to shake like a dog. I reach up with my hands to rub at my brows, snarling when Martika gently slaps them away. "You'll smear it."

"This better work." I scowl at Ghost as he saunters in with a crooked smile and bangs of burnished chestnut. The tips of his fingers are stained and there's an ink smear on his chin, but he's otherwise unscathed.

"Where is Dr. Barrows?" I realize I haven't seen him in the last few hours.

"He's got his own duties to attend to," Martika interjects smoothly, and I catch a strange look between her and Molly.

More secrets, but I decide I won't worry about them now. Maybe Ghost will spill once we're alone.

A wet dribble of ink slides out from underneath the towel. "Is this nearly done?"

"Should be close enough." Martika waves me over to a steaming basin of water. "We'll need to squeeze out the excess."

I sit on the stool, nearly wriggling as she unwraps the towel and blots at my face before taking a comb to my still-damp hair. I catch a shadowed reflection in the mirror, and then Martika's body blocks my view as she fusses with my locks for a few minutes.

"Hmm. It doesn't appear to have taken all the way," she says, "but there's no more ink left to try it again."

"I've become a regular piebald pony for my troubles, aye?"

"It doesn't look bad. It's really just a stripe here in the front."

Ghost's mouth twitches. "Suppose that makes you more of a skunk or a badger, then. Suits your temperament better anyway." He easily avoids the comb when I chuck it at him.

I stand up to get a better look at the results. It takes me a minute to recognize my face. So long hidden by a tangle of milk-white hair, my chin and my cheeks jut from the shadows of a careless mop top of the deepest black that curves past my jaw and just below my shoulders. Well, except for the silver streak to the right, emerging from my bangs and tucking artfully behind my ear.

A lump grows in my throat. I can barely remember what color my hair was before the metamorphosis into Moon Child, but it doesn't really matter. For this moment I can only see what I might have been if the circumstances of my birth were different. The potential of finally being seen as an actual person looms in front of me with terrible clarity.

"Something wrong?" Molly cocks her head at me, breaking my stare.

"It's nothing." I suck in a deep breath and pretend to wipe at the stained skin at my hairline.

Martika gives me a satisfied nod, gathering her supplies. Copper Betty appears a moment later to help clean up, and all three women depart in silence.

Ghost lingers in my doorway as though struggling to find something to say. "It's only hair, you know. It will grow back."

"I know." I shake out my newly shortened tresses, disliking the lightness of it. Restless, I pace in front of the dying embers in the fireplace. "Feel a bit naked without it, is all."

"Wait here a moment." Ghost ducks out the door.

I continue to wear a trench in the floor, staring out the little window with increased longing. I need a place to think, somewhere that isn't constrained by this room and its walls and its secrets. I had pried the nails out of the windowsill days ago in a fit of boredom, and I slide the window open to let the cool winter air roll through the room and over my face.

The dragon lands on my shoulder, its sharp claws digging into my skin, and whirs a hot puff in my ear.

"Aye." An easy swing of my legs and I scramble to stand on the sill, using the brickwork and the shutters to clamber to the roof. I'm not dressed for the night chill, but goose bumps are a welcome distraction as I settle against the chimney.

My fingers twitch for a smoke, but I content myself with watching the fog drift past the waning moon.

"Are you up there, Mags?" Ghost's voice whispers up at me from the window.

I reply with a soft whistle when I hear him climb up to join me.

"You're going to have to teach me those signals," he says, squatting down to my level. "Much easier than using words."

"I suppose." I glance up at him. "Would have thought you'd have picked it up by now, lurking about in the shadows as you do."

"Some," he admits. "Enough for a vague understanding, but there are some I don't know." He lets out a questioning trill.

My mouth purses. I mimic it but draw out the last note a few seconds longer. "You have to roll your tongue at the end there."

He brightens and repeats it, doing better this time. "What's it mean?"

"It depends. Each clan has their own signals, though there are some that are the same no matter what clan you belong to: Danger. All clear. That kind of thing. And Sparrow and I had a few we just made up when we didn't want anyone else to know what we were doing. But in this case, you asked me if I fancied a shag," I deadpan.

A huff of laughter wheezes out of him. "Not something I would have guessed."

"Well, if I said no—" I let out a short piping *twwisht* "—probably not. But I'm pretty sure you'd figure it out if I were so inclined."

"No doubt," he counters, amusement lighting up his eyes. "I'll keep that one in mind for later, shall I?"

I snort, unsure if he's teasing me or actually inquiring. I suppress a shiver at the cold breeze sliding down the back of my shirt. For all my dislike of the Pits, I hate waiting even more. Frustrated, I tap my head on the back of the chimney. "Shagging aside, there's been too much talk and not enough action, if you ask me. I just want to get this over with. The sooner I'm down there, the sooner I'm back, aye?"

"You're not wrong," he concedes, staring into the distance. "There's one more piece of it, but we'll have to wait until tomorrow for me to show it to you."

"Do tell," I drawl, nudging him hard with my shoulders. "You're nearly as bad as Molly with your vague hints."

"I'm sorry. Old habits." He flushes, glancing down at his hands. "You remember I mentioned recruiting you to unite the Moon Child clans? The truth of it is, I've already started the process. At least with the Twisted Tumblers. They're the ones working on the way to force open the Pits so you can escape."

I gape at him. Of all the things I was expecting, involving another clan wasn't one of them.

"My negotiations with them have stalled somewhat," he continues ruefully. "Not sure they trust me all that much—my being clanless and all. But I'm scheduled to meet with their leader tomorrow night, and I want you to come with me."

I've seen Josephine in passing but only during Tithes when she and Rory would hammer out temporary truces between our clans. The Twisted Tumblers are tinkers, making bastardized versions of Meridian tech with scrap the Banshees provide them with, and then they sell their devices in the thieves' market.

It said a lot that Rory had never attempted to cheat her. I shudder. "Not sure they'll be too happy to see a former Banshee in their territory."

"Oh, but you're so charming." He smirks as I whistle something rude at him.

"So what now? Fancy a trip to the sweetshop? I've always wanted to break into it and stuff myself sick." It's a halfhearted suggestion, and it fills me with melancholy. Without Sparrow there to enjoy it, the whole idea is suddenly hollow.

Ghost holds a hand out to me. "Come on. I want to show you something."

He pulls me to my feet, his callused fingers against my wrist. "Where are we going?" I ask.

"Just around the chimney."

We creep over the rooftop to the other side, the shingles sending chills up my naked toes and into my knees. A skylight nestles there, a twin to the one in my room, and he opens it easily, slipping inside with a simple grace.

I follow, descending onto the beam below and then onto the mantel and into a room much like mine. It's sparse, though—not nearly as lived in as I expected it to be. There's a bookshelf stuffed with papers and leather-bound volumes, but the rest of the space isn't particularly impressive.

A single bed leans against the wall beside the empty fireplace. Ghost is already there, lighting the tinder with a sparker rod that materializes from his pocket.

"A clever bit of Meridian tech, that." I hover over his shoulder to take a closer look at it.

"Nipped it off an Inquestor. It's a smaller version of one of those wands they use during the Tithes." He grimaces and passes it to me.

I roll it between my fingers. It's longer than a standard cigarillo and the width of my thumb, a jeweled blue button at the base. I press it, and a burst of lightning sparks from the tip. "If they catch you with one of these..."

"Now you sound like Lucian. Besides, you're one to talk, Dragon Girl." He rolls his eyes.

"Lucian?" I hand the miniature Tithe wand back to him and squat beside the fireplace to capture a bit of the warmth in my hands, rolling the name on my tongue.

"Dr. Barrows. That's what I've always called him." Something in the way he says it seems overly familiar, as though the two men have known each other for a very long time indeed.

The dragon uncoils from my neck and I pet it, one finger stroking its head. "He's a Meridian, isn't he?" The words hang there, thick and tight and terrible, and I almost wish I hadn't said them. Almost.

"Yes," Ghost says, his voice ragged. "And my brother." A weary relief settles over his face, as though he's set free something inside himself.

His answer rocks me to my bones. Sparrow would have been enraptured by the idea, but the whole concept makes me uneasy. For all my longing to reach Meridion, the citizens themselves seem so far out of reach as to be some sort of dream. Knowing I've been breaking bread with them for the better part of a month... It's a bit like discovering your dog can suddenly speak.

"But...how can a Moon Child be a Meridian?" I ask it slowly, trying to wrap my brain around the concept. "We're half-breeds by nature. That would mean...what, your mother was from BrightStone?"

"No. I was born on Meridion. Same as Lucian. We had the same mother. Same father, as far as I know. Same glittery skin at one point." He smiles wryly. "It's something to do with living on Meridion itself, I think. When you're gone for too long, the glowing effect fades. That's what happened to the Inquestors. Once Meridion stopped sending transport ships, they were just as trapped as Lucian and I were."

I chew on the inside of my cheek, pondering over this bit of information. "But that still doesn't explain why you're a Moon Child."

He shrugs. "And I have no answers for you. Lucian and I left Meridion under...bad circumstances. I was only about six or seven, and we had no choice but to disguise ourselves until the skin effect wore off. And then when I turned twelve..." He sinks to the floor to lean against the wall. "Well, it was a shock to both of us, let's just say."

I tug on my hair. "Explains your familiarity with the ink."

"My brother spent the first few years of my change trying to hide what I'd become, so sure he would be able to find a way to reverse it if he just worked hard enough. He's given up on that account. Mostly."

"I don't think anyone's really ready for it," I say softly. "My only saving grace was that Mad Brianna had seen it so many times by then that she knew how to wait it out until it was done. After that, she sold me off to Rory. I was a right bargain, to be sure."

He leans against the wall for a moment before pulling something out of a dresser drawer and pressing it into my palm. "I meant to give this to you earlier. Days ago."

I turn over my hand. It's Sparrow's necklace, made of tiny, green, teardrop crystals strung on a bit of leather.

"Oh," I choke out, my voice gone thick. Grief is such an empty emotion, and yet it's a bottomless cup, filling me to the brim. I slip the leather strap around my neck, fastening the clasp with numb fingers. It hangs at the hollow of my throat. It feels wrong that it's there at all, but it could strangle me to death for all that because I'll never take it off.

"Thank you." I turn away from him, holding back a quiet sob as I'm reunited with this last piece of Sparrow's past, clutching it like a talisman.

He's good enough to allow me a bit of time, poking at the fire with a piece of kindling until I manage to regain a sense of myself. "I've something else for you, too, if you want it?"

His words pull me from my melancholy. "Aye?"

Papers scatter everywhere as he riffles through the bookshelf. "Lucian really does have good intentions, but sometimes he can be a bit of an arse when it comes to thinking he knows what's best. You should have seen him fret when I moved out of his rooms and into this one. He's overprotective, which makes sense, I guess." He sighs.

There's so much I want to ask him, as though the reveal of this particular secret of his has somehow unlocked an odd curiosity inside me. What must it be like to have had a family before the change to Moon Child? I might even be envious about it on some level, but I cannot help but feel a twinge of relief that my own mother was long gone before I'd become what I am now.

"Ah. Here we go." A thin volume materializes in his hand. "Lucian's probably right about you not understanding it, but I'll help you read it, if you want." A wry smile captures his mouth as he gives it to me. "He wasn't technically lying about not having a copy, though, since it belongs to me."

I squint at the title, but I already know what it is, even as my lips move to try to sound out the words.

D'Arc's Manifesto.

A pocket full of promises
Too dark for me to keep
Lay me down in the cold, cold ground
To dream, perchance to sleep.

— CHAPTER NINE —

"'…and thus the Meridian sin of arrogance has been made very clear to me. Even I am not free of such an emotion, which has given rise to both my biggest success and most terrible regret…'"

Snowflakes drift past the window, a slow blur of white and silver against the darkness. Ghost and I sit beside the fireplace in his little room, poring over *D'Arc's Manifesto*. It's a short piece—about twenty pages or so—but there's a rhythm to the words that unfurls around me with quiet precision, even as Ghost guides me through it.

"Sound out this word here," he says. "Like this."

I try, wanting so much to get it right.

"Not quite. It's a longer *o* sound." He sounds it out for me again.

He's being oddly patient about my mistakes, and I'm grateful for it. Not that Dr. Barrows hasn't been considerate, but there's always a tension when he tries to teach me. I hadn't understood it before, but now it seems clear to me that for all his lofty ideals, what he really wants is to protect his brother. From the Inquestors, or the Pits, or just life as a Moon Child maybe. In some ways it feels cowardly, but was I any different when it came to Sparrow?

I stare at the pages for a few minutes more, but my eyes are drifting as my thoughts slide away, and I yawn. We've only gotten partway through the book, but it's not a bad start.

A light scratch at the door has us both glancing up, resignation flashing over Ghost's face. To his credit, Dr. Barrows merely sighs when he sees me.

"I might have guessed I'd find you here when you weren't in your room," he says.

"She deserves to know what we know," Ghost says firmly, but there's a hint of something darker in his voice.

"I suppose it's only fair." The doctor's expression becomes pained when he sees the book in front of us. "Just do me the favor of keeping it in this room. Best not to tempt fate more than we already are." His pleading gaze catches mine. "I'd prefer for Molly not to know we have this particular volume, if it's all the same to you."

The dragon huffs at him, and I nod, understanding he's given me a potent bit of information. If I were so inclined, I could have him arrested for its possession. The fact that Molly doesn't know fills me with a sudden rush of power, but it's short-lived.

"Aye," I say finally, shutting the book and handing it to Ghost. "I was about to leave anyway. It's been a long day, and I'm feeling a bit peckish."

"I'll have Copper Betty bring up something," Dr. Barrows offers, holding the door open for me. "If you wouldn't mind, I'd like to speak to Ghost alone for a bit, though."

Ghost gives me a nearly imperceptible nod when I glance over at him, and I take my leave, emerging into a narrow passage that leads to the third-floor hallway. Ghost's door has been covered up with a tapestry so I hadn't noticed it before, but it's across the hall from the doctor's room and directly next to my own.

Odder and odder that he would be concealed away like that, but perhaps it's only privacy he desires and nothing more. Or maybe

Dr. Barrows continues to try to hide his brother away from the world, even in the place they live.

My room is chilly when I close the door behind me. The window has been left open, and a puddle of melted snow sits on the sill. I shut it with a sigh, grateful the acrid stench of the ink is gone at least.

I pause in front of the mirror, blinking in astonishment again and trying to reconcile the reflection with myself and failing miserably. Perhaps my brain will make more sense of it tomorrow, but right now I'm mentally exhausted and too tired to think on anything else.

A change of clothes and a stirring up of the fire leaves me dozing in the overstuffed chair, the dragon behind me. Copper Betty comes and goes with a bowl of soup and a bit of cold chicken, which I quickly wolf down.

I spare a brief thought about trying to listen through the wall to hear whatever Ghost and Dr. Barrows are saying, but my gaze falls upon the map scrolls on the mantel. I unroll them on the floor, holding each corner down with one of the doctor's many books. As maps go, it seems fairly simple. Most of the chambers are squared off—some are labeled as sleeping quarters, mess halls, equipment rooms, and the like. Archivist Chaunders hadn't mentioned how long the miners stayed below during their work with the Meridians, though her father's notes would surely hold such answers.

For now, I simply trace each section of the mines with my finger over and over, lining it up with the gated entrance to the Pits. I can only imagine miles upon miles of inky blackness without a bit of breeze, and for a moment I don't think I can bear it.

I reach up to grasp Sparrow's necklace, sucking in a deep breath. "For you, aye. I'll do it for you," I whisper, curling up on the floor around the map.

Eventually my eyes drift shut, and I dream of finding my way through the darkness, shadowed by the fates of the other Moon Children who have gone before me.

"Another moment, if you would?" Dr. Barrows asks me.

I cross my arms but remain standing on the scale as he scratches out a new set of numbers in his notebook. He smiles up at me, pleased with my apparent progress this morning.

The scale creaks when I step off it and hastily throw on a loose sweater. "Eating enough for you, now?"

"Well, you're still dreadfully underweight, but it's a definite improvement." He moves to examine my face, lifting my lips to prod at my gums. "Still fighting some borderline malnutrition, but that's not unexpected given your circumstances. I'll inform Molly to include some additional vegetables in your meals. Don't want you getting scurvy, now do we?"

"As long as it's not rotting, I'll eat anything." I don't have the faintest idea of what *scurvy* is, but I probably don't want it.

"Well that's good," Ghost mutters from where he's sprawled on my floor, flipping through one of the miner's notebooks. "How do you feel about rats? There are instructions in here on how to make snares."

"Wouldn't be the first time." I shrug, ignoring the way Ghost pales. I roll my eyes. "Joking. Even as bad as things are here, I've yet to stoop to eating rats. Though I've thought about it awful hard a time or two," I admit ruefully.

"It's more of a pest-control entry, but seeing as we don't really know how the food situation will be, it might not hurt." Ghost waves me over, choosing to ignore that last bit of my response. "And you might want to take a look at these."

I peer over his shoulder at some pictures. "Mushrooms?"

"Yes. There are a few different types that grow in the caves beyond the mines proper. Some of them appear to be poisonous, so memorize it carefully so you can avoid those." He bookmarks the page for me.

"How reassuring." My mouth purses. "Suppose it's a good thing Archivist Chaunders gave us those books, aye?"

"Indeed." Dr. Barrows stretches, his gaze growing distant. "I took the liberty of paying a visit to her this earlier this morning. Fascinating lady, to be sure. Perhaps if I'd gone there in the beginning, we wouldn't be where we are now." He catches himself a moment later and shakes his head. "Well, there's no use on ruminating over the past, is there?"

Unexpected irritation skates through me. "Probably depends on your past."

Ghost flips to another page, glancing over at his brother. "Molly know you went?" he asks, wisely keeping the conversation focused on the problem at hand.

"Of course." The doctor gathers his things. "I've two patients to see to this afternoon and dinner with Chancellor Davis this evening, so I don't expect to be home until very late." His brows rise in sudden enthusiasm. "Hopefully with some of this new information, I might convince the Chancellor of our progress."

"Dinner with the Chancellor, aye? Someone's fancy." I mock curtsy at him, my wrists arched in a little flourish.

"Fancy is as fancy does," he retorts. The Mother Clock sounds out the hour in the distance and the doctor sighs. "Duty calls. I've left you some exercises on basic sums, Mags. See if you can't have those finished for me tomorrow."

"Aye." I give the sheaf of paper a sour look, resigned to what will probably be a long afternoon. The doctor snorts at my expression, exiting swiftly a moment later.

Ghost watches him go and then moves to follow. Disappointment swells in my belly. I'd hoped to at least have his company for a bit longer. The presence of another Moon Child soothes me, if nothing else.

"Are we still on for...tonight?" I ask, thinking of his meeting with Josephine.

He doesn't answer right away, peering out into the hallway before nodding at me, mischief flaring deep in his gray eyes. "Meet me up top when the Mother Clock strikes the eighth hour."

"Rooftop dancing, is it?" A little thrum of excitement ripples over my skin. "I'll be there."

The fog is thick this evening, frost nipping the air and sliding over my skin with icy fingers. Whatever snow we had earlier today is gone, but slick patches shimmer on the slate roof, glittering with the promise of a slip and a broken head if one should take the wrong step.

I wrap my coat tighter around my shoulders, foot tapping with impatience until Ghost finally appears just as the Mother Clock bongs out the time. He's got his cap pulled down on his head, a few wisps of brown hair sticking out near his ears.

He laughs when he sees me. "I suppose there's no need to ask if you're ready."

"What gave it away?" I head for the edge of the roof, blood suddenly boiling with the need to move, to stretch my limbs and run. "Which way?"

He grunts something noncommittal. "Maybe you should leave the dragon behind, aye?"

The dragon grumbles at him from my shoulder, but I reluctantly agree with Ghost. To tempt fate by leaving the Conundrum is one thing, but we cannot afford another close call with the Inquestors. I untangle the dragon's tail from the scarf around my neck and pry open the skylight to my room.

"Go on now. Find yourself a bit of space beside the fire, and I'll be back before you know it."

It clicks out a little snarl at me but slips off my hand to glide to its usual perch on the mantel. I shut the window behind it. "That's that." I brush my hands off on my coat and flex my fingers as my heart begins to beat faster. "How about a little race before business? It's been awhile; I need to make sure everything still works right."

He snorts. "Fair enough. First one to the museum, then. We have to head that direction anyway."

"Try to keep up." I wink at Ghost, my mouth curling into a private grin.

He bows mockingly at the challenge. "Lead the way."

I don't bother with a reply. I simply turn away.

One, two, three…

I leap into the fog. The wind whips through my shortened hair, the chill shivering over my scalp. I pay it no mind, save that the lack of weight has upset my balance and I struggle not to overcompensate.

A foot placed just so in the crag of a crumbling brick, my hands gripping a bit of pipe, a push here, a shove there. I call it rooftop dancing because that's what it truly is. A recognition of the rhythms of a city, the breadth and width of her bones given substance in structures of stone and iron and wood. But a waltz upon the roof requires more than grace and a pretty step. It's strength and flexibility, and the skill to turn or twist upon a moment's notice. You need to calculate leaps or falls, skid along slippery shingles, and scrape through a crack of an opening no wider than a flea's arse.

Ghost sprints in front of me, his movements easy and familiar; he knows these buildings as well as I do. I follow suit, tracking the fluid motion of his arms and the bob of his head, ears pricked at his slight exhalations, the grunts when his body collides with the structures.

My heart beats with a fierce glee at finally being set free, even if it's just for a night. I ignore the burning stitch in my side, the last remnants of my wound, and find myself grinning into the darkness despite it all. The fog has lifted for at least a short space, and the moonlight washes over us.

I take advantage of this sudden gift of visibility and climb higher, choosing a parallel path to Ghost's. A few seconds later I've overtaken him. He gasps something at me, but I can only laugh. Sparrow and I always played this game, but I marvel at how easy it is to fall into the familiar cadence with him, as though we've been doing it forever.

"Shit, but you're fast," he says raggedly when we finally take a rest upon the slanted shadow of a dormer window overlooking the square beside the museum.

My own lungs sting with the strain, but I merely cock my head at him when he slumps beside me, his chest rising and falling with exertion. "You've a keen grasp of the obvious, I see."

He kisses me suddenly. It's a clumsy brush of lips but earnest in its intent. The intimate intrusion catches me off guard, and after a moment, I pull away from the warmth of his mouth, feeling oddly empty. Confusion wars with longing and something else as we stare at each other, my thoughts drowning in silence, overcome by the staccato *tick-thump* of my heartbeat.

"What are you doing?" I swallow hard, unsure where this is going.

He lets out a sharp bark of ugly laughter. "Not the reaction I'd hoped for."

"Oh, aye? Should I swoon like in one of those penny romances?" I flutter my eyelashes at him, attempting to shift the mood away from the momentary hurt that flickers over his face. "You just caught me by surprise. Moon Children tend to be a little more direct beforehand, if you catch my drift." I let out the whistling trill I'd taught him before, my mouth twitching.

Shock rounds his eyes. "Gods, no. Just because I kissed you doesn't mean I want to...I mean, not *here*." He pauses. "Or is that how it is, in clans?"

"Often enough." I shrug. "There's not time for much else. Boy. Girl. That part didn't matter if I just wanted a few minutes to forget. We're sterile, after all." A sigh escapes me, and I sag against the brick of the dormer. "Not like it matters. There's no room for romance for Moon Children, Ghost. Not when your lover could be taken for a Tithe." My voice grows smaller, thinking of Sparrow. "Or for friends, even."

"I hadn't thought of it that way." His mouth quirks into a self-deprecating smile. "And I suppose my timing is off, given the circumstances."

"Considering I'm *trying* to be Tithed, yes," I agree wryly. "Was all this an elaborate attempt at seduction, then?"

He shakes his head. "No. Not really. Just taking advantage of the situation, as it were."

We sit in silence then, leaning against each other. Despite my previous statements, somehow my hand finds its way into his, and our fingers entwine. A skittering jolt zips up my arm. He says nothing, but the pulse at his neck jumps and I hide a smile.

"Was that your first?"

"My first what? Kiss? I grew up in a brothel, Mags. I don't exactly have a lot of firsts left, aye?" He nudges me. "First Moon Child kiss, though."

"Yeah? Want a second?" I'm half joking, though the weight of the Pits presses heavy upon me, making me more reckless than I should be. As distractions go, I'll take this one.

He blinks but doesn't wait to be asked twice. This time I meet him halfway, and a sudden flush of heat erupts beneath my breast, my pulse fluttering like a bird's wings. When he pulls away there's something unreadable in his eyes, a sort of grace that wasn't there before.

I exhale sharply, but he merely squeezes my hand again before scanning the square below us. "Come on. We're not too far from the Theatre Quarter. The Twisted Tumblers are expecting me."

I cock a brow at him. "All right, then. Show me."

The Theatre Quarter is bustling with a quiet frenzy. The nip in the air has driven most patrons indoors, but here and there, pockets of warmth and light spill out onto the cobblestones, punctuated by a cacophony of music and raucous laughter. The river doesn't flow through this part of the city, and I can't help but appreciate the distinct lack of salt stink.

I'm not as familiar with the streets here, but I try to avoid staring like a slack-jawed country cousin, my mind overlaying what I've seen of the Theatre Quarter with my memory of the map at the museum.

I haven't seen any other Moon Children yet; perhaps our disguises are the reason for that. Years of keeping within the boundaries of my own clan's territory is a hard habit to break, but I have to trust Ghost on this.

The Brass Button Theatre looms in front of us at the far end of a rounded park. The building is flanked by a pair of massive stone fountains with ethereal marble sculptures of men and women frozen in various acrobatic feats as if leaping through the water, their faces achingly lifelike. They're lit up by cunningly placed electric sconces, beams of gold and silver reflecting over the wet marble to give them an ethereal semblance, as though they truly dance upon the waves.

Patrons of the arts mill about outside, ignoring the damp as they light up their cigarillos and purchase fruits and candies from a nearby vendor.

"Intermission," Ghost observes. "They'll be out here for a few minutes."

"Must be nice to freely enjoy such entertainments."

He gives me an amused glance from the corner of his eye. "The Upper Tier gentry are as trapped in BrightStone as we are, you know. They're just better at hiding it. And clearly they've money to burn."

We watch them, wrapped in their furs and silken dresses, for another moment or two. These glittering jewels of the upper class are pretty, but it only serves to show how dreary the rest of BrightStone has become.

We walk the outskirts of the square, but I can't help lingering to look at the fountains just a little longer.

"You like those?" Ghost asks.

"I think they're beautiful," I admit, not sure how to explain it. "They look like how I feel when I'm up on the rooftops, when every step seems to lift me higher and farther away. Like I might jump and never come down."

"They've sculptures in Meridion that put these to shame. Larger too."

A scowl creeps over my face. "Is there nothing I can enjoy here without it being made less of?"

Confusion reflects in his eyes, and he dips his head. "It wasn't my intention to do so."

"Never mind." I wave him off, though the moment is ruined. I feel like a sham walking about the populace pretending to be something I'm not. Instinct insists I stake a claim somewhere safe that I can retreat to, and I'm tickled with a sudden longing to climb the nearest building.

But not here in the open.

Without another word, we drift up one winding road packed with sagging row houses and then another, cutting through a narrow alley before finding ourselves on the outer steps of an inn. The bedraggled, stuffed cormorant nailed to the stoop would give Hideous Lydia a run for its money.

"Charming," Ghost murmurs, but he follows me as I climb the fire escape to the windowsills and higher up until we reach the roof.

I resist the urge to pace, the relief I'd felt only a short while ago now gone, as though it's the very city strangling me. Above us, Meridion is lit up, glittering like a cluster of stars and just as far out of reach.

Something prickles my shoulder, and I flinch, nearly sliding from the roof. I lean on Ghost for balance. "The hells take it," I say as I realize what it is when a puff of steam warms my ear.

"How did it get out?" Ghost frowns at it. "And more importantly, how did it find you all the way over here?"

The dragon's ember heart glows, but if the little monster has answers, it's not sharing.

"Maybe it went up the chimney again. We'll have to be careful going back if we don't want anyone to see it."

Ghost's frown grows deeper, but he's not looking at the dragon. "We've got company."

I hear the scrape of footsteps from the nearby rooftops and catch the glimmer of pale hair beneath the moonlight.

"Don't move," a reedy voice calls out from the next roof over.

Ghost raises his hands. "It's all right. It's just me."

A puzzled silence follows, and a scruffy boy peers around a chimney, his hands cradling a crossbow. Judging by his apparent age, he must be newly changed. His pale hair twists tightly about his soot-blackened face in a series of tiny braids.

"Ghost, is it?" the boy confirms. "Aye. Josephine's been expecting you for days now, but she never said nothing about no lady coming with you."

"Mags isn't a lady," Ghost retorts, grunting when I kick him in the shins. "She's one of us, as you can see from her delightful manners."

The boy lowers his weapon and slinks out from behind his perch. His mouth drops when he sees the dragon on my shoulder. "Are you bringing *that* to trade?"

"We'll discuss that with Josephine," Ghost interjects before I can say anything. He gestures at the boy. "This is Tin Tin, one of Josephine's errand runners."

"Lookout," Tin Tin insists, scowling. "They let me take the bow tonight. See?" He waves it at me, and I duck out of the way as the point swings by my head. A sheepish grin splits his lips. "Sorry. It's not cocked."

On closer inspection, I see he's right, but I still don't want it aimed at me. It's not a standard crossbow, but it's not Meridian tech, either. Rather, it's a bastardized custom job with a mechanical auto-cock and a pistol trigger.

I make a noise of appropriate enthusiasm. Tin Tin beams at me, a scrappy little bulldog of a lad with a puffed-out chest and slightly bowed legs.

"Right. We're all settled, then?" Ghost winks at me when Tin Tin flushes. "To the Rookery, if you'd be so kind."

"Follow me. We're to use the north door this evening." He slings the crossbow over his shoulder and shimmies down a drainpipe.

Ghost waves at me to follow and then brings up the rear as we find ourselves in a dark corner of a dead-end alley. Stacked barrels and a crate of empty bottles are piled on one side. Tin Tin gives one of the barrels a careless shove, exposing a rust-encrusted grate nestled within the cobblestones.

My nose wrinkles at the faint whiff of piss. "The stink pipes? Really?"

"It's the only way to the north door," Tin Tin says cheerfully, tugging a key from his vest and squatting down to fiddle with what must be a lock, though I'm damned if I can see it. "Besides, these have been abandoned for a while. They only fill when the river overflows."

"A regretful fact," I say, trying not to breathe too deeply. "They smell like they could use a good cleaning."

A second later the grate creaks open to reveal a tunnel. I shudder when Ghost pulls out a lightstick and drops straight down without hesitation, swallowed by the darkness. I stifle a shudder, but I see the outline of his silhouette at the bottom. It's not too far.

I slide down the hole and land beside him, my knees bent for the impact. The two of us move to the side to let Tin Tin through after he somehow manages to hold on long enough to relock the grate.

"Come on." Tin Tin jogs off down the tunnel, one foot on either side of the narrow trench that runs down the center. A sluggish rivulet courses down the trench, and whatever liquids it holds within, I'm pretty sure water isn't one of them.

I sigh and follow, Ghost bringing up the rear again. It's a maze of pipes and tunnels down here, and the darkness presses hard upon me. Is this what the Pits are like? Endless passageways of shadows and shit?

I shiver into my coat. "The gods can have it."

Tin Tin lights up an electric lantern hanging from his belt and whistles low when we approach a metal panel set within the center of one of the walls. Two short bursts and one long.

The dragon hisses in my ear, and I catch a faint knocking on the other side of the panel. Tin Tin raps on the door in response, and it swings open. I grind my teeth when I spot yet another tunnel, but a pair of Moon Children wave us through.

"Josephine's in the workshop," the taller one says, his gaze flicking over Ghost. He seems unsurprised at the change of hair color, which can only mean Ghost has done this before.

Tin Tin nods, turning off the lantern. No need for it here anyway, as the corridor is fitted with a strip of softly glowing lights, running the length of the floor to illuminate the passage.

Ghost sees where I'm looking and points to a control panel in the wall. "They skim off the theatre's power supply."

"Bold," I mutter, impressed. Rory would never have dared such a thing.

"I'm so glad you approve," Josephine drawls from the doorway at the end of the passage. I startle, flushing when her mouth curves into an amused smile.

I study her as she and Ghost exchange their greetings. She's older by several years, two thick braids framing her face, held back by a thick pair of welder's goggles. A wide scar rivers over her cheek to cut through her left eye and slash through her mouth. Based on her reputation, I'm unsurprised at it, as well as at the square jaw and the nose that's obviously been broken multiple times. She's short, like Penny, but her curves aren't due to excess of flesh; rather, she's built like a brick wall, the bare arms on display rampant with sinewy muscle.

No wonder Rory wouldn't cross her. A flick of her leather-bound wrist and she'd break him in half.

She rubs her forehead with a greasy hand, tucking a wrench into the apron tied around her waist. "And here I thought you'd be a no-show, Ghost. You're overdue by at least a week."

"I brought him, just like you told me," Tin Tin says proudly. "And wait 'til you see what the lady has for trade."

Josephine sucks hard on her lower lip when she spots the dragon. "Indeed. And who might 'the lady' be, I wonder?"

"Raggy Maggy. Formerly of the Banshee clan," I snarl, ignoring Ghost's warning cough. Stupid to blurt it out like that, but something about the way she cracks her knuckles makes me think honesty really is the best policy here.

"Oh yes. I've heard of *you*." Her mouth purses, and she crosses her arms, leaning against the door. "You look remarkably well-fed for a corpse, I must say."

Refusing to be cowed, I cross my own arms, mimicking her pose. "The mind boggles. I've a cat's own luck, and I shed lives like skin."

"That doesn't explain why you're standing here now." An edge creeps into her voice. "I don't recall extending this invitation to any but Ghost."

"There's been a change of plans." Ghost steps forward to place himself between me and Josephine, but somehow it feels like it's all for show. "She's a part of this now."

"So I see." Josephine stares at me a moment longer, her gaze resting heavily on the dragon. "All right, then. If Ghost vouches for you, I'll let it go. But heed me, Raggy Maggy. If you bring the Inquestors down upon me or mine, I'll make sure the only skin you have left will be the one mounted on my wall."

I can only nod at this. Ghost hasn't elaborated on exactly what we're doing here to begin with so I've no choice but to accept her terms, such as they are. And they're fair, considering I'm technically trespassing.

Whatever she sees in my face must be good enough for her because she opens the door behind her and waves us through. Tin Tin trudges after us.

I stifle a groan when I see more passageways. By this time I'm so mixed up there's no chance I'll ever find my way out without help. We pass a boiler room and then another, finally coming to stop beside what can only be her workshop.

A steaming furnace blazes at one end, enveloping us in a thick wave of heat as we approach. Piles of tech and gears are scattered about on benches and the floor, like scavenged bones in the cave of some mechanical predator.

"What did you bring me this time, Ghost?" Josephine asks.

He fishes in his pocket, pulls out the miniature Tithe wand, and tosses it to her. "Thought you might be interested in one of these."

She snatches at it in midair, a sudden eagerness in her expression. She presses the button, and a fork of tiny electrical pulses erupts from the business end. "Impressive."

I raise a brow at him. "So you steal Meridian tech for Josephine?"

"*Steal* is such a harsh word." Josephine turns a knob on her goggles so they light up, and she peers at the wand as if she's mentally dismantling it. "Ghost 'acquires' things I have need of to fulfill my contract with the BrightStone Chancellor. And in return, I allow him passage into my territory and the occasional bits of information I pick up here or there."

I study my fingernails. "Contract?"

"Of course. There's a rebellion coming. Maybe not today or tomorrow, but soon enough. The only chance we have of winning is to beat the Inquestors at their own game. That means taking apart their tech to see how it works and developing our own weapons from it."

Anger seeps through me. That Rory had never mentioned such to me or the others means nothing. He might not know or he'd simply chosen not to share the information. That's his right as clan leader. What bothers me now is how many intrigues my current housemates seem to be involved in and what they're not telling me.

Josephine watches me process this new bit of information with an appraising eye. She reminds me of Molly, the way I can see her mind whirring with thought. "But it begs the question, what have *you* to offer me? You're clanless, yes, but that doesn't mean you have free rein to trot about my territory. There's a price to be paid."

"She's with me," Ghost snaps. "We've been through this; if you want something from her, say it."

Josephine grows quiet for a moment and then dismisses Tin Tin, waiting until he sourly disappears up the hallway. She raises a brow at me. "So you're the one they've suckered into this little adventure, aye?"

"For whatever that's worth, aye," I say. "Not that you sound like you approve much."

"I approve of the plan to overthrow Meridian rule. Just not the way you're all going about it," Josephine tells me.

Ghost rolls his eyes. "Well it's not like you've come up with anything better, anything that would actually *work*," he retorts. "Stealing a ship and cutting through the chains anchoring Meridion to the ground so it floats away is not our goal. Not to mention those chains are impossibly thick; we'd never manage it with the tools we have now."

My gaze darts between the two Moon Children. This is clearly an old argument and not one I have any desire to involve myself in. Yet I snicker at it anyway. "Well maybe we hold that one in reserve, aye?"

"At least you've got an open mind," Josephine says begrudgingly. "Oh, I nearly forgot. Assuming we go with the original idea of sneaking you into a Tithe…" She gestures toward me and pulls the hair from the nape of my neck to take note of my brand. "It might take a bit of work to convert this to one of ours, but one of my clan has a similar number. I'll make sure she's offered for the next Tithe, and we'll do a last-minute switch before she's taken to the Salt Temple. And with a bit of luck, you'll be on your way."

My stomach twists into a sickening knot. How quickly these last few pieces have fallen into place. Whatever brave words I might have said to Ghost or Dr. Barrows or Molly feel so terribly hollow. To be discussing an actual brand change and a Tithe?

It seems my fate is sealed.

I sigh. "Tell me something. I've never quite understood how can you be so cavalier about offering up one of your clan to the Tithe. You seem to care about your people, far more than Rory ever did about us."

The other woman grows very quiet. "I hate it," she asserts. "With every fiber of my existence. That's why I do my damnedest to ensure my clan doesn't get tapped any more than they have to be. Have you never wondered why the Banshees have so many of their number offered for Tithes?"

I shrugged. "I don't know. I figured the Inquestors hated us more, maybe."

She snarls, mouth crooked. "No. Because Rory allows it. He's grown too used to the kickbacks from the Inquestors. As long as his creature comforts are seen to, what does he care how many of you are sent to the Pits?" Her eyes narrow. "And I was just as happy to let him do it. After all, each Banshee chosen was one less of mine."

The bluntness of her words strikes me hard, but honesty is like that sometimes. "I wish I knew that the last time I ran into him," I mutter.

Josephine's eyes grow intense, staring deeply into mine. "I am curious, though. What could have possibly convinced you to take on this particular challenge? Altruism doesn't exactly run rampant among Moon Children, if you haven't noticed."

Ghost's mouth opens as though he's about to say something rude, but I wave him off. "I owe him and the others a life debt," I tell her. Technically it's true, even if that's not really the reason I'm doing it, but it's one she'll understand.

Something a bit like respect flickers across her face, and she abruptly turns away. "Fair enough. Both of you, come with me. I need to show you something."

Ghost and I share a puzzled look. Josephine ignores us, tapping a button beside the furnace. A panel in the wall rumbles, sliding sideways to reveal a smaller room within. She pats down her apron, her jaw stiff.

I crane my head, eyes widening when I see what she's hidden away. It's some sort of harness, fitted with leather shoulder straps attached to a metallic engine. Pistons and cogs and what look like brass...feathers?

"Wings," I breathe. "You're building wings?"

Ghost slips past me to inspect the harness more closely. "Are you out of your mind?"

Josephine thrusts out her chin. "Do you have a better idea for getting up to the top of the gates to unlock the Pits? If so, I'd love to hear it because I've been beating my brains out on this issue for months, and right now, this is the best I've got."

"But you actually know how the locking mechanism works?" Ghost's voice takes on an excited tone.

"Aye. It's simple enough from what I can tell—nothing that a blowtorch won't cut right through. I've been studying it from a distance with a scope during the Tithes, and really, it's just the issue of getting *up* there that's the problem." She rolls her eyes. "The Inquestors are sloppy as all shit, but that's arrogance for you."

I reach out to touch the webbing of one the wings, my skin burning with a flutter of longing. What would it be like? Not to simply leap from rooftop to rooftop, but to take to the air in truth... "They're amazing."

She turns toward me. "You must understand. I've nearly got it working, but I can't get the thrust quite right." She points at the dragon, nonplussed when it bares its teeth at her. "If I could study that, figure out how it's put together..."

I still beneath her scrutiny. A terrible desperation fills her eyes, and for a heartbeat, I can see past the rough facade to the woman beneath. Somewhere along the way she's been backed into a corner from which she can't escape.

Would I be any different?

"Study it, how? You aren't going to dismantle it, are you?" I nearly take a step away from her, but she lets out a bark of laughter, tempered with all the gentleness of grinding bricks.

She opens a metal box from beneath the forge and unlocks it. "That won't be necessary. I found one just like it years ago, but it's too fragmented for me to try to repair."

Ghost and I peer into the box, its contents a mishmash of bits of glass and metal. It takes a moment, but I recognize them as the scraps of the other dragon, the broken one, I found near Architect Jacobs. "Where did you get it?" I ask.

"Stole it," Josephine says brusquely. "And don't ask for the details. It was stupid, and a lot of people were killed for my arrogance...But some things are worth the sacrifice. And that's what that dragon is: freedom." She runs her callused fingers over the bent curve of one of the wings of her device.

Ghost looks at me. "Mags?"

My gut twists. "How long will you need?"

"I want to sketch out its structure and observe how it actually flies. I won't hurt it, if that's what you're asking. I could even fix that wing if it lets me." Her mouth quirks up slightly. "A couple of hours, at the most."

It only takes me a few moments to decide, brutal practicality winning out over whatever sentimental attachment I seem to have acquired to the dragon over the last few weeks. Regardless of how I get into the Pits, making sure the others have a way to unlock the gates is the only way I'll have to get out. If a few hours here helps me to that end, then I'll take it.

I unwind the dragon's tail from around my neck, ignoring its growl of protest. "Done." The dragon squirms between my fingers, but I tap it on the nose. "Hush. You go with her now." It huffs at me and jumps out of my hands to land on the harness, its ember heart flaring hot.

Beside me, Ghost shifts uncomfortably, and I can tell he's not entirely sure I've made the right call, but what harm could it do to let Josephine study it for a short while?

Ghost gives my hand a tight squeeze before turning to Josephine. "We'll wait until you're finished, if it's all the same."

"I expected you might." She gives me a smile as she pulls out a charcoal stick and notepad of parchment. "We'll even feed you, if you like. I'll have Tin Tin escort you to the Rookery proper, shall I?"

The Rookery is apparently on the roof of the Brass Button Theatre—or at least that's where Tin Tin takes us. From here we can see the whole of the square and the surrounding buildings, and lights shining down below. It's easy to watch the familiar rhythm of the city unfolding. From a distance, chaos becomes nothing more than patterns, groups of people moving in clusters, alighting from place to place like squawking birds.

But it's nothing Ghost and I haven't seen before, and it doesn't hold our interest for long. From up above, everyone looks the same anyway. Equality in size, if nothing else.

The rooftop itself is ornate, a gilded crown of statues and lights encircling the top of the theatre. It's enough cover to prevent anyone below from noticing the goings-on and that suits me fine. Not that it's my clan, but old habits die hard and Moon Children tend to be more secretive than most. It's rare to find a place where we can simply...be.

Moon Children linger in every corner, eyeing us with quiet caution, but I don't sense any of the animosity that Rory would undoubtedly show if the tables were turned. Tin Tin gives us a cheery nod and leads us to a large cooking pot perched above a merry fire. He passes each of us a bowl and ladles a serving of what appears to be stew and a hunk of bread into each one. I don't have to be asked twice, and Ghost and I find our own perch on the rooftop, sitting to eat our meal with an eagerness that surprises me.

"They must be doing well," I muse, sipping straight from the bowl. "Looks like they've even got real vegetables."

"Not common fare for the Banshees, I take it?"

"No. Oh, every once in a while Rory would open the larder, but usually we were on a daily food stipend, and it wasn't much. We'd have to come up with the rest ourselves." I glance around at the other Moon Children, noting that they seem far less gaunt than the members of my former clan.

"We'll have to tell Lucian about our meeting with Josephine," he says. "He'll be pleased about Josephine's progress. Might be less happy that I brought you here with me, but given how close we are to enacting our plan, I suspect he'll overlook it. All that's really left is changing up your brand, and Lucian will do that once Josephine gives us the right design. He should be able to give you something to make most of the procedure painless."

"Yeah. Painless." An emptiness washes over me, the future seeming to hurtle forward with uncompromising clarity.

"Are you scared?" He snorts softly when I don't answer. "I'm sorry. That's a stupid question."

"Maybe." A sad little laugh escapes me. "I'm a simple person, Ghost. I'm not used to thinking beyond where my next meal is coming from. A shag and a smoke and a nipped bit of ale—that's my life. Nothing more. Protecting Sparrow gave me purpose, but without that?" I shake my head. "Maybe that's really why I took you up on your offer. It sounded better than living in the shadows, always wondering if I'd be caught. At least this way I might control my destiny a bit, aye? If I throw myself off a cliff, well…at least no one can accuse me of tripping."

His expression turns pensive. I can't look at him anymore as a wave of bitterness sweeps into my belly. I don't know why admitting to any of this bothers me so much, but showing any vulnerability in BrightStone is usually an invitation for trouble.

Keep your head down or you expose your throat to the wolves.

It's an old saying that Mad Brianna used to cackle at Sparrow and me whenever we would leave to work the streets. But if you don't look at anything other than your feet, sometimes it's too easy to get lost.

A light touch on my hand pulls me out of my woolgathering. He gives it a small squeeze, his mouth opening as if to say something, but he seems to think better of it. What was there to say, really? Platitudes fill my belly no better than flattery.

"How long were you watching me and Sparrow? Before, I mean." The question slips out before I can stop it, but it's been eating at me for quite some time.

He's quiet for a bit, and then he sighs. "Off and on the last few months. Like I told you before, I was looking for recruits anyway. I simply happened to stumble across you more than once and took advantage of it."

"Oy. Stumbling, aye? More like spying, I'll bet. I see how it is." I poke him in the ribs with a sly grin. "Sounds like something one of you perverted Meridians would do."

He flushes. "It's not like that. We couldn't tell just anyone what we were planning. You two seemed to be the most...I don't know. Willing to go against your clan leader?" Troubled, he frowns at me. "You have to trust me when I tell you I never wanted either of you to come to harm over it."

A deep furrow takes root across his brow, and he pinches the bridge of his nose. How much guilt has he carried since Sparrow was killed that night? We had been headed to the Conundrum anyway, but I'm not Mad Brianna; I can't read the future in the fog. In the end, things are what they are.

"Trust is a bag of cats," I say slowly. "It's all tangled up in knots, and I don't know how to untie it or if it will bite me if I do."

"I know. And I'm sorry for that. And maybe there was more to it than mere recruitment," he admits. "I'm lonely, Mags. For all my brother's attempts to protect me, for all the sacrifices he's made, there's a part of him that resents me." His eyes fixate on my hand, brimming with a loss I'm not sure I understand. "I'm a Meridian. I'm not...not supposed to be like this."

"You certainly seemed cozy enough with Josephine," I point out.

"It's not the same thing. That's a business transaction, and one set up between my brother and the Chancellor. I'm their go-between so the Chancellor doesn't implicate herself directly if any of this information surfaces. Hells, Josephine's *never* invited me up here before. But one introduction to you and here we are."

"Infamy has its perks."

"Maybe." He shakes his head. "You know, I tried to convince Lucian to let me go into the Pits myself, back when he started planning all this. Told him I could dye my hair, steal a mask and a robe, and sneak into a Tithe as a Rotter."

"I imagine *that* went well." Given what I know about Lucian's protectiveness of Ghost, there wasn't a chance he'd allow it unless the situation in BrightStone was so dire they had no choice.

Ghost snorts. "Of course not. And he had a point, even if rubs me wrong to admit it." A crooked half smile turns up one side of his mouth. "I've never had the chance to be part of a clan as just myself, to know who or what I'm truly supposed to be. I've got no inner knowledge of clan politics, no cultural background. If there are any surviving Moon Children below, they aren't going to trust me. I don't belong anywhere."

I nudge him gently, taking his hand. "Makes two of us, aye?"

His fingers entwine tightly around mine. "Aye."

Stew bowl now empty, I lean against him, content to eat the last of my bread. Without Sparrow these last few weeks, I've been drifting. How could I explain the loss of someone who had been the other part of my soul, a sister beyond blood?

I tug on her necklace, grateful beyond measure to have it, though it's a pale substitute for the way her presence drifts through my memory. I side-eye Ghost. His name is oddly fitting, considering the circumstances.

A soft, lonely sound carries over the breeze—mournful strains of a fiddle from the other side of the rooftop. The other Moon Children go silent as they listen. I can't see who's playing from here, but it doesn't matter. Living above an actual theatre obviously lends itself to an intrinsic knowledge of music and dance.

But the song... Oh, the song. It's not one I know by name, but the vibrato of it rolls deep and thick in my bones. It's not quite a dirge, but there's an undertone of regret and loss, and a hunger that stirs something in my gut.

Beside me, Ghost exhales sharply. I don't need to look at him to know he feels it, too. One would need to be made of ice not to.

He takes my hand again, and this time an electric jolt skims the surface of my palm. Our fingers thread together, and a breath of regret slips through me. The music fades away for a moment, and the tension builds all around us, expectant. Perhaps a clan ritual, then.

Before I can move, the music explodes into something lively. All around us Moon Children break into laughter, bodies sliding in a circle around the cook fire. I don't hesitate, pulling a slightly taken aback Ghost behind me as I move into the whirling mass.

If there are steps, I surely don't know them, but it doesn't matter. Moving is the important thing, and even if Ghost and I start off awkwardly, before long the impromptu dance falls into something akin to a contest. Leaps and jumps, flips and spins, and balancing on the crested peak of one of the statues—rooftop dancing, in truth.

It might seem odd to an outsider, but living under the knowledge that our very existence is an illusion makes for hard living. Taking our pleasures where we can offsets that just a tiny bit.

I find myself smiling at it all, exchanging grins with Ghost. He backs up a few steps and gestures at me, then holds his palms up. I run toward him and reach out, vaulting onto his hands with my own so he's holding me balanced, upright, and upside down. His arms tremble slightly as he lifts me, tossing me higher so I arc overhead. I land neatly behind him.

"Not too shabby," I observe, letting him pull me to my feet. "A few more days of practice and we could take our act on the road."

"We get through all this and maybe I'll take you up on that." He laughs, and it takes me by surprise. "Panhandling Moon Children on the streets of Meridion. We'll make a fortune."

"Can't wait." We pause in the relative calm, breath fogging in the air between us. "Since we're getting everything out in the open, any other big secrets I should know about?" I ask.

"At least one," he says, not quite looking at me. "In for a penny, in for a pound, right? It's about Martika. She's not who you—" He stiffens, staring over my shoulder. "Something's going on. Look."

I turn around, realizing the entire rooftop has gone quiet. Shadows slide past us to get a better look, and voices are raised in alarm. I glance back at Ghost, but he's already steering me toward the overlook.

It's chaos below as herds of people are pulled from their nightly distractions. But my only concern is watching the pairs of Inquestors sweeping the streets to usher them along and the faint hint of smoke in the air...

But it's not coming from the rooftop cook fire.

"What is that?" Ghost points across the river, where a terrible golden light shines through a wave of oily smoke rising from somewhere in...

"Market Square," I breathe. "It's on fire."

The man in the moon came down too soon
Burned by the light of the sun.
The blood red sea swallowed his spoon
And left him hungry and numb.

— CHAPTER TEN —

Ghost's eyes widen. "We have to go. The Conundrum..."

Not bothering to wait for me, he throws a leg over the edge and starts climbing down.

"Oy!" I shout after him. "What about the dragon?"

Ghost doesn't answer, and I glance behind me. The other Moon Children are too busy watching the spectacle unfolding below to pay attention to anything else. I grind my teeth together. I have to trust that Josephine will keep the dragon safe, that she'll honor the agreement between us.

"Bag of cats, aye," I mutter, clambering down after Ghost. Normally I'd never be so obvious about scaling a wall, but the townsfolk have far more to worry about than us.

Ghost has reached the streets and heads for the river, ducking in and out of the mass of people with an uneasy swiftness. I follow suit, several hundred yards behind. Above us, the engine of an airship whirs. It's low and loud, and the propeller fans stir up dust and garbage as it glides down the main street, its spotlights sweeping over us all.

I squint beneath the lights. Ghost has disappeared like his namesake again. Desperation is likely lending him speed, but I know where he's headed. There's a trestle track linking the Theatre

Quarter to Market Square, and it's the quickest way to get across the river via the roofs. It doesn't run anymore, and the support struts are about as substantial as a cat's whiskers, but if it's timed right, a clever Moon Child can easily make his or her way across.

I find myself on top of a tavern, its chimney slick with grease, and I lose my footing. I twist to keep my balance and slice my palm on a rusted bit of pipe. Pain stings my skin. I can live with it, but the blood will make my grip unsure. I'm forced to stop to bind it, tearing a strip off the hem of my shirt for a makeshift bandage.

Ghost is too far for me to catch up. "Slow and steady now, Mags... And let's hope he doesn't leap arsefirst into the fire." I whisper it under my breath, the words an odd comfort.

A second airship emerges from the fog, and I press myself flat against the chimney, sliding out of sight as soon as I dare. It passes without hesitation, its destination clearly somewhere else.

I flex my fingers on my wounded hand until I'm satisfied the bandage won't slip off and head for the trestle. Three blocks up and four blocks over, and then I'm balanced at the edge of the bridge, the river running thick and black beneath me.

The orange blaze of the fire is easy to spot now, shadows of airships circling around it dropping buckets of water. A thin sliver of relief traces its way up my spine. At least they're not simply letting it burn.

I suck in a deep breath and step onto the trestle. The actual bits of train track are long gone, stolen or melted down, leaving only bare, half-rotted boards and a thin bit of railing. The Meridians aren't particularly interested in the upkeep of BrightStone's transportation infrastructure, but even if the trestle were intact, only the citizens of the Upper Tier have the resources to keep such a thing running. And why would they? They have their private carriages to attend them and no need to rub shoulders with the rest of us.

I launch myself, my feet flexing along the narrow passage in an effort to balance my weight evenly. There's a groan and a crack as something gives way, but I don't slow down. When I get to the center where the worst of it is, I swing from the rail and over the side, taking refuge among the girders.

Beam to beam, I keep my limbs loose and flexible to adjust for any potential give, but I reach the other side without additional incident. There's no sign of air patrols or Inquestors over here, but there's no sign of Ghost, either. The smoke is thicker on this side of the river, a dark miasma clinging to my skin.

I wrap my scarf around the lower half my face to keep out the worst of it and continue on. It's easier going now. I know these buildings, and the ins and outs of them without thinking—which roof has the missing shingle or the squeaky drainpipe, which alleyway is clear to descend into and which ones are nothing more than dead ends.

Movement flutters from the corner of my eye. Another Moon Child making her own way, but she's fleeing in the opposite direction.

Not a good sign.

I whistle at her. *What news?*

A cautious reply echoes back. *Flee to the Warrens.*

And then she's gone.

"I'll take it under advisement." I decide to chance it on the ground; some of the airships are floating by a little too close to the roofs for my liking. I emerge from an alleyway and slink toward Market Square. Worried faces peer out of shuttered windows and cracked doors, and snippets of conversation stream about me, my ears straining to pick out the relevant bits of information.

"—said the museum has burned down to the ground..."

My heart skips a beat when the words start to sink in. I begin to run openly now, shoving past clusters of people and narrowly avoiding being spotted by a pair of newly arrived Inquestors who begin shouting at people to go inside.

The smoke grows darker and thicker as I get closer to the square. By the time I arrive it's nearly impossible to see, and my eyes tear up at the grit. Airships buzz over the square, water streaming from a series of hoses tethered to large water tanks on their decks. As one empties and departs, another ship moves in to take its place.

They're currently working on the sad remains of the haberdashery; all that's left is a smoldering husk. Next to it, the sweetshop is scorched but mostly intact, though the damage to the upper levels is substantial.

And beyond that...

There's far too much smoke for this one building to be the only victim, but the rest of Market Square appears to be relatively untouched, save for the falling ash upon the wind and the chaos of overturned vendor carts in the center.

A crowd of people huddles at the far end of the square, closer to the Conundrum, and I rush toward them.

Crack!

My knees slam into the cobblestones as I'm shoved from behind. I shake it off, trying to stand when a burst of white heat shunts its way through my body. Every bit of me shudders, my bones trying to slip themselves out of my skin. But I can't cry out or do anything but topple over.

A Tithe wand. Someone's hit me with a jolt from one of the Inquestor's pig-stickers. The pain recedes for a moment, leaving me sprawled upon the cobblestones, my ears ringing.

"The hells," I mumble. Inquestors only use Tithe wands during actual Tithes, so what are they doing?

A flash of red swirls in my vision, and I'm dimly aware of the Inquestor as she circles around me. I slur something rude at her and struggle to get to my feet. She raises the wand again.

Ghost barrels out of the shadows, slamming the Inquestor to the ground. They roll, twisting against each other. I kick the Tithe wand out of the Inquestor's hand and it skitters across the cobblestones, but it's already too late. One of the airships is flying toward us, two more Inquestors on foot.

Ghost has the Inquestor pinned beneath him, his knee pressed hard against the woman's throat. "Go! Get out of here!"

"But I can't just leave you—"

His head snaps up. "My brother will know what to do. Find him."

Before I can respond, he's struck by an electrical shock of his own, the other Inquestors swarming over him in a flood of billowing crimson.

I run.

Coward, coward, coward.

The phrase beats in my mind with every step, but he's bought me a few seconds and I can't waste them.

The spotlight of the airship dogs my trail, but I lose it quickly, pelting down the alleys with a speed born of fear. I half run up the nearest wall to jump a sagging wooden fence and rocket through a gap between two houses before somersaulting to my feet.

The whir of the airship engines grows louder, chasing me through the narrow streets as I sprint toward Bloody Bay, rounding back on myself to come out on the wharf. I don't pause to look over my old stomping grounds, which are eerie and quiet.

I clamber down the length of the pier. The tide's low so I don't have to worry about falling in, and from here it's only a leap to reach the stink pipes. The large pipes empty into the bay here, a thick sludge dripping into the water below.

I clamp my hands over my mouth to keep from gagging and press inside. There's no way to avoid the raw waste, and after five heartbeats, I stop trying. Oily liquid sloshes into my boots, soaking my trousers to the knee. It's clammy and awful, and a moment later, the stench hits me and I vomit, the remains of my stew slopping into my scarf.

For the love of the gods…

But I only dare to release the scarf a little, wiping at my mouth with the only dry spot I can find.

The airship sweeps past the dock, spotlights shining. I can only hope they're going to pass me by, but a distinct thud upon the docks has me retreating even farther into the pipe. Heavy boots march over the wooden boards, voices issuing commands I recognize only too well.

No choice, then.

I make a run for it, a hand on either side of the pipe to keep my balance in the slippery stuff. The air is nearly intolerable, but I aim for what appears to be a bend.

Get there and turn the corner. They won't come in here looking for you. They won't. They can't.

The pipe narrows somewhat and curves. I nearly throw myself around it, just as a beam of light illuminates the inside of the tunnel.

"What a stink!" The owner of the voice coughs.

Shadows play along the walls, and I flatten myself out of sight, praying they don't attempt to look any farther along. A few seconds later the light fades, leaving me in the shadows again. The vibration of the airship propeller continues to rumble above me, though; they're hovering while the Inquestors do their search. If I try to leave now, they'll spot me for sure, so I've no choice but to stay where I am, crouched in shit and coated with vomit.

When it becomes apparent that they're not leaving anytime soon, I grow desperate, staggering farther into the darkness until I reach a grate. It's clogged with debris, but the openings are far too small for me to get through anyway, and I have to trudge back the way I came.

I'm half-dizzy by this point, creeping to the entrance of the pipe to take a whiff of air that's only slightly cleaner than what I'm standing in. The tide's starting to turn; if I wait too much longer, I'll be trapped here until it lowers again.

I risk a glance behind me and shudder.

Not a fucking chance in all the deepest hells.

Swallowing hard, I slip out of the pipe to slink over the jetty beneath the pier. The rocks are slick with foul-smelling seaweed and tiny barnacles so sharp they cut my fingers nearly to the bone.

"Fuck, fuck, fuck." I cling to a piling, nails digging into the rotted remains of a mooring. The salt water laps at my thighs, the chilly dampness running up the length of my trousers until I'm shivering so hard I nearly let go.

But it's better than the stink pipe, by a thousand-fold.

At last the dock grows quiet. The airship takes off, leaving me to drag my wretched self to the nearest ladder. By now I'm nothing more than a weary bag of bones encased in a cocoon of wet shit and saltwater brine. No one would possibly recognize me for anything but the lowest piece of street trash, but with the reek rolling off me, there's little chance anyone would willingly want a better look. I abandon the scarf as a lost cause, but instinct has me pulling my hood up anyway, a choice I regret two seconds later when it traps the stink pipe stench about my face.

I decide to risk climbing to the rooftops, but it's a slow process. My hands and feet are stiff and chilled from the water, and my palms are burning from my various cuts. There's nothing else to do but press on, clinging to the shadows as best I can.

Inside, my clockwork heart clatters with a wretched sort of terror. Have I learned nothing from Sparrow's death? What will Dr. Barrows say when he discovers I left his brother behind? A hot flush of guilt and anger washes over me.

Your fault. Again.

Swallowing down a sob, I continue limping my way along. This time I give Market Square a wide berth. The crowd has thinned out; all that's left are pairs of Inquestors making rounds in various corners.

Smoke still swirls in the distance, but I can't make out its source. At this point I no longer care about anything but finding my way to the Conundrum, besides. I scramble over to the skylight window above my room, hoping beyond hope that somehow Ghost is there, that he escaped.

A quick glance inside reveals nothing but the soft glow of the fireplace embers. I pry at the latch of the window with numb, shaking fingers. An awful rush of relief sweeps through me when I slide it open to slip inside, balancing on the beam as I pull it shut behind me.

From there I've only got enough strength to lower myself to the fireplace mantel and then to the floor. It's not a graceful landing, and I wince at the resounding thump of my boots on the hardwood. It's as though all my energy has been sapped, and I sink to my knees.

The doorknob rattles, and Dr. Barrows rushes in, wild-eyed and disheveled. He hits the lights, and I squint at the sudden brightness. His face registers surprise as he realizes who I am.

"Mags?" He squats down beside me, recoiling when he catches a whiff.

I ignore his reaction. "Is Ghost here?" My guts are coiling snakes, constricting in knots so tight I can barely breathe.

"No. I thought he might have been with you." His voice is a thinly veiled mix of fury and anguish, the words trembling in the space between us.

"The Inquestors took him," I whisper hoarsely. "He took me to meet the Twisted Tumblers, so we were in the Theatre Quarter when he saw the fire…"

"Stupid boy!" He wheels and punches the wall so hard the plaster cracks.

The violent motion is so at odds with his normally gentle appearance, and it shocks me into standing. My coat slips from my shoulders, and I kick it, unable to bear touching it anymore.

"He told me to find you. I couldn't save him. There were too many Inquestors..." My voice trails away. "What happened?"

He pinches the bridge of his nose as though trying to calm himself into coherent thought. "The museum was burned to the ground, and it was *not* an accident. Whoever did it got sloppy, and it spread too fast for them to control."

I taste blood on my lips from where I've bitten down, fear flaring deep inside me. "What are we going to do?"

"I don't know." He whirls on me. "Where's the dragon, Mags? The Inquestors were here tonight looking for it."

"Looking for it? Here?" My eyes dart toward the door, half-ready to launch myself back out the window.

"Aye." Molly Bell enters the room, her lips set in a grim line. She points at Dr. Barrows. "*You* need to calm down. I've girls nearly half-sick with hysterics already. They're jumping at shadows as it is, and you stomping about up here isn't helping matters."

He stops pacing, letting out a long, slow breath. "I've inquiries to make." Without another word, he stalks from the room, his footsteps heavy upon the stairs.

Molly stares at me for another moment and then sighs. "If half of what I just overheard is true, I'm afraid you have a lot of explaining to do. But that's going to have to wait until you get a proper bath. I'll have Copper Betty meet us downstairs." She winces. "And I'll be burning those clothes."

I can only nod at her, my eyes drawn to the doorway. "Do you think he'll find Ghost?" I ask, my voice barely above a whisper.

Molly cocks a brow at me. "For your sake, you better hope he does."

Hot water trickles over my shoulders and down my back, infusing me with warmth. But it's hollow. Each sting of cut and bruise is a pinprick of a reminder that I've no right to enjoy any of it.

I've been taken to the bathhouse below the brothel. Upstairs, the evening crowd should have arrived by this time of night, filling the bar with the appreciative cheers of men applauding the way the ladies dance for them. But it's all quiet, the evening's events lending everything an air of melancholy.

The bathroom is sparse, with copper pipes heating the floor from below in what I can only assume is typical fashion. A wooden bench sits beside the pool, a pile of towels folded upon it. I sit on the steps, not daring to go much deeper than the third step down.

Copper Betty pours another basin of water over my hair, her robotic eyes somehow impatient. She gestures at the soap and then points to where the deep water foams and bubbles.

"No," I tell her. "I can't swim. I'll not let you drown me for the sake of clean hair."

The automaton shakes her head in mechanical exasperation, but I stay where I am. She'll have to make do with me dunking in the shallow end. I have my doubts as to how clean I can actually be, soaking or not. The stink pipes leave a mark that is hard to rub off.

The soap is harsh but effective, and I scrape at the grime on my flesh with a wet cloth. Beneath the dirt, my skin's true color appears, which is less of a dusky gray and more of a golden brown. I raise my arm to stare at the way it shines beneath the lantern light. Apparently satisfied, Copper Betty clanks away to fetch a large towel and gestures for me to get out of the water. She's barely wrapped the towel around my shoulders when she starts dragging a comb through the tangle of my hair.

"Ow!" I cry. "Not so hard, you great metal monster!"

"Imagine how much worse it would be if we hadn't cut it earlier," Molly says, watching impassively from the doorway.

I flinch, hiding deeper into the towel. "So what now?"

"So now we wait. Dr. Barrows will try to find out whatever information he can through the...channels available to him." Her tongue darts out and lingers in the corner of her mouth. "As will I. Once I've managed to clean up the mess the Inquestors left behind."

She gives me a sour look and ushers me upstairs to my room. Copper Betty remains below to take care of my filthy clothing and has orders to bring up something for me to eat.

Molly leaves me alone in my bedroom, returning only to throw a nightgown at me. "This is the last one," she warns. "Anything else and you'll have to buy it yourself. I'm not a seamstress to outfit you."

"Technically the last ones were from Dr. Barrows," I point out absently, pulling the gown over my head. It's too big and hangs down nearly to my ankles. "I look like the mast of a ship about to set sail."

"You're lucky I don't put you to work down below. It will take me weeks before I can repair the damage those red-cloaked bastards did. They tore up every single one of my seat cushions. Every. Single. One."

I sink onto the bed, her accusatory tone washing over me. "Dr. Barrows said they were looking for the dragon."

"Not that they said so in so many words." Molly's eyes narrow. "Inquestor Caskers already knew we were aware of its existence the other night. This was a warning for me to keep my mouth shut."

"But they were willing to burn down the museum. Why not this place?"

"Professional courtesy." She sniffs, studying her perfectly polished nails with a tired smile. "I guard and sell many secrets here. They need me, as much as they hate to admit it. Besides, my girls only charge them half price for their services."

"A lofty ambition, I'm sure."

Molly shoots me a withering look. "Whatever you think about my profession, my girls are more than mere bed warmers."

"Oh, aye," I agree. "So they trade themselves for information."

"Somewhat like that, yes."

"Nice work if you can get it." I pace to the window and glance down at the alley. Behind me, Molly coughs hard into her fist. "I'm not lying," I snap. "You think I would turn down work that got me a warm bed and decent food? And for what? Spreading my legs for some Upper Tier fob with a wrinkly sad sausage for a cock? As opposed to going down to the Pits? Aye, I'd do it."

"Indeed." She fixes me with a sloe-eyed stare, but the laziness is deceptive, the way a cat is quiet before it pounces. "Where is the dragon now, Mags?"

I hesitate, not sure I want to tell her. I slump into the mattress. "I lost it," I say finally. "When the Inquestors were chasing me."

The lie slips from my tongue easily enough, but there's a calculated gleam in Molly's eyes that I don't like.

"Well, maybe it's for the best. I doubt the Inquestors would have been too friendly if they *had* found it here, secrets or no." She taps her fan against her palm, staring out of the tiny window at something only she can see. "I suggest you get some rest while you can. I've a terrifying amount of work to do and I cannot be distracted by your whereabouts. If you might curtail your nocturnal activities and spare us any further wrath from those above, I'll be quite in your debt."

I stiffen at her tone but busy myself with lighting a fire in the fireplace, shifting the logs about until the blaze shakes the chill from the room.

A dull clanking from the hallway heralds Copper Betty's appearance, complete with a tray from the kitchens. My stomach rumbles, loud enough for Molly to smirk at the sound.

"I'll leave you to it. We'll figure out what's to be done in the morning. Perhaps Dr. Barrows will have had some luck finding

Ghost." And with that she strides out the door, leaving me to my own devices.

Copper Betty places the tray at the foot of the bed, staring blankly at me until I dismiss her. I fight the urge to slam the door behind her, unsure why she unnerves me so, but it's easier to lose myself in shoveling a roll into my mouth than investigate my own shortcomings.

Ghost weighs heavy upon my thoughts, though, and before long I'm pacing a trench in the floorboards in front of the fireplace, replaying what happened over and over in my mind until I'm half-sick with the memories.

Somehow, I need a plan. Maybe Dr. Barrows will find his brother. But maybe he won't.

"He's a Moon Child, after all," I mutter at myself. "And it's your fault. So it's only fitting you try to find him in your own way."

Satisfied with this, I retreat to the bed to eat another sweet roll. As much as I want to search for him immediately, going to ground here for the night is the best course of action.

"But tomorrow? Tomorrow's a new day."

Somehow saying it out loud only solidifies my resolve, as though the walls might take my words as commitment.

There's no answer, and I don't expect one. In the end, I turn off the lights and stare at the flickering of the fireplace until something like sleep swallows me up.

Maggy, Maggy quite contrary
How doth thy garden grow?
With zombie maids and bloody staves
And death flowers all in a row.

— CHAPTER ELEVEN —

Wake up, Mags."

There's a light pressure on my face, and then I'm staring into the bloodshot eyes of Dr. Barrows. There's a haggardness within that wasn't there before; an empty despair clings to his skin with all the sharpness of stale smoke.

I struggle to sit up, wiping away the grit of sleep. Not that I'd gotten much. My chest aches as though suddenly remembering what had happened yesterday.

Ghost.

"Did you find him?" I only ask it out of courtesy. Surely if he had, the bitterness would not run so deep in his gaze.

"He was rounded up with several others by the Inquestors. Supposedly as suspects in the museum fire, but my usual sources are being rather tight-lipped with their information. Someone's paying them off," he says grimly. "I couldn't even get the Chancellor to see me."

I blink, thoughts churning. Fear makes me foolish, but Ghost won't be helped if I lose my head about it now. "But why? They were just attacking us for standing there...and they were using Tithe wands."

He sinks into the overstuffed chair, resting his temple upon his fingers. "I can't possibly imagine what they're trying to accomplish. To shut down the museum would be one thing...but this? It makes no sense at all."

I bite my lower lip hard, drawing blood. "Archivist Chaunders? Did she survive?"

He nods slowly. "Yes. But she was very badly burned, Mags. They're keeping her at the Salt Temple."

I exhale raggedly. If she's under the mercy of the salt priests, there's nothing to be done for her. "I want to go see her."

He hesitates. "I'm not so sure that would be the best idea. The temple is bound to be crawling with Inquestors. If one of them recognizes you..."

"I don't care," I say, shaking my head almost violently. "She's my friend. I've already lost two of my clan sisters, and Ghost, and now I'm about to lose her, too!" I choke on a sob.

And whose fault is that?

I swallow down a thick lump of anger at myself. "Please," I whisper.

After wordlessly watching my sudden outburst, he sighs softly. "All right, Mags. Perhaps it might be better if I go with you, though. You might garner less attention that way."

The warning beneath the words is clear. No rooftop dancing today. And what can I do but agree? Every decision I've made so far has been wrong.

A tired smile touches his lips, but his eyes remain empty. "Give me some time to break my fast and wash up. Try to find something suitable to wear to the temple, if you would?"

I glance down at my nightshirt and remember that the rest of my clothes were destroyed the night before. There's little doubt as to what he means by *suitable*.

His mouth purses at my expression. "I'm sure Martika has a dress you can borrow. Let me see if I can talk her into it."

My ears perk up at that, and I hear Ghost's voice in my head, repeating that cryptic statement about who Martika really is, but I quench my curiosity quickly. My focus right now needs to be on providing comfort to my dying friend and finding Ghost. Secrets can come later.

I glance down at my hands, rubbing at the thick calluses on my thumbs. "I'm sorry...for everything."

He squeezes my shoulder when he passes. "Me too."

The scent of smoke still hangs thick around Market Square as Dr. Barrows and I emerge from the Conundrum. The Mother Clock bongs out the early morning hour with her usual low chimes as we walk. The sound feels heavier than it normally does somehow, sinking into my bones with a mocking rumble.

Vendors are out and about, greatly subdued as they wheel their wares through the streets to whatever spots they choose to claim for the day. Several Inquestors remain posted outside of the ruins of the haberdashery.

"To prevent additional looting," Dr. Barrows notes.

The doctor is dressed in a long, brown wool coat and a scarf of cobalt silk about his neck. His derby hat is perched rakishly on his head, as though he couldn't quite expend the energy to right it, but it doesn't seem to bother him.

And I...I am wearing a skirt. Ill fitting and plain, it's woven of dark-green wool and lace trim, seemingly borrowed from Martika's closet. I escaped being tied into a corset by hiding within a loosely belted blouse and a hooded gray cloak that hangs to my ankles, hiding a multitude of fashion sins, including my lack of coiffure.

I don't have time for that sort of nonsense anyway. The skirt itches me something terrible, and I can only squirm within its confines.

Dr. Barrows scans the crowds and raises a gloved hand. "Don't fidget."

"I can't possibly walk to the temple in this," I say, pulling the cloak tighter over my shoulders to hide the fact that I'm scratching at my arms.

"Indeed. And I'm far too tired to travel by foot at this point. Hence my hailing a cab." He whistles shrilly a moment later when we reach the corner of the square, sighing when one of the horseless carriages pulls up from the queue.

It's a worn contraption, probably built before Meridion made its first appearance. Great gouts of steam puff beneath its rusting metal belly, and the driver holds the side door open for us. Dr. Barrows nudges me inside.

The whole thing stinks of rotting leather and sagging cushions stuffed with horsehair. The bench creaks as I take a seat. Dr. Barrows explains something at the driver and climbs in to sit across from me.

I glance out the window, watching the streets slip by in a blur of foot traffic and the occasional vehicle. Not all the BrightStone streets can accommodate such inventions—and the Meridians have forbidden public carriages from entering the Upper Tier without a permit—but Market Square and the Theatre Quarter are open to transport.

Looking up at the rooftops, I can't help but retrace my steps from the night before, a shiver taking root in my spine when we cross over the Everdark on the Sacred Bridge. BrightStone's founder must have been a religious chap, given the names of the five main bridges of our city, but it all seems like a mockery to me.

We take a sharp left after the bridge, skimming alongside the river until the cab comes to a sudden halt, the brakes squealing in seeming horror as they're applied hard enough to finally tip me off the bench. Dr. Barrows moves to catch me but doesn't manage it until after I've nearly cracked my nose on a low-hanging handle.

I straighten my skirts, trying to descend from the carriage without looking like I've been tumbled.

The cabbie holds his hand out, but I leave it to Dr. Barrows to pay him. It's not like I have any jingle anyway. Instead, I study the crushed white shells crunching beneath my feet.

The carriage steams off, backfiring twice as it disappears, and is swallowed up in the remaining haze. "I wasn't sure if you'd have him wait," I say, crouching down for a better look at the shells and marveling at their brightness. I can only guess how nothing tarnishes them, even here.

"Yes, well. We can certainly pick up another one later. Let's see how this goes first." He tugs me to my feet.

I nod and let him lead me to the entrance of the temple. The main doors are recessed quite far into the building itself, past a series of yellowed pillars shot through with veins of copper. An awning of weathered metal hangs over the walkway, pockets of corrosion evident everywhere I look.

A single Inquestor stands beside the main door, her crimson robes stark against the pillars. She draws her spine straight as we approach, but Dr. Barrows takes my arm as though he is merely escorting me.

"State your business here," the Inquestor says softly, her gaze sliding between me and the doctor. I refuse to cringe before her bold stare.

"We have come to pay our respects to the archivist," Dr. Barrows says. "She is an associate of ours."

"Is she now?" The Inquestor spits the words like she's tasted something foul, and I know she'll never let us in. But the door creaks open and the wizened face of a salt priest peers out, rheumy eyes squinting at our presence.

"What's all this, then?" he asks.

"Visitors for the archivist," the Inquestor reports smoothly. "Claim to be *associates*."

The salt priest grunts. "What of it? The temple is for any who wish to seek solace within her walls. The end to this poor woman's suffering can't come too soon. Surely you have it in your heart to grant her a few final moments among friends?"

I must have made some small sound of distress because the salt priest opens the door wider, his gray robes billowing in a sudden updraft. "Come in, my dear."

Dr. Barrows wastes no time and steers me forward, one hand splayed against my back. The Inquestor sniffs as we pass but makes no move to block our way. An uneasy relief floods through me when the priest closes the door behind us. I have no love for the salt priests or their sea gods, either, though, and the clink of the door closing only sounds like a cage locking.

An odd dampness clings to the inner walls of the temple, and a moment later I spy a large bubbling pool in the center of the rotunda. Intricate knotted carvings curve around the border of the pool as foam swirls within.

Another salt priest stands before it, an acolyte dressed in faded blue robes. He stirs a driftwood paddle clockwise in some esoteric fashion. He's a younger man, with only the mere tufts of a beard sprouting from his cheeks, but his face brightens when he sees us.

"Would you like a closer look?" The acolyte gestures me forward. "A saltwater spring allows us to purify all those who seek the wisdom of the gods."

"No," I say.

Disappointment tightens the corners of his mouth.

"But thank you," I add. No sense in aggravating them when they're actually trying to help, I suppose.

The old priest who let us in tugs at my cloak with a trembling hand. "This way to see your friend. We have her in the Room of Respite."

"That sounds promising," I mutter darkly, but it's the fear of what I'll see that spurs me to say it.

If the salt priest heard me he gives no sign, leading us around a curved passage made of bleached limestone. Myriad fossilized shells wink from within the porous walls. I suppose it's meant to be pretty, but I suppress a shudder, imagining death by slow suffocation only to have my bones put on display like some morbid peep show.

Several arched doorways branch away from the hallway. Other rooms of healing, perhaps, but the drawn curtains that flutter at our passing remind me of shrouds.

A bird-masked Inquestor peers out from one of the rooms and then turns away, swallowed up by the shadows. A Tithe Collector, come to find those with the Rot. I catch a glimpse of a dark-haired girl with hollow eyes sitting on a bed, and she looks up as I pass. A soft buzz vibrates from within, and I catch the faint whiff of ink. She's being tattooed with a Tithe mark on her forearm, a formal indicator that she'll be Tithed to the Pits soon.

Our gazes meet, and her despair pierces me so abruptly that the breath stills in my lungs.

But then we're moving down the hall, pausing outside an open door. The salt priest coughs. "She's in here. Do not tarry long."

Dr. Barrows is kind enough to take the first step into the room. Somehow it's easier to bear if I can stare at the polish of his boots instead of the body on the bed. My mind doesn't quite recognize her as human, and I can only gape at the ruined remains of her face, the charred scalp and blistered flesh.

The doctor has no such issue, and he studies her prone form with a cool and practiced gaze. She's wrapped from the neck down in what look like wet bandages, the cloth slick and shiny.

"Cooling gel," Dr. Barrows observes. "To help numb what's left of the skin."

I flinch from his clinical observations, shutting out the rest of his words to concentrate on her face. Small details jump out at me, from the swollen eyelids and the naked brows, the rattling sigh of her breath and parched lips.

I pause, realizing I have no idea what her first name is, and I settle for clearing my throat. "Archivist Chaunders?"

She stirs, a moan sighing from her lungs. "Mags?"

"Aye." I kneel beside her, unsure what to do. I don't dare touch the fragile membrane of her skin.

Her eyes crack open, revealing a bloodshot brightness that makes her gray irises shimmer with an otherworldly essence, as though she's already passed on to whatever plane of existence remains for her. Her body shudders. "The...In...questors. Know I..."

A lump forms in my throat. "I'm sorry," I whisper.

"Not...your...fault." Her entire body stills, only for her chest to rise again suddenly a few moments later. "The dragon, Mags..."

But whatever else she is about to say is swallowed up by a gurgling cough. Immediately the salt priest kneels at her side, his gnarled fingers tracing some esoteric sign upon her forehead with a pasty substance—salt flour.

Dr. Barrows rests his hand on my shoulder, squeezing gently. "It's time, Mags."

But I can't leave. Whatever she said, this happened because of me, and I need to see it through. I have to be here for her when she leaves this world. When the acolyte enters, I only shuffle a few steps, watching as the two holy men intone their prayers, my mouth trembling.

Once again, I've lost a friend.

Once again, it's my fault.

My vision seems to narrow into a gray space, wavering as I try to focus on what's happening, but it's lost in the shaky wobble of my legs. I press my palm against my lips to keep from giving voice to the wail that threatens to erupt from my throat, swallowing back a choking sob.

Boots scuff on the floor outside the doorway, and I glance up to see the bird-masked Inquestor staring at us. My first instinct is to run for it, but Dr. Barrows tightens his grip upon my shoulder, warning me to stay still.

"I've come to collect the remains," a metallic voice hums from behind the mask, muffled and without empathy.

"But why?" The question squeaks out of me despite my fear. "She didn't have the Rot."

The Inquestor ignores me, his hand brushing over the Tithe wand hanging from his hip.

Outrage boils through my blood, so hot I nearly expect my fingers to be on fire when I step forward. "She's not even cold yet, you vulture! You can't just take her! She didn't do anything wrong."

"I am sorry about your friend, dearest," the elder salt priest interjects before the Inquestor can react. "But the possibility of contamination is too great a risk."

"Contamination from what?" I snap.

"It is not for us to determine the sins of those who have passed," the salt priest intones soothingly, as if that would help. "But the Inquestors feel it would be best if they oversaw her arrangements."

The bird-beaked Inquestor presses his hands together in an odd gesture of helplessness as he turns to the priest. "We cannot allow others to fall into sin."

The salt priest nods sagely. "Indeed. The Moon Children will be busy atoning for this poor woman's weakness. Eating the sins of the damned is no easy feat. It is only a pity we do not have more of them to go around."

He says this so seriously, I have to choke down the ugly, furious laughter that bubbles in my chest. I'm supposed to be a common BrightStone citizen, after all. He doesn't know who I truly am under this dyed hair. I also know that blinded by his religion, he has no knowledge of the truth in which Moon Children live, but to have him preach it to my face?

"If you're so concerned with sickness, then why let us in here at all?" I challenge.

"Quite." The Inquestor's voice darkens. "And we left instructions that none were to be granted entrance, but it would appear the priest's judgment was lost in a moment of foolishness." A pause. "You have paid your respects, as you would. It's time for you leave."

The curt dismissal leaves me seething, the lies tasting bitter on my tongue. But Dr. Barrows merely nods in acquiescence. "So it is. Thank you for your compassion in this matter."

"A courtesy in name only, I assure you." The Inquestor turns his back to us, leaving us with little else to do but retreat.

The curved walls press down upon me, the pale whiteness heavy and thick and cloying. My breath comes in soft gasps. I'm only a few sobs away from bolting out of this place, Inquestors or no.

A glance behind me reveals Dr. Barrows, his mouth set in a grim line. His lack of reaction only spurs me on until I'm running. I burst through the doors, ignoring the sudden exclamation of the Inquestor standing guard outside.

Shells grind beneath my shoes, and for a moment I want to see them stomped into dust, but all I can hear is my poor friend's death rattle as she took her last breath. I can't shut it out no matter how hard I clamp my hands over my ears.

Dr. Barrows shouts something after me, but I don't care. The skirts tangle around my legs, forcing me to hitch them up to keep from tripping. I only stop when I come to the edge of the square in the center of the Theatre Quarter, the Brass Button Theatre perched on the other side with its statues and fountains, and its illusions that somehow there is civility in this world.

I sink to my knees in the dust, vomiting noisily. Images of those I've lost in just the past few weeks waver before me. Sparrow. Ghost. Archivist Chaunders.

"Mags." Dr. Barrows has caught up to me, carrying his hat in his hand. His face is flushed and awful, and I know he's imagining Ghost in the same situation because that's what I'm thinking, too.

"We have to find him." My voice is thick against the lump in my throat, and I wrap my arms around myself, rubbing at a chill that I can't get rid of.

"I've currently exhausted my avenues, at least until I'm able to meet with the Chancellor." He sighs, hoisting me up with one hand and patting a handkerchief against my mouth with the other. "Here. Let's find you a little something to eat."

"All right." I sniff, wiping my nose on the cloak. He winces but takes my arm anyway.

"Small steps. Calm steps. Running attracts attention, and we don't want that. I am but an uncle escorting his favorite niece to one of her daily distractions."

"Favorite niece, nothing," I say. "I'm your only niece."

It's a poor attempt at a jest, but his mouth twitches. "That's the spirit."

We stroll around the square, nodding politely at all those we come across. The tension here is not as tight as in Market Square, but a nervous confusion lingers in the faces of most of the BrightStone citizens. Dr. Barrows slips easily into the visage of the put-upon aristocrat. I attempt to do something similar, but it's easier to withdraw into the hood of my cloak.

An airship patrols overhead in lazy circles.

"What if the Chancellor can't help?" I ask quietly.

"Then we try something else." He coughs abruptly, as though he doesn't want to discuss it anymore. We stop at a fruit vendor, and he buys me an out-of-season peach that costs more jingle than I normally make in a week.

I thank him and eat it without tasting it, the juice sticky on my chin. When the peach is nothing more than a pit, I roll it between my fingers. My thoughts wander to the Twisted Tumblers, but Josephine was pretty firm about not wanting me to bring attention to her.

On the other hand, she has my dragon. A dragon that led to Sparrow's death, the burning of the museum, and the death of the archivist. I owe her a warning.

"What about Josephine?" I give Dr. Barrows a sideways glance, but he barely seems to acknowledge my question.

"Ah, yes. You did mention you were out this way last evening." He shakes his head. "Foolish boy."

"Well at least he's been trying to show me *something*, instead of hiding everything away for my own good. Incidentally, we *were* going to tell you that Josephine had a way to get me into a Tithe. And she's nearly solved the issue with making sure the gates will be open so I can escape the Pits." I give him a small smile. "Surely that's worth something?"

"Not without finding Ghost first." The doctor's eyes shutter, dismissing me.

"Don't be such an arse." A grunt escapes him when I elbow him in the side. "He sacrificed himself so that I could still do what you need me to do. What I promised I'd do. Don't cheapen that by letting all your plans fall by the wayside in a search for him. I want to find him as much as you do, but Josephine has the dragon. If we want it back we're going to have to reach out to her anyway," I point out. "And if she can command the other Moon Children to look for Ghost, we may find him that much faster."

He grits his teeth, swallowing whatever he was going to say, and sighs. "So how do we contact her? Ghost was our only method of communicating with her, which leaves *me* out of the loop on this one."

I don't want to try to scale the Brass Button Theatre to the Rookery. Anyone climbing such a visible and well-known building in the middle of the day will stick out like a sore thumb, never mind a woman in a skirt. Chances are Josephine keeps it tightly guarded anyhow. Even if anyone up there does recognize me from the night before, they won't exactly be keen on me giving away their position.

And if they don't recognize me at all? A perceived assault upon a clan's headquarters usually results in death, and that's not something I plan to risk.

On the other hand, even if I can unlock the stink pipe we used last night, I'll be lost in moments. Which means I'll have to go looking for Moon Children directly, assuming they haven't all fled to the safety of their clan home by now.

I gaze down at my skirts and then up at the rooftops, wondering how I'll manage to scale the buildings without ripping something. And not that I care about the skirt all that much, but just once, I'd like to return to the Conundrum with my clothing intact.

Dr. Barrows watches me with a raised brow, and I scowl. "Don't think you're going to stand here while I do all the work."

"Wouldn't dream of it. What would you have me do?"

"Be my lookout. You're going to keep watch for any Inquestors that happen to wander by. Signal me quiet-like if you see anyone getting too close. At least until I get roofside." He frowns, and I roll my eyes. "You can whistle, can't you? Like this." I demonstrate, sounding out the two-note warning Sparrow and I had used so often in the past.

His lips purse, repeating the signal until it's passable. "Do you need a boost?" he offers.

"No. Climbing here is too obvious, especially in daylight. We'll split up."

"How will I know you've made it up there all right?"

I whistle a different set of notes at him. This answer seems to satisfy him because he strolls off, lingering at the front window of a tinker's shop.

I walk in the opposite direction, both to give us some distance and to find the best place to climb. I end up in one of those dead-end alleys with a convenient set of stacked barrels. It's only a question of rucking my skirts up and tucking them in about my waist. I'm not wearing much in the way of smallclothes, but there's none here to see anyway.

Balancing atop the highest barrel, I scrabble up the brickwork to a slip of a windowsill and then a rotting bit of trellis. Despite my best intentions, my skirt catches on a nail, the cloth ripping with a disappointing cheerfulness.

But there's no time to worry about that now. A rush of blessed relief slides over me when I finally reach the safety of the roof. The sun is fully up now, burning the haze with a vengeance and making the nearby shadows starker.

I take refuge in one and sit against a chimney to get my bearings. The sounds of morning with the familiar clinks of crockery and the rising calls of the street vendors. A dog barking a few streets over. The distant buzz of an airship. Everything that falls within the realm of normal, even if everything feels terribly subdued, as if the entire city is waiting.

When I can't stand it anymore, I creep from one roof to the next, taking extra care not to make too much noise, pacing myself to hide in the rhythmic beats of life unfolding all around me.

I let out a series of questioning trills. Soft at first, but growing a little louder on the third round. I don't know the Twisted Tumbler signals, so I stick with the common notes, slurring them together so it nearly sounds like birdsong.

What news? Danger danger. What news? Danger danger.

Below, Dr. Barrows continues his easy stroll of the street. He holds a steaming drink in his hand and sips it slowly as he pretends to browse.

I whistle at him softly. He makes no sign that he's heard me, save a gentle tap of his hat. Good enough.

After a minute or so, I change position, moving to another rooftop and then another, timing them so the average listener might not pay much attention. By the third time I whistle my call, I'm growing frustrated.

Technically, Josephine had given me leave to be in Twisted Tumbler territory. Might as well put that to the test. I let out a more aggressive set of signals, essentially the equivalent of calling everyone suck-tit bastards and cowards.

I sigh at the sound of a weapon being cocked. "Finally," I say.

"Should have known it was you," Josephine drawls from up above, flanked by two other Moon Children. There's soot on her cheeks and arms. Clearly, I've interrupted her work, and if the scowl on her face is anything to go by, I probably don't have much time to convince her of my reasons for being here. All three of them hold crossbows like the one Tin Tin was using the night before, and all three are pointed in my direction. "When my scouts said a townie was up here singing war songs, I blew them off, but here you are…"

"It's not exactly like I knew where to go," I remind her. "You didn't give me a way to contact you."

She climbs down to where I am and waves the others away. "No offense," she says bluntly, "but this isn't the way to make an impression. If you needed to find me, you should have let Ghost do it."

"That's the problem," I say, not wanting to get into a pissing match about protocol. "Ghost was taken last night."

Josephine's face darkens as I explain what happened with the Inquestors. Her gaze grows hot when I mention the Tithe wands. "I *knew* you were trouble. You and that dragon."

"I'll be happy to take it off your hands," I snap back, a chill skittering down my spine. "That's what the Inquestors are looking for." My voice is hushed, the archivist's death terribly fresh in my mind. "That's why they burned down part of Market Square, and that's why they'll probably kill you if they find out you have it."

"Well, there's the rub," she says dryly. "It's gone. Disappeared this morning, in fact."

Dismay floods into my gut, hot and tight. "What do you mean *it's gone?*"

She answers me with a shrug. "As I said. When we realized you and Ghost had left last night, I figured I'd keep it until I heard back. I stepped out to look at the damage in Market Square for myself, but when I returned, it wasn't in my forge. The good news is I was able to make enough notes to carry through to a working test model of the wings, so we're still on schedule as far as that part's concerned."

"Convenient," I mutter. I'd be less inclined to believe her if I didn't know the little metal beast had its own ideas, but it didn't make me feel any better. "So now what?"

Josephine rubbed her chin, leaving another soot mark dimpled upon her skin. "I don't know as far as the dragon goes…but seeing as Ghost was rounded up by the Inquestors, I think I might have a way to find out what happened to him."

"Move over. Your elbow is in my face," I hiss. Tin Tin grumbles something under his breath, but shifts all of two inches to give me a better look through the air vent to the private theatre box below.

Everything is rich velvet and intimately lit, with twin doors on both sides of the box. One leads to the balcony overlooking the stage and the other to the main hall of the upper level of the theatre. The vent is barely wide enough for my shoulders to squeeze through, but it's enough to let me lie flat.

"Are you sure he'll be here?" I can't help the sting of annoyance from filling my voice. Tin Tin has wriggled his skinny self partially over my body, peering through the vent opening. And it's not that he weighs much, but he's got sharp little elbows that dig into my back.

"Josephine said so," he whispers. "The High Inquestor always attends the theatre about once a month. There's an actress performing tonight who he favors."

I sigh. Nothing for it, then, but to wait in this small, dusty duct. As compromises go, it's not the one I would have chosen, but given the circumstances, it's the best I can hope for. My dismay at Josephine's loss of the dragon is overshadowed by her complete inability to trust Dr. Barrows in the slightest, Ghost's brother or no.

Dr. Barrows is on his own, forced to buy his own ticket on the off chance he can find out anything from his end. But the only person who matters to me right now is the High Inquestor. Josephine insists he often conducts business in his private box, so with any luck we'll be able to learn something about where they took Ghost. Failing that...

My jaw tightens when the door creaks open, but it's merely an usher, dressed in a gown of black lace. She plumps the pillows, fills a carafe with cold water, and sets out glasses beside a bottle of brandy. Sliding open the balcony door reveals the stage below, lights shining in a blur of shadowy colors.

Any other time would have found me staring at the goings-on in fascination. The theatre was outside of Banshee territory so we never had the chance to sneak into a show, but now the stakes are too high to pay more than scant attention to it.

Someone is singing, strutting about with exaggerated motions. I suppose it must be considered beautiful, but it grates on my ears like so much wailing.

"Where are they?" I whisper. "The show has started. Maybe we're in the wrong box."

Tin Tin grunts when I shift beneath him. "This is the one he owns. He's always late, aye? Half the time he never watches the show anyway."

But I have no more time to answer, because the door slides open again, and this time a man enters. His face is hidden beneath his hat, but even from here I can see how fine his coat is and the gleam of his sharply polished boots.

"That's not him," Tin Tin breathes in my ear. "I think it's…"

Lord Balthazaar.

I've only seen the man a few times from a distance, but there's no mistaking that saunter, that prideful air of power that seems to drape over him like a cloak. He lingers at the door closest to the stage for half a minute before closing it. The sound is muffled immediately, and I swallow hard. My breathing seems loud and terrible now. I might exhale and an explosion of dust will shower down upon the man to reveal us all.

A flare of light shines bright and hot. He's lit a cigarillo, puffing expertly as he takes a seat upon one of the benches. Time seems to tick by even slower as he waits, and my clockwork heart beats out the seconds with perfect precision.

Tin Tin stifles a cough, straining to keep quiet, but Lord Balthazaar takes no notice of anything, save the pile of ash in the crystal tray beside him. As slow as it feels up here, he's only partway through the smoke when the door opens again.

This time an usher enters, bowing as a crimson-robed figure arrives, the fabric at his shoulders gilded with a gold trim the only indicator of his rank. The High Inquestor.

The two men exchange glances and dismiss the usher with a wave, the High Inquestor pouring himself a glass of the brandy. He's a tall man, with an aristocratic face, but his expression is all but hidden in the shadows.

Lord Balthazaar taps the cigarillo against the tray, his nostrils exhaling a large puff of smoke. "Why do we bother continuing this farce?" he asks, but I can't tell if he's angry or bored, the lack of inflection in his voice at odds with the sneer upon his lips.

The High Inquestor closes his eyes for a moment, listening. "Hush," he murmurs, as the singing grows higher in pitch. "My favorite aria."

"It is Lydia's, as well."

"A pity you do not share her opinion of it. It's a fascinating piece if you're aware of its history." The High Inquestor smiles, but it carries a savage edge to it.

"As you say." They remain quiet for a long while as the rise and fall of the singer's vibrato fills the hall. My limbs grow stiff beneath Tin Tin's weight. Sweat trickles into my eyes, but I don't dare attempt to wipe it away. I blink against the sting.

"The Chancellor is growing impatient with your shenanigans." Balthazaar pours himself a glass of brandy. "We shall have to hurry this little scavenger hunt along if we're to keep her in ignorance."

"What can she do?" The Inquestor is unconcerned, sitting lazily in his chair with one foot stretched out onto a small table.

"Well she's certainly been knocking at my door with regular frequency." Balthazaar drops the cigarillo into the tray. "Was burning half of Market Square truly necessary? She's going to be pestering me for charitable donations for the next six months."

"We were acting on additional intelligence that turned out to be incorrect. One of my Inquestors indicated a Meridian dragon was in the museum. We found no such evidence, but my men were a tad...overzealous. Pity about the archivist, though. She could have been useful to us."

White-hot anger blazes through me at how dismissive they are of Archivist Chaunders's life, as though she had merely been a potential tool left out in a trash heap. My hands fist tightly, knuckles pressing hard against the sides of the vent as I force myself to continue listening.

"For a city with such amazing technology, you all seem to have damned little responsibility of it," Balthazaar snaps. "I care nothing about it. Forget these petty games of yours. You chase shadows and act surprised when they slip from your fingers. What of your promises? When will I have my wife back?"

Brandy sloshes over the sides of the snifter when he slams it on the table, but he takes no notice of the mess.

"You know better than I do how things are coming along in that particular area." The Inquestor sighs. "When a breakthrough has been made, you'll be the first to be notified. Surely the blood infusions are working for now?"

The other man scowls. "As little as they ever did. It barely keeps her alive. No more."

"Ahh. That's a shame. Perhaps Georges needs a nudge. I'll look into it."

"Whatever you must do. All I get are complaints at the quality of the subjects." Balthazaar waves his hand impatiently. "Our stock appears to be dwindling."

Stock? Subjects? Infusion? Their words seem to blur by me as I struggle to make sense of them. Dr. Barrows would know what they mean, of that I have little doubt, though so far none of it seems particularly helpful when it comes to Ghost.

"Yes, well, things are a bit different these days, aren't they? The new regulations have been in place for quite some time. And that's even going beyond trying to find someone willing to rut with the common slatterns they have down here. We rounded up some suitable brood mares among the BrightStone dissidents last night.

We'll make sure they're well compensated for their trouble once they produce their brats. "

Moon Children...They're making Moon Children.

I nearly choke at the casual way they talk of breeding hapless women on the off chance a Moon Child results from the union. Even if my own mother had died upon my birth, there had always been some small part of me hoping I might find my Meridian father, that there had been *some* reason I'd been born. But they make it sound as though it's nothing but a faceless shag. Their disdain shouldn't surprise me, but it stings far more than I expect.

The conversation devolves into political small talk, but my thoughts whirl with the repercussions of their discussion and the need to try to remember as much of it as I can. I want to slither out of the vent while it's all fresh in my mind, but I don't dare move. Tin Tin's breath is hot on the nape of my neck.

The two men have gone quiet now, listening to the music. Another usher knocks on the door and enters, bearing a tray of fresh baked trifles. My mouth waters when the scent wafts our direction, imagining powdered sugar and cinnamon melting upon my tongue.

The High Inquestor thanks the usher and takes one, nibbling at it daintily and wiping at his mouth with a cloth every few seconds. Tin Tin makes a soft sound of longing, and I nudge him sharply.

Another knock at the door, but this one isn't nearly as polite as the usher's. Before either of the men can react, the door slides open, revealing a tall, well-dressed woman. Her hair is pulled up into something stark and severe, and she glares at them from behind a thick pair of violet spectacles.

The High Inquestor reacts first, giving her a charming smile. "Ah, Chancellor Davis. To what do we owe the pleasure?"

Without bothering to reply, she strides into the box and takes a place on the bench beside Balthazaar. In her hand she's clutching a scroll, fury rolling off her in waves. "Explain to me how my investigators have discovered that arson is responsible for last night's tragedy? A fire that points to Inquestor involvement and that resulted in several deaths, as well the loss of goods and businesses in Market Square, not to mention our last existing historical archive."

"Perhaps this conversation would be better suited for your office," the High Inquestor suggests, a soothing tone to his voice.

"A meeting I have tried to arrange numerous times this morning *without any reply*," she snaps. "What other choice do I have but to force myself into your presence?"

"Indeed." Lord Balthazaar raises his hands. "I've nothing to do with any of this."

Chancellor Davis lets out a snort. "Of course not. You practically live in his back pocket, but you're obviously the victim here."

"Have a care what accusations you make without proof," he snarls, getting to his feet.

She moves to block his leaving, her cheeks flush with anger. "Citizens were rounded up last night by Inquestors without cause. Where are they? I've families looking for their loved ones without any way of contacting them."

"They are being detained while we question them," the High Inquestor explains. "Have no fear for their well-being. They will all be released by the end of the week."

"That's not good enough! I insist you release them into the custody of the BrightStone city guard, and we will perform our own investigation. Arson or not, it falls under BrightStone jurisdiction."

"Ah, but there were biological agents in the museum, were there not? Samples from ill citizens? Are you suggesting your people are equipped to deal with the fallout, should something happen?"

She deflates. "Your own record on such matters has little to show for it. Nearly twenty years and the plague remains—"

"Exactly," the High Inquestor interrupts, though the hitch in his voice indicates her words have hit their mark. "If we can barely manage, how can you possibly expect to?"

The Chancellor looks unconvinced. "I'm going to need something a bit more formal than your word. I want a complete report of what your men were doing at the museum last night."

"We had just been talking about this very thing," he replies, indicating Balthazaar with a small gesture. "In fact, there will be a fete at Balthazaar's estate...shall we say two days hence? Perhaps we might conduct our business there, in more pleasant surroundings? I shall provide you all the information you need in the meantime."

Something dark flashes over Balthazaar's face, but he gives the Chancellor a strained smile. "A charity ball, if you like. To help with city repairs from the fire."

"I will talk with my advisors on the matter," she says, clearly reticent. "But if that is the best I can hope for, then so be it."

The High Inquestor bows. "I will have the reports sent to you in the morning. I'm sure you will be more than content."

Her jaw tightens. "I shall await your counsel on the morrow. Until then, it would be greatly appreciated if your Inquestors showed more restraint when it comes to the civilian populace. There are rumors of possible riots, and BrightStone can ill afford a lack of stability during the winter season."

After several repeated assurances from the two gentlemen, she finally takes her leave, but her lack of satisfaction on the matter is more than apparent. I've never given much thought to the political dance that holds BrightStone within its sway, but I find it oddly comforting to realize that not everyone remains beneath Meridion's thumb.

"Bothersome woman." Balthazaar slips on his overcoat, buttoning it with precise fingers. "And I'll be expecting compensation for hosting your little party, mind. The food will have to come from my private pantry on such short notice."

"A great hardship," the High Inquestor agrees, laughing. "She won't show anyway. It would undermine her honor to do so. And how are your new guests, incidentally? Wouldn't want to be called a liar by our lovely Chancellor."

"Alas, all but one appears to have contracted the Rot. Undoubtedly sinners of little remorse." A sly smile plays over Balthazaar's lips. "They have been sent to the Salt Temple to be Tithed, as planned. The last one has a rather stubborn immune system, it seems. He's remained disgustingly healthy, despite the injections."

My blood turns to ice. Ghost. They're talking about Ghost. Who else could it be?

He's alive, my inner voice babbles, a sick relief flooding my stomach.

"Might be worth a look at his blood to see if he's built up an immunity." The High Inquestor squeezes the other man's shoulder. "Imagine having a cure for your Lydia, right under your own roof."

Balthazaar nods with a quiet malice. "Until the charity ball, then?"

"Wouldn't miss it."

They share a soft chuckle that ripples with secrets, but their good humor is like the festering skin growing over a wound gone rancid—just as pleasant, too.

By the time they leave, my arms and legs are so stiff I can barely move. Tin Tin and I wriggle our way backward to the main level of the heating ducts. We spend a few minutes uncramping in the wider pipes. I'm in no hurry to leave until enough time has passed that I'm sure Balthazaar and the High Inquestor are gone.

I look at Tin Tin, whose face has grown pale.

"Oy," he says. "That weighs heavy on the mind, aye?"

"And it's not likely to get lighter in the telling." I wipe the sweat from my brow, nose wrinkling at the stink of my fear. "To think they killed the poor woman, and for what?"

Tin Tin stares at me, unsure what to do in the face of my wrath as my knuckles crack into fists. "We have to tell Josephine. Even if she chooses not to get involved, we have to let her know. We have to let them all know."

But what about Ghost? A flutter of panic beats itself against my chest at what he's being subjected to.

Tick. Tick. Tick.

It's all falling apart around me, and I've no way to sort it out except to run.

And I can't do that anymore.

"Dr. Barrows is waiting for me. Tell Josephine what happened here, and if she should stumble across the dragon, send me a message by way of Molly Bell at the Conundrum."

I'm uncomfortable relaying messages through Molly, but I see very little choice in the matter. And this is too important to waste any more time.

We scramble out of the vents, emerging in a subbasement of the theatre near the furnace. Tin Tin looks uneasy, and I realize we're probably very close to some hidden entrance of the Rookery. But I can find my way out of the theatre from here.

"Make sure you lie low for a few days," I remind him.

Tin Tin nods, his too-old eyes wide and troubled. "Aye. Be careful, Mags."

"And you, my friend. And you."

Ring around the rosie
Pockets full of posies
Ashes, ashes, blood, and bone
My dress is torn, and I'm all alone.

— CHAPTER TWELVE —

Dr. Barrows is nowhere to be found outside the theatre. I try not to linger, sweeping through the square as quickly as I can. Night will be falling soon, and there's nothing for me but to make my way back to the Conundrum, hurrying through the streets with steady purpose. I'm still in the wretched dress Martika lent me earlier, and there's no way for me to travel with any speed over the rooftops wearing *that*.

By the time I make it to Market Square, the Mother Clock is tolling out the hour and the streets have gone silent, citizens scattering into their homes or whatever bits of shelter they can find. I go through the servants' entrance of Molly Bell's and up the stairs. The hallway is quiet, but there's a light beneath my door and shadows wavering beyond.

Dr. Barrows pacing, no doubt.

The doorknob rattles as I stride in, relief washing over me at the now-familiar scene. Molly is draped lazily over the stuffed chair filing her nails while Dr. Barrows moves with anxious energy in front of the fireplace, his boots dirtying up a section of the hardwood floor.

He jumps when he sees me, his eyes full of questions. He doesn't voice them, but he doesn't have to; it's burning from him, this need to know if I've discovered anything, and I'm not so cruel as to keep him waiting.

I exhale sharply, my voice ragged. "Balthazaar. He has Ghost."

He pales, frozen as my words sink in. But it's the cold fury emanating from his face that alarms me most. I quickly relay the rest of what I learned, and by the end of it, Molly merely seems pensive. Dr. Barrows has slumped against the wall, his head in his hands as though he can't quite believe it.

"So when do we go rescue him?" I'm not sure I expect an answer so much as I'm trying to fill the swiftly stifling silence.

Molly lets out a bark of laughter. "We don't. Or rather, *you* don't. You're staying here."

Now it's my turn to laugh. "And how are you going to keep me inside? I'll just follow you up there." I point to the skylight. "He's rich, right? A noble? I'll sneak in through a window, easy peasy."

Molly lets out a sigh. "Balthazaar's manse is set aside from the main part of the Upper Tier, close to the Frostfells. There are no rooftops for you to get there or back. And if Ghost's injured? What then?"

"Ghost is the best rooftop dancer of all of us. And I can scale a wall as easy as—"

"This isn't some tumbledown shack in the Warrens, child. There are guards and dogs and other protections." Her gaze lingers on my face, roaming over my body in a measuring fashion I don't much care for. "Did you mean what you said earlier in the baths? Would you spread your legs to save your friend?"

"Oy. What are you getting at?" I clench my teeth at the thought.

"Answer the question. Would you let yourself be used thusly?"

I scowl at her but nod. "If it comes to that...yes."

"You cannot be serious, Molly. No one would ever mistake her for one of your courtesans. Look at her." The doctor flushes a moment later, but I can only agree.

"You said it yourself: no one wants to see a broomstick in small-clothes. If it's a tumble he wants, aye, I can do that, but I doubt he'd find it worth the money." My mouth compresses.

"'Tis true," Molly says. "But you will not be alone." She circles around me, but now she's feeling down my arms with critical fingers. "Trying to slip her in as one of the regular girls would be a disaster, but I've found the more outrageous a spectacle I present, the easier it is to hide something in plain sight." She gives me a sour look. "With the attention on my courtesans, no one will give you enough of a second look to realize you don't really belong."

Dr. Barrows frowns. "Risky, Molly. You'd only be able to pull that stunt off the once."

"Once is all we need." She taps those pointy teeth of hers with the tip of her fan. "Not that we could show up unannounced, of course. But Lord Balthazaar is rather fond of our services here." Molly continues to pace, circling, circling. "I'll secure an invitation to his upcoming fete...and offer our resources to be at his disposal."

"And you would have me find Ghost that way?" I ask, a brow raised.

"I don't actually expect you have to go that far, no. But I needed to know if you were truly committed to playing the part. There is always a possibility that it would become necessary."

I snort, looking at my dirty fingernails. "I don't think it's my acting skills that will be called into question, aye?"

Molly smirks at me. "Don't worry, Moon Child. I have the utmost faith in Martika. If she cannot transform you into a flower of the night, I'll go dressed as a Moon Child myself."

"I'm sure she'll find that most gratifying," Dr. Barrows says, sarcasm dripping from his words. "Shall I fetch her?"

Molly's mouth splits into a broad, toothy grin. "Aye. And have Copper Betty draw Mags another bath. We've got some work to do."

This time I'm allowed the courtesy of toweling myself off. Though whether that's because I've scared off Copper Betty or because Martika doesn't want to be bothered is anyone's guess.

She eyes my hair critically, running careful fingers through the tangles. "Hmmm."

"What? Are there lice up there?" I smirk. "Wouldn't be the first time."

Her face wrinkles in disgust. "Gods, no. Just the ink has diminished some. It's not all that noticeable yet, but since you'll be wearing a wig anyway, it shouldn't matter much."

She doesn't point out the obvious. If the ink is fading from my hair, how soon before Ghost's becomes obvious? And what would Balthazaar do to him if he found out?

"Too bad we can't use the hair you cut off." The irony leaves a flat taste in my mouth.

"Even if Molly allowed it, it wouldn't be a good idea. The other lasses will be wearing wigs, and yours would look too authentic. We don't want you to stand out."

She ignores my scowl and frames my face with her hands. "Curls," she says firmly. "Pulled away from your face and bound behind your head. So you can move freely. But first things first: we need to get you fitted properly."

"A dress?" I sigh, even though I knew this would be the case when I agreed to the plan.

She nods. "And a corset and appropriate shoes. And we keep you at the back of the group so you're less likely to be spotted."

I shudder. Being forced to mince about in pointy little heels has my heart clinking with despair, but I've only myself to blame. "As long as I can wear boots, aye?"

"I'll see what I can do, but we need to take your measurements. If you would?"

I fall into step behind her, clutching my towel around my shoulders. "What about the other girls? What will you tell them?" I don't want my life to depend on Molly's word or the words of the women working for her.

"You're new. Molly's trying you out for a few weeks to see if you fit."

"Not much chance of that," I mutter.

Martika says nothing but ushers me into a small fitting room on the second floor. The room is draped with cloth of all kinds—silks, satins, brocades—and I sneer at the luxury before me. She has me stand on a chair and begins fussing with a cushion. It seems to be a heart made of velvet, but a horde of silver needles bristles from it like a prickly pig.

"How long will this take? Are you making me somewhat from scratch?" I know naught about seamstressing, but surely we don't have time for this.

"Heavens, no. Molly would never allow for that sort of waste. We'll simply take one of the other girl's existing dresses and fit it to you. Now stand still. The less you move, the faster we'll go."

Grinding my teeth, I do as she asks, my arms held out stiffly at my sides. Before long, she's fitted me into a simple shift and a pair of silken hose. I hate the way the hose feels, like the slick skin of a snake constricting me within. "Is this necessary? I'm not planning on lifting my skirts for aught."

"You told Molly otherwise, but either way, you need to appear the part. At least we don't have to shave you. Moon Children appear to have wickedly smooth skin, lucky things."

"How would you know what I told Molly?" I narrow my eyes at her. "Listening at doors, are we?"

Martika's mouth quirks into a smile but she avoids looking at me all the same. "She told me, of course." It's said so smoothly, but I know she's lying. I can't read the pulse point of her neck because it's covered, but I see her swallow.

I study her from beneath my lashes for a moment. Ghost had been about to tell me something about her before seeing the fire in Market Square: *She's not who you—* I roll that idea about in my mind. Who I, what? Think?

I'm still not sure what to make of it, but I'm not about to start making accusations just now. She's holding needles, after all.

Martika measures out a length of the shift, marking something on the floor in chalk. She takes in the shift tighter around my hips and deftly pins up the hem. "I imagine this is going to be a new experience for you."

I squirm as she wraps a tape measure about different parts of my body, poking here and there. I don't pay any mind to that until she starts mumbling about plunging necklines. "We'll have to do something with that panel on your chest."

I bristle, though I'm not sure why. I'm hardly one to care what people think of my appearance. "You can't take it off, if that's what you mean."

Martika glances up at me and shakes her head. "We don't want you so easily identified if something happens. Maybe we can hide it beneath a bit of lace." She finishes with the last pin. "Ah, well, there we are. I've got your base measurements now. With a little help, I'll have it ready for you by tomorrow. Molly should have a plan of attack worked out by then."

She hands me a set of frilly smallclothes. "Here. You may as well get used to wearing them." Wordlessly, I take them from her; I have no intention of putting them on, the ridiculous things. Amusement flickers over her face as she helps me out of the shift and hose.

"I'll try them on later," I tell her, my mouth pinched.

"I'm sure you will." Her cheek twitches, but she leads me through the twisting hallways and up the stairs. "I'm tempted to have you room with one of the other girls tonight," she muses aloud, "but I'm afraid that will lead to too many questions. If only we had more time…"

I snort. "You're telling me."

Martika pauses in the doorway of my room. "I'll have Copper Betty bring you supper. If I were you, I'd get some rest. We've some long days ahead of us."

I pace over to the window, pulling the damp strands of hair from my neck. "Aye," I agree, though I don't really mean it. It's going to be a long night because there's no way I'll be able to sleep. I hate not knowing what the plan is. I hate not knowing what's happening to Ghost. I hate not knowing any of it.

The door shuts behind me, leaving me alone with my thoughts. I throw the underthings on the bed, still not inclined to try them on. The wooden floorboards creak beneath my feet as I pace.

Scritch. Scratch.

Something scratches at the window, glittering through the pane. I walk over to it, and my eyes go wide. I jerk the window open and dodge the metallic dragon as it hurtles itself into the room, circling once before alighting on the mantel.

"And where have you been?" A gasp of hysterical laughter lodges in my throat, as though I'm unsure if I should be happy or terrified that it's here. I think of the archivist, and my stomach twists until I'm choking down a quiet sob, the wretched remains of her body seared into my memory.

"A great bother you are," I say to the dragon. "Wrapped in secrets and death." It hisses, its wings flaring out. "I see you've had that wing fixed. Make sure the theatre doesn't get burned down for the kindness, aye?"

I glance out the window, but the streets are silent with barely a lamplight to chase away the darkness. Tempting to get up on the roof myself for another look-see, but I'm still only wrapped in a towel.

The window slides down with a shudder, the chill night air cut off with a click, leaving my face itchy and hot. I let the towel drop to my feet as I rummage about the room. Somewhere along the way I've been gifted with another pair of trousers and a shirt, left folded neatly on the chair.

At this rate I'm going to start owing Dr. Barrows a clothing stipend. My skirt from earlier was left in the baths; I'm just as happy to leave it behind, welcoming the comfort of the well-woven trousers. I rub a fold between my fingers. "Say what you will about the Meridians, Mags, but they've lovely taste in clothes."

And best not get used it, the voice in my head adds.

But first…

The dragon whirrs at me, its tail twitching like a cat's. I toss it a piece of coal from the fireplace. "I suppose we ought to tell the good doctor that you're back, aye? Maybe it will help ease his mind somewhat that there's at least one less thing to worry about."

Its ember heart pulses as it swallows the coal. I hold out my arm, wincing when it clambers to its usual spot around my neck.

I poke my head out into the hallway, but there's no sign of anyone. A clock on the landing ticks out the minutes, but somehow it seems like the loudest thing I've ever heard. The door to the doctor's rooms is shut. I creep my way there, my ears pricked for any sound.

"Oy. Doctor?" I tap on the door a few times, spying through the keyhole when there's no answer. Except for what appears to be the barest hint of candlelight on the other side, I can see nothing at all. I try the doorknob, not surprised to find it latched, but it's easy to jiggle free with a little luck and a clever twist.

A moment later the door creaks open, and I slip inside.

In the daylight, I can only imagine this room to be nearly as humble as mine, but in the candlelight, there's something oddly comforting about it. Stacks of scrolls and books perch upon a desk like birds made of parchment, as though they'll take flight into the darkness to scatter upon the floor if I breathe too deeply.

I give them a cursory look over, but there are very few pictures involved, so I won't learn anything from them. I let them be, giving myself leave to roam. It's somehow odd being here, given the intimacy of wearing his clothes, and yet not knowing much about him. The fire pops on the hearth, a spark leaping onto the floor. It begins to smolder so I stamp on it quickly. I barely feel the ember through the hardness of my naked heel, but that's not what attracts my attention.

Everything is neat and in perfect order—the bed made neatly, the books organized on their shelves, the pictures hanging just so upon the wall. There are maps of Meridion and other places I don't recognize, and upon the mantel, decorative baubles and instruments glitter copper bright.

Meridian-made, I'm sure of it. And also worth a small fortune.

One of them whirs in time, an assortment of tiny spheres circling one another in an odd little dance I can't quite figure out.

Thief? No. Opportunist? Without question.

The thought dips into my mind as reflexively as the way my fingers twitch. Letters are carved into the base of the device, and I peer at them, my brain struggling sluggishly to make them out even as my lips move. "C...onstant as the...stars."

"*Ahem.* I would much appreciate it if you chose not to abscond with my orrery. It has a great deal of sentimental value." The doctor's voice pulls me from my imagined fistfuls of jingle, the dragon snarling as I jerk upright to face him.

Only he's not standing in the doorway to the hall but in front of a small opening beside the largest bookshelf. A fake panel?

"I was only looking," I say weakly, hiding my hands in the oversized shirtsleeves.

"Reassuring," he retorts, his dry tone indicating he believes nothing of the sort. His glasses are resting on his forehead, as though he's hastily pulled himself together.

I flush. "I'm sorry. I shouldn't be in here."

"No, you shouldn't. But since you are, you might as well see the rest of it." He thrusts a weary hand through his messy hair, turning toward the other side of the room. He pauses, eyeing the dragon. "Where did that come from?"

"It was outside my window." Its tail tightens ever so slightly around my neck. "Must have found its way back."

"So it would appear. I don't know how I'm supposed to keep up with any of you. All this coming and going..." He shakes his head and gestures. "Come on. It's through here."

I hesitate for a span of a few heartbeats at the invitation but push past him with a brazenness I don't quite feel. "What's all this, Doctor?"

"There's no more need for formality, Mags." His mouth quirks into a self-mocking smile. "Call me Lucian." The name rolls off his tongue easily enough.

"Your brother told me. I wasn't sure..."

"Ghost talks too much." He snorts, but I barely hear it as we step into the next room. Unlike the warmth of his bedchamber, this room is cold and callous. Sterile and pale and empty. In some ways, it's the exact opposite of Martika's cozy little seamstress room, though there are nearly as many needles scattered about. Syringes, scalpels, and beakers filled with stinking fluids and puffs of smoke.

A cage full of mice sits on a large table. Test subjects?

"Not what you were expecting, I take it?" The humor has fled the doctor's—Lucian's, I correct myself—voice.

"Not exactly a lady's fashion closet, no." I'm only half joking, but he cracks a smile at me.

"Clever girl," he murmurs. "But this is the real reason no one else is allowed up here. We tell the girls it's to give me privacy, but..."

I move closer to the cage for a better look. There are about ten of the little things, some piled into sleeping balls of fur, but a few have been cordoned off into separate compartments. Two of them stare with dull, dead eyes as they stagger about, their faces pressed against the bars so that their teeth chatter madly at the ones who seem normal.

I recoil in disgust. "The Rot? You've got mice with *the Rot*? Are you mad?"

"Some might think so," he concedes.

"I didn't even think animals could carry it." My mind reels with the implication. "If one of these things gets out..."

"I take the utmost care, Mags. And that's why you must never come into my chambers without an express invitation. I cannot risk the chance of discovery."

"So why are you showing *me*?"

"Better to make explanations now than to apologize later." He raises a brow at me. "And you're immune, so you've nothing to fear from them. If anything, I may have you assist me on further experiments if there's time."

"Aye. Because getting bit by the little shitbags is exactly what I want."

"Oddly enough they're mostly docile. The Rot doesn't change who you are so much as it accelerates the aging process, from what I can tell. Eventually their mental faculties fail them, and that's when they tend to bite." He shrugs. "It's more of a tactile thing, I think, like how an infant puts everything in its mouth."

My stomach churns. "Ghost never mentioned anything about this."

"That's because he doesn't know." A pained look crosses his face. "For this very reason. Now that he's been taken, he cannot reveal that of which he isn't aware."

I cock a brow, my gaze drawn to the mice, wondering at what he's really saying. Ghost isn't stupid; he had to have suspected his brother might continue his work in such a way. But samples or secrets, it doesn't change the fact that I'm merely a means to end.

"What's that?" I point at a drawing on a piece of parchment. It's got spindly little legs leading to a narrow coil of body and a giant crystalline head. "Some breed of Meridian spider?"

"In a manner of speaking. It's the virus that causes the Rot. Or at least a diagram of it."

"You're daft. I think I'd know if I'd seen one of *those* running about the streets." I poke at the sketch. "We could step on them like stink beetles. No more problem."

He sighs. "If only it were that simple. They're too small to see, Mags."

"Oh, I'm sure. Invisible stink beetles, aye." I glance about the room as though I might catch one crawling up the wall.

"That's not even the whole story. It's all about the macrophages. The way the virus injects itself into the body's natural immune response..." A rueful smile kicks up the corner of his mouth at my blank expression. "Perhaps we'll save the lecture for another night?"

I tip an invisible glass at him. "Of course. And maybe after a few drinks, I'll be able to see what you're talking about."

A soft chuckle escapes him, and he gestures for me to follow him back into his bedchamber. He shuts the little door behind us, pulling down a worn tapestry to cover the opening before retrieving a decanter of brandy from a small cabinet.

The amber liquid gleams as he pours us each a glass. I stare at it warily and then shrug. I don't usually get to drink anything stronger than the watered-down ale of the docks. It's the only thing I can afford, but even if it weren't, indulging is a poor choice. Rooftop dancing is hard enough sober. Drunk, and my chances of kissing the cobblestones after plunging several stories becomes much higher.

I'd rather have a smoke, but I sip it anyway. My nose wrinkles as it burns down my throat, and he laughs. I toss back the rest of it in two swallows out of spite and set the glass down on the bookshelf next to the copper device with the spinning spheres.

"What's an orrery?" The unfamiliar word rolls off my tongue in a slur so it sounds more like *orrrerrrrery*. Dr. Barrows is kind enough to ignore it.

"It charts the course of the planets—the relative time it takes for our world to orbit the sun, in conjunction with that of the moon and the other heavenly bodies with whom they dance." He gazes fondly upon the piece. "A gift from my beloved."

"You were married, then?" I blink, wondering what such unions mean upon the floating city.

"Not exactly. Many marriages on Meridion are arranged. Limited bloodlines give us scant choice in the matter if we wish to avoid inbreeding. But in my case, it matters little enough. Jeremiah was unlikely to get me with child," he adds dryly. "Nor I, him."

"I suppose not." A wry smile curves the corners of my mouth. "I've never had to worry about that, either."

"Something we have in common." He pours himself another drink.

Inwardly, I sigh. I don't like knowing this much about people. It makes it too easy to care. But for some reason I feel a strange tug toward Lucian, just as I do toward Ghost. A sort of kinship I've only ever felt with Sparrow and Archivist Chaunders.

"I'm sorry you had to leave him behind." It's an awkward thing to say, but I don't know how else to express it. Matters of the heart belong to those who have room in which to bear them, and mine is only made of metal.

Lucian smiles. "We were young and bound by propriety. Given my family situation, I cannot blame him for not following me when I left. Well, that and I was under suspicion of murder at the time."

"Murder?" I nearly laugh aloud at the thought, but the sadness reflected in Lucian's eyes stops me. "I'm sorry, but you hardly seem able to hurt a fly, let alone kill someone."

"Tragic circumstance, I suppose you'd say. In either case, no, I didn't kill anyone. But the damage had already been done. My name was cleared eventually, but our family estate was in ruins. Ghost and I had no other choice but to come here in a sort of self-inflicted exile. I don't regret the choices I made, but that doesn't mean I can't be melancholy about it." He stares down at his hands as he swirls the brandy in his glass. "I miss him. Terribly."

"But Ghost comes first," I say softly.

"Always." He drains the glass quickly but makes no move to fill it a third time. "My biggest fear has come to pass, and I've no way to hide him behind me this time."

A bitter laugh escapes me. "But you'll hide him behind me, is that it?"

"To save him? Yes."

Red-rimmed eyes meet mine, and relief threads through me. The truth, then. At last. Or at least more of it than before.

I turn away from the orrery and walk slowly about the room, pretending to study a map on the wall. I must make some questioning sound in the back of my throat because Lucian joins me a half second later, his face flushed.

He traces his finger over the coastline, pointing out the inlets and bays, towns I've never heard of filled with trees and forests, deserts and oceans. All of it might as well be a nursery rhyme.

"...Never been there, of course," he drones on, as though hypnotized by his memories. "Here, past the Frostfells, there's the greenwoods of Elwynn. And over here, the Niordians live on the steppes."

"Is that where you come from?" I interrupt. "Meridians, I mean?"

"No. We originally came from across the Goldglimmer Sea, but that was before my time. There was a war..." He pauses for a beat. "Meridion was built in an effort to escape it. I suppose we've been wandering ever since." He glances upward and shakes his head. "I was raised on Meridion, and it is the only true home I've ever known."

The longing and despair wavers in his voice, but my own sympathy dissipates with his next sigh. "And what of me, or any of the other Moon Children? Don't we deserve a bit of that home?" I gesture about the room angrily, only to have the brandy glass slip from my fingers. It shatters on the floor and the two of us wince, Lucian retrieving a towel from his nightstand to soak up the brandy.

I make a move to help him, but he waves me off, and I shake my head. "While I appreciate your 'melancholy,' as it were," I say as sincerely as I can, "please forgive me if I find it chafing that Meridians care so very little for their half-breed offspring as to let us starve in the streets, only to bury us before we're truly dead."

"I'm sorry for that, Mags," he says hoarsely. "Meridion is not full of bad people—just self-absorbed ones. I am trying to undo it, these injustices my people have thrust upon yours, but I cannot do it alone."

I hear the question beneath the words, the fear that I will leave him to find Ghost on his own. The terror that he might not be able to do it.

Both our heads snap to the door when we hear a firm rap upon it. "Is everything all right?"

Molly.

"Yes." Lucian gathers himself and straightens his shirt before opening the door to let her in. "Mags dropped her glass. That's all."

"How very unfortunate." Molly hovers in the hallway, poking her head in for a brief moment. Her gaze narrows when she sees the dragon upon my shoulder. The points of her teeth show when she grimaces at the shattered remains of the snifter on the floor. "I'll have Copper Betty come clean up the mess immediately."

"Much obliged." Lucian nods at me. "Thank you, Mags. That will be all."

I bite the inside of my cheek at the dismissal, but the weight of the day is heavy on my shoulders and I am out of ideas.

"Good night, Lucian." I slip out the door before Molly can say anything else, leaving the two of them staring after me in silence.

Four-and-twenty magpies baked in a tart,
A spoonful of blood and a still-beating heart.
A mouthful of feathers and bristling bone,
A song for a penny, and a king for a throne.

— CHAPTER THIRTEEN —

"There now, that should about do it." Martika steps back, a self-satisfied smirk twisting her mouth. "Fairly impressive, if I do say so myself."

"Indeed. She nearly appears to be female now. Well done." Molly applauds her with an oddly polite clap, and she flashes her teeth at me. "Go on, lass. Take a look."

I swallow any comeback and turn to face the mirror, the dress swirling at my ankles. And I immediately stumble in the high-heeled boots that encase my feet. Martika reaches out to steady me, amusement glittering in her amber eyes.

Eyes like Dr. Barrows's eyes, I realize.

Perhaps they were cousins? But no, that would make Martika a Meridian, as well.

Still.

I glance at myself in the mirror, and any thought of odd family connections flees with the last of my breath.

I am...

"Beautiful," Martika murmurs.

Molly gives her a sharp look, but I'm not paying any attention to anything but the girl before me. The white, powdered wig hangs in luscious ringlets to my shoulders, long enough to cover the brand at my neck, and a feathered fascinator glitters from the top. My skin is luminous, golden; my lashes curled and eyes kohled; cheeks smudged with rouge. My lips part in surprise at the emerald corset and ruffled skirts, the bustle and striped hose, the laced and low-cut bodice. I still have no bust to speak of, but somehow Martika has cut the thing so I've got the actual beginnings of curves, my heart panel neatly enshrouded behind the wall of lace. An elegant shawl finishes the look, delicately wrapped over my shoulders.

"Martika, it's amaz—" I start, awe in my voice.

"Not bad for a painted whore, eh, Mags?" Molly interrupts, her words bouncing off my reflection and marring the illusion.

I shift within the corset, a sudden itch tickling my rib cage with no way to reach it.

Molly pulls my hands down as I attempt to reach into my bodice. "We'll have to cover these up. There's not a manicure in all Meridion that could possibly hide these horse hooves."

It's a fair cop. No matter how long I soaked them, my nails remained coarse, the calluses thick at the tips of my fingers. "We could put false ones on," Martika suggests, but I make a face at her.

"And if I need to climb? You think I'll have time to take them off?" I flex my fingers experimentally. "And that's assuming I can move around in this bit of frippery at all, let alone shimmy up a roof." I pull at the skirts experimentally, exposing part of the frilly underclothes.

"That's the spirit!" Molly slaps my ass with a wink. "Put her in gloves, then."

"Thanks," I retort, fussing at the tightly cinched bit of torture.

Molly glances at the clock on the mantel where the dragon remains. "If we had any stones at all, we'd send you with that around your neck. But that's too brazen, even for me." She pauses. "Which reminds me...That little beastie is far too wily for its own good. We can't have it slipping away and following you. Do me a favor and make sure it's contained before you go?"

I nod.

"Ah, well, I'm off to check on the other ladies," she goes on. "You've got about twenty minutes to finish up here. Meet us down in the main hall."

"Are you coming with us?" I ask.

She shakes her head. "I'm needed here this evening. We've a full house down below, and that means business. Besides, I never attend such events. It tends to limit the...interactions."

"It reminds them why the girls are there, you mean," I say, trying hard not to squirm when Martika tightens a loose ribbon at my shoulder.

"That too." And with that, Molly whisks out the door, the scent of rose perfume trailing behind her.

I give my dragon a sour look and retrieve the cage from beneath my bed. Ghost had left it behind that first night I had finally agreed to help them in their plan with the Pits, but I hadn't bothered to use it before now. The dragon snarls but does as it's asked, and I slip it another bit of coal before I shut the door. "Sorry. But you *do* have a way of showing up in odd places." And the last thing I want is to attract more attention to myself.

Martika hands me a pair of satin gloves draped between her perfectly manicured fingers. Her nails are short and squared. Practical. She nods in approval when I wriggle my hands into the tight-fitting cloth. "There. Think that should about do it."

"They make my hands hot."

"Oh, the horror," she mocks, even as a smile tugs at her lips. "Somehow I think you'll manage. Now run along downstairs and meet the other girls. I'll be there shortly."

I didn't think they'd have me mingle with the other girls directly, but I suppose I should get it over with. "Are *you* coming with us?"

Martika gives me a tight smile. "Yes. Sending bouncers would be considered impolite, but I'll make sure propriety is satisfied. Such as it is." She gives me a gentle nudge. "Now go."

I let myself be pushed out the door and follow Copper Betty down several flights of stairs, my hands gripping the railing for dear life. I hope to the Hells I don't have to run in these damnable boots.

A snort escapes me. Ask me to leap across rooftops or climb a wall and I don't have to think twice, but walking in heels?

"Monstrous devices," I say aloud.

Copper Betty pays me no mind at all. I study her smooth movements and the delicate slide of her hips, the way she carefully steps with each foot, and I mimic the motion until I'm no longer staggering like a drunken elephant.

An uneasy shiver roils through my belly as we step into the main lounge. The bar is in full swing, the men deep in their cups. In my own clothes, I am shielded. But hiding myself openly is more frightening than I thought it would be. I'm being weighed and measured on a scale I don't even belong stepping on.

And stare, they do.

Bored, interested, curious—their gazes linger on my hair, rove over the curve of my hips and the stretch of my legs. It's like ants crawling over my skin, and I bite down on my lower lip to keep from screaming.

I see mouths slide open in grins, revealing tongues and saliva and teeth. Some are chuckling and dismissive with their opinions, and others seem quite willing to tear me apart. The girls on the stage begin to sing, drawing the hungry, hollow stares back to them.

That's when I make my escape to the main entrance.

Almost.

A set of wandering fingers boldly strokes up the inside of my knee. My hands are already clenching and I'm turning, whirling around with my fist drawn up. The man jerks in his seat, his greasy hair falling into his eyes. His terror stops me short, but I don't ask what he sees.

Molly Bell descends upon me like a murderous crow, snatching me backward so I stumble into the doorway and nearly fall into the sitting fountain. "Control yourself," she snaps.

My face flushes at the rolling wave of titters from the other girls, but Molly is making her toothy apologies as I attempt to straighten out my skirts.

"Ye must be new, aye?" One of the whores tosses her wig of pale hair over her shoulder, her smile soft as honey. Her gaze glitters with a chilling hardness. All business, this one. "Ye best not come anywhere near me when we get to the fete. Pull that stunt and we'll all be out of a job and walking home. Except you. I'll make sure you're left in an alley somewhere."

I scowl at her, fussing with the one of the toggles on my skirt. "Try it and see where it gets you."

"Ladies." Martika inserts herself between us. Her gown has been changed into something just as severe but with a bit more lace. She looks like an oversized lampshade in her dress, but no less intimidating for all that.

The whore sniffs. "I'd heard you'd found a lover, you old biddy. Keep her up above in the lofts like a bird, feeding her sweeties on the sly."

A lopsided smile crosses my face. I know this song. Posturing among the hierarchy happens all the time among Moon Children, and her words slide off me like rain. I don't really have time for it, and I've no interest in fitting in here.

I let one gloved hand drift behind me to brush over Martika's face. The matron stiffens. "I'm her Magpie, sure enough."

The whore scoffs at me. "Magpie? What kind of name is that?"

"I like pretty things." I move slowly toward her. I'm sure it looks like I'm stalking her, but the deliberate motion is only to keep me from falling. My fingers rub together. "Jingle. Jewels. And eyes."

"Eyes?" She crosses her arms.

"Aye. Shiny. Fun to pluck out." I let my own eyes go half-lidded, as though I'm becoming seduced by the idea.

She takes a step back from me. Martika coughs abruptly, but I've already stopped. There's no need for violence; I've made my point. The others give me a wide berth when I move to the far side of the fountain under the pretense of tightening the laces on my boots.

Martika's face is unreadable in the sideways glance I give her. But there's no time to talk about it, as Molly is clapping her hands and steering us out the front doors of the Conundrum. A shining horseless carriage is parked in the street by the entrance, long and massive, and I can't help but stare at it.

Not that I haven't seen one before, of course. But this particular model is monstrous, stacked double. It sports no fewer than eight wheels of chrome and brass, and the large, silver wolf crest that belongs to Lord Balthazaar.

One of the whores giggles as I'm shoved forward to mount the velvet stairs. The door swings open and we're herded into the belly of the thing, and all I can envision is my little dragon in its cage upstairs. Is this what it's like to be swallowed?

Inside, the carriage is plush and beautifully appointed. Leather benches. Valises filled with cigars. Bottles of brandy and crystal goblets and small trays of sweetmeats. A twisted stairwell leads to the upper level where, undoubtedly, another assortment of enchantments are waiting. Not that I'm going to try my luck in these shoes.

The other girls squeal in delight, rushing forward to fill the seats and pulling out the brandy to pour themselves a drink before heading up the stairs in fits of laughter.

"Like wee birds in the nest," I say dryly, but I help myself to one of the cigars. Martika watches me with a sour face as I light up, sucking on the tip. I flop into one of the seats and take a long drag, stretching my legs out on the seat across from mine. "I might be able to get used to this."

"My Magpie?" She arches a brow. I can't tell if she's amused or annoyed. I'm not sure it matters.

"It makes for a nice explanation. They accept it. No more wondering why I'm here or why I'd be talking to you."

"Indeed. Magpie it is." She crosses her legs and stares out the window, seemingly lost in thought. Above us, the other girls continue to laugh and make merry. I flick the ash from my cigar into a silver basin as the carriage lurches forward.

I expect the ride to be rough over the cobblestones—something this large should be unwieldy—but it's smooth as silk. Beneath us, the pistons hum and churn, but aside from a slight rocking motion, I barely notice we're moving at all.

Outside, the streetlights flash past. I stare at my reflection in each hazy, golden glow, wondering at this stranger who lights up with every passing street. I suspect even Rory wouldn't know who I was if we crossed paths this evening.

Disguises have never been my forte; I'd never had the opportunity or the resources to pull it off. But here, in this place, I am a painted whore, not a Moon Child.

A nudge along my leg brings me back to myself. "Did you hear anything I just said, Magpie?"

I blink at Martika. She sighs, frustration flitting over her features, and she smacks me hard on the knee. "When we get there, follow the other girls' leads but try not to get too caught up. I'm assuming you've never been to one of these affairs?" She catches herself the moment she says it. "Of course, you haven't. Anyway, it's not like it is at the Conundrum. You're expected to mingle. Everyone will assume why you're there, and the Moon Child costumes are going to cause a stir."

"How will I find him?" My palms sweat in the gloves, and I struggle not to remove them. I stab the cigar into the silver bowl. "I fail to see how I'll manage to get away to search without being terribly obvious." I exhale sharply, trying to swallow my panic. "This is a crap idea."

"It's the best one we've got at the moment."

It's supposed to sound reassuring, but her answering smile doesn't reach her eyes. I'm not sure if she's trying to convince me or herself, and there's nothing particularly optimistic about that.

I glance out the window, not recognizing any of the streets we're passing now. I've never traveled this far from the Warrens. The houses here are massive, made of brick and stone and stucco. They are set back from the road, ensconced on plots of land and flanked by the rotting remains of trees, their branches wavering in the shadows. Bones of the earth, poking through the sooty skin of the city.

We have no trees in the Warrens. Not even as much as these relics.

The rest of the carriage has grown silent, the other women quiet. Are they preparing themselves for what they must do? Or perhaps it's merely anticipation. I lick my lips, grimacing at the taste of the paint Martika applied.

"Don't," she says absently. "You'll smear it." She points out the window. "Look. We're slowing down."

And we are. The hum of the carriage has become a discordant *putt putt putt* as the brakes are applied and we turn onto a gravel road. In the distance, Lord Balthazaar's house looms, lit up on the outside with a great many lanterns.

Molly was right. Even if I can manage to get Ghost and me onto the roof of this place, we'll have very few choices as to how to get down, and nearly all are exposed. I scan the second and third levels. Would they keep him upstairs in an attic, perhaps? Or below in the wine cellar? Or maybe they merely hold him hostage in a bedroom.

My mind veers from other possibilities. I've got enough to try to manage without worrying if he's injured, too. My lips compress, but the carriage pulls into a curved courtyard, coming to a halt with a great puff of steam. We're here now. Anticipation fogs the inside of the vehicle as the ladies gather themselves.

Martika nudges me. "Remember to smile. Protocol among the gentry requires discretion, so you can expect a bit of courting before anything is expected to happen. Do your best to slip away when you can."

"Aye." I attempt to open my fan experimentally. It snaps shut on my fingers, and I grunt. There's no more time for talk. The carriage door swings open, and I catch a glimpse of the bowed head of a footman outside.

Martika exits first, exchanging a few words with a manservant standing at the door. He nods and disappears into the manor, and she gestures at us to come forth. I let the others go before me and linger at the stairs leading down to the ground, trying not to gape at the extravagance.

Heavy stone walls surround the manor, and golden light pours through thick glass windows, as if Lord Balthazaar has somehow managed to capture the sun within his home. There are no torches here—everything is electric, from the wall sconces flanking the austere, wooden front doors to the massive crystal chandelier hanging in the foyer.

I can barely take in all the rampant largesse as the footman assists with my descent from the carriage. My booted heels wobble in the gravel, and I lean on the poor man heavily to keep from tripping. His face flushes, and I abruptly let him go.

Led by Martika, our little band of ladies sweeps into the foyer. I bring up the rear. A murmur of surprise greets us. All around us are men and women of the Upper Tier, all sumptuous fabrics and glittering jewels, polished boots and neatly oiled mustaches. Their gazes sweep over us, filled with amusement or outrage, and sometimes a combination of both.

"Oh, how deliciously scandalous," snickers an elderly matron, sitting in a wingback chair, a thick walking stick resting upon her lap. She tracks us with an eager smile, her wrinkled fingers clutching the stick.

"She's looking to beat one of us," one of the younger whores whispers to me. "I've seen her before. I'd avoid it unless you're into that sort of thing...or she pays a fair bit."

I shudder. "I'd rather not."

"Ah, well, here." She presses a sachet into my palm. "In case you find yourself in a situation you can't get out of."

"What is it?"

"You *are* new, aren't you? Molly Bell's a strict madam, but that doesn't mean she's keen on having us raped. Ruins the merchandise, if you know what I mean. A bit of this blown in someone's face will knock them out long enough for you to run away. It's not much but it will do in a pinch, and it's better than the alternative, aye?"

I don't have to be told twice. I tuck the sachet into my bodice and give the girl a nod of thanks before we're herded into what appears to be a ballroom. No one is dancing, but a string quartet made up of automatons plays a subtle melody oozing with sedate properness. The light shimmies off their swiftly moving mechanical fingers. Their cogs whirl quietly, and they're as neatly dressed as the gentry, hiding their emotionless faces beneath wide-brimmed hats.

What would Copper Betty think of her higher-class brethren, I wonder. And then I realize I'm standing by myself. The other girls have dispersed into the crowd in a swirl of long legs, swaying hips, and glittering smiles, working their trade; Martika is nowhere to be seen.

Damn her. I'm being studied curiously by a mutton-chopped man in a wool suit, probably because I'm staring at everything like the street rat I am. I turn toward him and give him my best attempt at a seductive smile, scowling when he abruptly changes direction, his face paling.

So much for that.

I sigh and head for the far end of the room where there appears to be a buffet laid out.

One of the fine ladies sniffs when I approach, nibbling a crust of well-buttered bread. The amount of food is staggering, almost obscene with its freshness—breads and cheeses, vegetables and choice cuts of meat.

"Taking advantage of the buffet, are we?" a masculine voice drawls. A gloved hand swoops past me to snag an apple from a silver bowl. "As do we all."

I stiffen. It's Inquestor Caskers.

Swallowing the fury and fear that threatens to erupt from me, I keep my face pointed down. I am merely deciding which apple to choose. Will he recognize me? He thinks me dead, but he's not stupid.

And that's assuming Rory didn't go and tell him I was still alive in an attempt to curry favor...

The corset seems to constrict around me, a cage of whalebone and laces, and I pray he doesn't see through the smoke and mirrors that are lace and rouge. I take an apple, biting into it to hide the tremble of my jaw. The juice runs down my chin, and I murmur something noncommittal at him, chewing slowly as I lift my face.

He's in full regalia; metals and pins and stripes that must mean something to someone adorn the smart fit of his crimson uniform. A decorative sword hangs on his hip, but there's no sign of his pistols, which means he's here for pleasure and not business.

He squints at me for an instant, and I can see those beady, black rat eyes working it through. It's clear he knows he's seen me before, but he can't quite place where. Finally, he simply hands me a handkerchief to wipe my mouth with.

He bows before leaving me to my own devices once more. I clutch his handkerchief, my heart pattering over and over with an ugly whirring *hitch-click* of a beat.

The music has somehow grown louder, and couples are taking to the dance floor, their steps perfect and precise. One of the whores cocks a brow at me when she sees me wallflowering, but I can't dance. And hells…no one is coming to ask me anyway.

Back to my mission. I linger in each room, munching on my apple in a way that hopefully makes it look like I'm too busy to participate in idle chatter. Martika is still nowhere to be found, and a thread of fear inches its way down my spine. Surely we haven't been found out already?

A low hum of anticipation ripples through the crowded hall, and I turn to see Lord Balthazaar striding into the center of the room. There's a handsomeness about him, but it's the kind that's accentuated by his surroundings—from the oiled hair to the manicured fingers to the smartly trimmed beard. He's dressed in sumptuous clothing, too—a fine linen shirt and a silken waistcoat, a fur-lined cape draped over his shoulders. He carries a goblet of wine in one hand and a silver-tipped cane in the other, an ornate wolf head adorning the top. Its sinister eyes are glittering rubies, at odds with the cheerfully seductive illumination of another great crystal chandelier hanging from the ceiling.

Aside from at the theatre, I've never seen him up close, but sometimes he would make random inspections at BrightStone's main gate when a food delivery was arriving. It paid to linger about when he did so as occasionally he would share his largesse, throwing hats full of copper pennies into the air. I'm not ashamed to admit I'd scrambled over the muddy cobblestones with the rest of the crowd, ignoring his spiteful chuckles as he smirked at us from his private carriage.

But tonight he plays the proud host, nodding and greeting the guests with all the airs of a Meridian. From the responding simpers, it's clear everyone knows where their bread comes from. He beams more and more with each tip of a hat or curtsy, collecting their fawning gestures like coin. If I hadn't overheard how little he wanted to be holding this particular party, I would assume he was delighted to be here.

His smile falters a bit when he sees me and the other girls, but he hides it quickly. "How droll. I shall have to thank Ms. Bell for being so very...insightful."

He takes a seat in a high-backed chair at the far end of the room. It's not a throne exactly, but it might as well be for all its golden inlay gleaming from the woodwork. One of the manservants approaches him with a platter of fruit, but Balthazaar waves him off. He sets his drink down on the small table beside him and beckons to one of the other whores, his smile growing cruel.

Before she has time to think, he snatches her onto his lap, gripping her arm tightly enough to bruise. To her credit, she barely makes a sound. "Well now, aren't you a lovely bird," he croons, tugging at her wig so it nearly falls onto the floor. The girl wriggles inside her corset and swishes her skirts, showing an expansive bit of thigh as she does so. The men whistle appreciatively and even Balthazaar's brow raises.

As a distraction, I'll take it. I slip through the crowd, only to have my own wrist snatched by a drunken guest. "Here now, this one's trying to leave! Come on, girlie," he slurs. "Show us what you can do."

I shudder in distaste at being touched, but I keep a smile plastered on my face all the same. With any luck, I'll scare this one off as easily I did the first.

"Here, lass." An arm cuts between me and the other man, steering me away from the others. I glance up to see Lucian standing there. I raise a brow at him, but he feigns ignorance at my recognition. Inwardly, I sigh. More subterfuge. If any more comes my way, I'll drown in it.

Lucian gives me a courteous bow, introducing himself as though we've never met, and pretends to give me a moment to fix myself up. He thrusts a goblet of wine into my hand. He's dressed in dapper fashion, his waistcoat made of cloth several degrees nicer than what he normally wears, complete with a top hat and scarf to rival the fashions of many of the other guests.

"Not that I don't admire your sense of style, Magpie, but you make a lousy spy. The idea is *not* to attract attention to yourself, right?" He rolls his eyes, but the amused tone softens his chastisement.

Wait a minute...

"What did you call me?" A sharp thrill runs through me. I've caught him at last.

He stills. "Magpie," he says weakly. "It's what we all agreed to, wasn't it?"

"Is it?" I sip at the wine. "Mmm. Don't recall seeing you in the main hall of the Conundrum when I made that particular announcement. Martika was the one who agreed to it in the carriage." An impossible thought slams into me. "For that matter, I don't recall a single time I've ever seen the two of you together... One of you always leaves the room to retrieve the other. It's a tad suspicious, wouldn't you say?"

He gapes at me and lets out a gasping chuckle. "You're ridiculous...and right. I'm sorry for the deception."

I raise an eyebrow at him. "It's all right, you know. I'm sure I don't care if you like prancing about in ladies' smallclothes. After all"—I gesture at the other guests—"some people like to pretend they're futtering Moon Children. Perhaps you might want to consider giving that one a try, as well?" A strangled sound emerges from his throat, and I bite back a small laugh. "Your secret is safe with me."

"I suppose I owe you an explanation." He swirls his glass, rubbing his thumb over the brim. "And I *don't* prance. It's a necessary disguise."

"How so?"

"It started out as a method of hiding when Ghost was small. When I ended up with Molly, it seemed only natural to continue the charade a bit longer, and before long, Martika was but another of her employees. Molly finds the conceit rather quaint, I think. Hiding me in plain sight appeals to her vanity." A grimace crosses his face. "The voice modulator is a tad uncomfortable, I'll admit. There's a reason I always wear high-necked dresses."

"Seems like an awful lot of trouble to go to, if you ask me." I roll my eyes.

"Like everything else I've tried, I'll admit it's spun out of control. But how else would I have attended this party? I certainly didn't have an invitation. This way I can poke about without too much interference and change again before we leave." He bows gallantly and takes my hand in an elegant gesture. "No one will associate my dour alter ego with the dashing doctor who danced with the Moon Child whore after purchasing her services for the evening..."

"And you have, so to speak." I down the rest of my wine. "In a moment. My boots have come loose, stupid things." Lucian waits while I tie the lacings again. He plays the bored paramour well, sipping his wine with a dull expression on his face as he continues to scan the crowd.

The other whores have dissipated into the mass of gentry again, but none of them appear to be hurting from lack of attention. Even Lord Balthazaar deigns to acknowledge me with a curt nod, but after a short amount of time, he removes himself from the ballroom.

An uneasy suspicion creeps over my skin, and I share a look with Lucian.

"Come on." He grasps my hand tighter. "Follow my lead and play along."

He pulls me onto the dance floor but ignores my feeble attempts at waltzing with a grace I don't deserve. The steps make no sense to me. What time have I ever had to learn? But it doesn't matter anyway. The doctor guides us across the room in as polite a fashion as we can manage, wincing when I crush his toes beneath my boots.

"Dancing lessons next time," he mutters in my ear.

"When *you* can climb on the rooftops, I'll consider it," I retort, earning me an amused snort in return. "Don't suppose you discovered the whereabouts of...?"

"Not exactly. I've poked about here and there, but I suspect we need to check below. I've noticed a rather sharp increase in his personal guard lingering about the stairs to the kitchens."

"Maybe he's guarding the food," I jest. "If I were here on my own, I'd have pillaged an entire hamper of sausages by now." My stomach actually rumbles thinking of it, echoed by Lucian's soft chuckle.

"Yes, well. Not all of us are as practical as you."

When we reach the place where Balthazaar disappeared, I expect us to split up, but Lucian surprises me by keeping a tight grip on my hand. "If anyone asks, I'm your patron for the evening. We're looking for...er, a quiet place."

"Don't expect anything fancy. That's extra." I blow him a kiss.

He lets out a stuttering cough, and I hide a smile, nearly stumbling when he stops suddenly. I glance up to see Lord Balthazaar walking down the corridor with the High Inquestor at his side. The two of them turn the corner and are out of sight.

The doctor stares in their direction and then squeezes my hand. "After them."

Together we amble down the hallway, as though merely strolling without purpose. His arm wraps about my waist, fingers lingering over my hip. The only one who sees us is a frazzled-looking scullery maid, her arms full of dirty plates as she hurries toward the kitchens.

There's no sign of Balthazaar, and I'm beginning to worry they've found a private room where we can't follow, but then the low murmur of deep voices has me flattening against the wall. The shadows of the two men dance opposite from the alcove where they hold council.

"...Tithed as soon as this little charade is over. I'll inform the Salt Temple in the morning."

"And the anomaly?" Balthazaar's voice burns with a curious anger.

"Needs to be made an example of. Moon Children masquerading as common citizens is a recipe for disaster." I share a look with a rapidly paling Lucian.

"But the Chancellor—"

"Has no jurisdiction over Moon Children," the High Inquestor says. "Don't worry about it until I come for him tomorrow. You've had him moved from the wine cellar?"

"Yes. He's with...her. Too many people sniffing about tonight, and her wing is off-limits to guests."

"To be sure." The Inquestor's voice is soothing, almost seductive, and the dark warning behind the words has my skin growing clammy. "But you do understand why this is such a sensitive issue, do you not?"

"Of course I do, you pompous windbag." Balthazaar's shadow is shaking his finger in the other man's face. "And do *you* understand that I don't care? Meridion and their damnable politics can go to the Pits and the Rot take them, too. Until my wife has regained her...her health, I don't want to hear about whatever conspiracies the Inquestors are involved in or so-called rebellions you're trying to stop."

The High Inquestor says something I can't hear, but a shift in the shadows indicates they're moving again.

"This is bad, Mags. Very bad." Lucian grips my shoulders tightly, fear lighting up his eyes. "Listen. I've got to go warn the Chancellor. If we've been compromised…"

Panic rushes through me, but I scowl at my own weakness a few seconds later. Ghost is the only important thing right now. "What about your brother? You can't possibly be leaving this all to me?"

"I have to, Mags." Despair fills his voice. He leans forward, his lips brushing my forehead before I can react. "I'll send a carriage for you as soon as I can, but…" He hesitates. "Don't risk yourself if you can't do it covertly. I don't want any undue casualties."

A scowl twists my lips into something ugly. "The way Sparrow was a casualty?"

This time he flinches, but he doesn't look away. "Yes. Like Sparrow. I will be back for you, Mags. I promise." He bows, regret on his face, but it doesn't slow his feet any as he backtracks his steps.

The hallway is all the emptier without his presence, but I straighten my shawl and pull down on my skirts. It's a nervous motion, I suppose, as though I'm adjusting armor of another kind.

For the first time in several weeks, I am truly alone.

I press my palm against the panel on my chest, willing the *hitch-click* beating of my heart to calm, even as my fingers brush over the sachet of sleeping powder the young courtesan had given me earlier.

"Right," I mutter, the beginnings of a rudimentary plan taking form. "Let's see just what sort of mischief a Moon Child can really do."

A drop of blood upon a bit of snow,
Crimson wishes that come and go.
The fairest of mirrors reflects only these,
A crown of thorns and a coat made of bees.

— CHAPTER FOURTEEN —

O f course, plans or not, wandering about aimlessly will only attract attention, so I do the next best thing and head for the kitchens. It's easy enough to find—all I have to do is follow the stream of chambermaids and pages, serving lads and butlers, all moving to and fro like fish in a river of soot, sweat, and alcohol.

The key to appearing unobtrusive is to act as though you belong. I've been avoiding eyes my entire life so it's no great trial to grab a tray of glasses from a sideboard and a bottle of brandy. I'm just a whore finding refreshment for my patron, after all.

Most of the servants pay me no mind, too occupied with their own tasks, so I slip away. In the distance comes the swell of laughter; the party is clearly still going strong. Good enough for me, anyway.

Given Balthazaar's comments about Lady Lydia in the theatre and his reference to Ghost being kept in a specific, off-limits wing of the house, I can only assume I'll have to go poking about even more.

Eventually I find myself in a parlor with lounges and chairs, a well-stocked brandy chest, an empty fireplace, and an upright piano. A place for highborn ladies to gather, no doubt, freed from their boorish counterparts as their husbands are entertained by bawdy house companions and foul-smelling cigars.

A thin layer of dust indicates the room hasn't been used for quite some time, but the door on the far side leads to a series of halls that are far more luxurious than the previous. Rows of tapestries and fine wooden doors line the corridor, and there are no crowds of maids and scullery wenches in which to hide.

I turn the corner and pause when I see two guards standing outside a large door. They wear Balthazaar's livery, so it's more than obvious that these must be Lady Lydia's chambers.

I move to duck back around the corner, but I've already been spotted. All I can do is tip my chin up and march toward them. I hold out the tray with the brandy.

"What's all this, then? You shouldn't be here." One of the guards frowns at me. He's older with a weary face, but the younger one gives me a slow wink with an appreciative look at the brandy.

"A nightcap for you, courtesy of Lord Balthazaar." My mouth curves into a smile as I pour them each a glass. "You know, since you're missing the party and all."

They hesitate, and I cringe inwardly, not sure what I'll do if they turn me down. But the older one sighs. "What the hells," he mutters, swiping the closest glass. He sips it carefully, even as the younger guard reaches for me.

"And are you part of the nightcap, too?" He leans forward as though to steal a kiss, and I smirk at him.

"That all depends on you, my lord." My eyes drift sideways toward the older guard, but he's too preoccupied with his drink to pay much attention to his compatriot, even going so far as to relieve me of the tray and bottle to pour himself another glass.

Well and good, then.

I suck in a deep breath when the younger guard pulls me back so he can nuzzle my shoulder. My fingers find the sachet still nestled in my bodice and manage to loosen the drawstring to carefully pour a bit of the powder into my gloved hand.

I tip my head as though to blow him a kiss, and the powder puffs at his face in a soft haze. His eyes widen in confusion, but in moments, they roll back into his head and he slumps into my arms.

"What's going on?" The older guard nearly drops the tray as I sink to the floor to lay my would-be paramour gently on his side. He kneels down beside me, turning the younger man over for a closer look.

"Ah, perhaps he couldn't handle his drink," I murmur, snatching another handful of powder and throwing it at the second guard when he looks over at me. He grunts, tumbling onto me, and I shove him to the side.

My skirts tear as I get up. "Of course." Though, I suppose I should be happy they've lasted as long as they have.

I try the door to the bedchamber but it's locked, and I rummage through the older guard's coat, rewarded with a key ring. The largest key, a bit of brass and silver, fits easily.

"In and out," I breathe as the doorknob turns, and I duck inside, praying Ghost is really here.

Like the parlor, this room is dark with only the dim light of a bedside lamp on a nightstand. As rooms go, it's plush and comforting, with an intricately carved headboard atop a massive four-poster bed and thick green curtains framing the windows.

It's not the room that holds my interest so much as the person lying in the bed, chest rising and falling with a labored dissonance. Each gasp is a struggle, but there's something routine about it. These lungs have fought this battle for an eternity. I cannot help drawing nearer for a closer look, but it can only be Lady Lydia.

A sliver of cold steel presses against my windpipe. "Move and I'll slice you open." I freeze, but I know the distinctive timbre of Ghost's voice well enough by now. Inwardly, I sag with relief.

"Well, that would be a plum shame, given what I've had to do to find you," I retort.

He pauses. "Mags?" His hushed tone is disbelieving.

"Indeed." My hand is at his wrist, gently shoving the blade away from my skin. Not that I think he's going to attack me now, but still. Dead's dead, accidental skewering or not.

"But you...you look like..."

"A girl? Aye. Molly's idea. Good to see I'm so convincing." I thrust my chin at the knife. "Planning on gutting the guards when they came in?"

"They won't. They're too scared of the Rot. I was hoping to snag the Inquestor who comes in to care for her." His gaze snaps to the form on the bed and back to me. "She's had a sleeping draught, but she drifts in and out of consciousness."

I reach out to steady him when he nearly stumbles. He manages a weak smile, and it's then that I see the bruised cheek and the swollen eye squinting at me from beneath the fall of his hair.

"A few love taps, courtesy of our fine lord's accommodations. I'll be all right. It's my leg I'm worried about." He grimaces, shifting his weight, and I realize he's bleeding through his clothes, his filthy trousers soaked to his skin.

I kneel down for a closer look. He's bound it with a makeshift bandage—what looks to be part of his shirt. It's not the worst wound I've ever seen, but it will need a bonewitch for sure. "Can you climb with it?"

"Probably not," he admits, gritting his teeth when I give it a careful poke. "I'll not be dancing the rooftops with this tonight. Walking out of here will be challenge enough. But that's assuming I can get out of the chains first. I'm a bit limited in how far I can go."

"Chains?" My gaze follows where his finger points. His ankles are chained loosely together and bound to an iron ring on the fireplace. I snatch the key ring from where I dropped it, trying each one until the tumbler gives way. "There we are."

He rubs at the spots on his ankles where the manacles were. "Thanks."

"Hmpf." I lean my ear against the door. There's no sound from the guards, but we need to move quickly. Someone's going to discover them, even if they don't wake up soon. I shuffle out of my shawl and remove my skirt so I'm only in my corset and shift.

"What are you doing?" he hisses. "I mean, you're pretty and all, but I'm not shagging you here."

"Tempting, but I had escape pegged as a slightly higher priority." I hold the skirt up to his waist. He's a fair bit taller than I am, but that can't be helped. "Here, put these on."

He immediately does as I say, awkwardly sliding on the skirts and the shawl. "This isn't going to fool anyone."

"Not if they slip a hand up your arse, no." I pull off the wig and toss it on his head. My natural hair sticks out in a ruffled mess, but hopefully no one will pay attention to a couple of drunk party guests in various states of disarray. "Now hold still." An open bottle of wine rests on the nightstand next to a small bowl. I take a long pull myself before deliberately spilling some down the front of Ghost's shirt. He clutches the shawl awkwardly, and I bite my lip against a burble of laughter at his ridiculous expression.

"I'm going to get you for this," he mutters, but the corner of his mouth twitches all the same. He sucks down a few swallows of wine himself and sighs. "That Balthazaar is a tricky son of a bitch."

"Tell me about it," a slurring voice says from the bed.

My attention swivels toward Lydia. She's a frail thing, and on first glance, I might have only taken her for an invalid, brought down by some common sickness. The coughing fever, perhaps. But the telltale signs of the Rot are there, etched in a complexion that's a little too mottled in some places and too bloodless in others. A bit of her hair pokes from beneath a lace bonnet, but it's wispy stuff, nearly nonexistent. The dry lips and sallow, wrinkled jowls hang from her face, as if she might shed her skin entirely.

And yet her eyes open to reveal jaundiced orbs, the iris a dull heliotrope in color. But there is nothing faded or lost in the way they narrow when they see me gaping at her.

She coughs, but it's more of a brittle laugh. "If you're here to do something useful, you might do it now. Kill me, if you like. Smother me with a pillow."

I frown at her. "You want to die?"

Another hacking laugh. "Do you think this is living? I'm already dead. Balthazaar just can't seem to accept that, the tiresome old prick." Her lips tremble into a sneer. "So proud, those Meridians, to try to find the key to immortality. They found it, all right. Too bad about the living death part, eh?" Spittle flies from Lady Lydia's mouth, and she raises a gnarled hand. "Vanity and arrogance, my lass. This is what comes of it."

"I don't understand...I thought it was virus." I frown at her. This is the first I've heard anything about immortality. I glance at Ghost, but he shakes his head.

"Breeding Moon Children doesn't work," she says, ignoring me, her words a muttered ramble. "Tell that man...tell him to stop... Their blood doesn't work..." Her voice drops to a dull slur until I can no longer understand her at all. My head reels with the implications of the words I did catch, even as the door rattles behind us.

"Time to go!" Ghost snatches my hand, and we limp-run past the bed and out a set of doors onto a garden patio. It's a large indoor courtyard full of leafy trees beneath a great glass roof, and the scent of growing things hits me full in the face. It's like a dream of damp soil and soft grass, and for a terrible moment I have the urge to strip and roll upon it.

"So...*alive*." I can't help the longing sigh from escaping when I reach out to brush the bark with my fingers.

"We're going to be less alive if we stay here," Ghost points out. We duck through a thick cluster of bushes and head toward a set of doors on the far side. "We've got a little time while they gather their courage to follow us, so let's not waste it. For such well-armed fellows, they are rather cowardly."

"You don't think Lydia will tell them where we've gone?"

"I doubt she cares about anything but death," he says bluntly. "And frankly, neither would I if I were in that state."

"Ghost...The others you were captured with—"

"They had us in cells down below. Injected us with what must have been the Rot. The others fell ill very quickly, and the Inquestors took them. I'm not sure what he was going to do with me when it was clear I was still healthy." A grimace tightens his mouth.

"You're going to have to go to the Chancellor. You and your brother. Surely now you have proof as to what they're doing." I swallow. "Do you think she meant it? Breeding us...as a cure?"

"I don't know. It's the first I've heard of it. But we can discuss it later. Assuming we can get out of here in one piece." He winces as he attempts to put weight on the bad leg. "Let's find the way out. And go slow."

I throw his arm over my shoulder and clasp him about the waist so he can prop his weight on me. "Just keep your head down and let me do the talking."

"Aye." He catches my chin in his free hand and presses his mouth on mine for an instant. He tastes of blood. "For luck."

I kiss him back hard, letting the moment sweep past us in a wave of longing. This time his fingers trail over my jaw to cup the back of my head. My hold on him grows tighter, the realization that I've found him finally sinking into a fierce relief. The desperate ache that's been clenching my stomach this whole time finally loosens, replaced with a slightly hysterical optimism. If we somehow play our cards right, we might just pull this whole ridiculous charade off.

He retreats first and cocks his head toward the door. I grit my teeth and quietly crack it open to peer into the hallway. Everything still appears quiet.

And yet...

The laughter coming from the ballroom is strained. Definitely time to leave. "Come on," I whisper, and together the two of us limp toward the kitchens. A serving girl stares at us and nearly drops her platter, but I give her a drunken smile.

"My sister imbibed a wee bit too much, aye? We needs us a drop o' fresh air to strengthen her spirits up for another round."

Ghost makes a coughing sound in a rough falsetto, as though he's going to puke his guts up right there in the hallway.

"Th-that way, mum." The girl points down another corridor and flees in the opposite direction.

"At least she didn't scream." Ghost grunts when his bad leg brushes against mine.

"Small favors," I say. "Moon's blood, man. What have you been eating that you're so damn heavy?" He shifts so I'm not under the brunt of so much weight, and we turn the way the serving girl indicated.

This time we do get a few odd looks, but most of the servants are still too busy to pay us much mind as we slink into the kitchens. But then we're chased outside by a monstrously large cook, her face ruddy from the fire and her hands coated in flour. Not before Ghost manages to pocket a couple of biscuits from a tray, though.

"I haven't eaten in two days." He shoves one into my hands as we catch our breath, leaning against the brick wall enclosing the rear entrance to the estate. "Now what? We're not going to be able to hide out here for long, and we're too far from Market Square to hire a carriage."

"With any luck those guards will be too embarrassed to report that one girl managed to best them." I tear into a piece of the biscuit without really thinking about it. "And Lucian said he'd come back for me, but I don't think we'll have time to wait for that."

"Lucian is here?" He blinks, relief on his face.

"Mmm. Well, *he* was last I saw. For all I know Martika will be the one leaving as she arrived."

He looks away. "There's a reason for the deceit. So much rides on our ability to hide..."

"One day you're going to run out of excuses." I press a finger to his lips. "Hush now. Explanations later."

He swallows the last of his biscuit and gives me a bemused smile. "Quite the little commander, Mags."

"Come on," I say finally. A broken garden hoe lies beside the door, obviously meant for disposal. I snap off the bent blade and hand the rest to Ghost to aid him. If things take a turn for the worse, maybe he can beat someone with it.

The courtyard is lined with small stones and leads to a graveled walkway that undoubtedly allows servants to perform their outside duties without being seen by the people who live within. Ghost's breath becomes labored as we move along, but he doesn't ask to rest and I don't offer to stop.

Gardens and storage sheds branch off from the main thorough-fare, and once or twice voices approach us and then fade out again. Guards, perhaps, but an uneasy thread twists it way through my gut.

I stop suddenly and have to catch Ghost when he continues moving forward. "What is it?" he asks.

"I need a better vantage point. I don't like stumbling around in the dark like this. Let me head up for a better view so we have an idea which way to go to avoid trouble."

Ghost leans against the wall. "We need to figure something out fast. I'm bleeding again."

"Damn." We're not going to be able to hide a blood trail for long.

"Leave me here, Mags. If what you've said is true, there's no sense in both of us being caught. I'm only going to slow you down."

"Just...wait here a moment." A trellis hangs beside us, covered in withered vines. Whatever fruit grows on them has long since given up. The trellis bends beneath my weight but holds steady as I climb.

There's no cover here except the darkness itself, but I need a view from above to figure out the best course of action. Maybe I can spot us a proper bolt-hole to hide in.

My boot scrapes on the crenulations of the gutters at the first landing, and I freeze, my arms aching something fierce from my previous exertions. No cry of alarm is sounded, and I ease my way to the nearest windowsill. The curtains are drawn, but I still go slowly. People accustomed to noises in their houses are very much in tune with sounds that are not, and even though the party is going on strong below, I can't afford to be careless.

I spare a glance at the ground, but Ghost has sunk into the shadows as best he can. The whites of his eyes glitter up at me, and I catch the wince of an attempted smile.

My shift snags my heel, ripping when I scale the outside of the window. I catch my breath on a dormer roof, and I'm off again a few seconds later. I don't intend to go all the way to the top. The first roof level stretches out toward the front of the manse, and I follow it toward the well-lit courtyard.

Instinct sends me flattening against the roof as a beam of light sweeps past from the window beside me. It creaks open, a shadowed head poking out.

"Could have sworn I heard something," a familiar voice says. "No matter."

Inquestor Caskers? My neck aches with tension as I try to see.

The only answer to his words is a muffled grunt. From this angle, I can only assume it's Lord Balthazaar. Common sense tells me now is the time to return to Ghost, to make our escape while the two of them are preoccupied, but the next words root me to the spot.

"And when Balthazaar comes back, we'll make sure your whore gets a front-row seat. Did you think Molly wouldn't warn us about what you were doing, hiding in that disgusting flesh house?"

I'm a gargoyle, perched on a house made of bricks, but it's all shit. Shit and piss and death, and the rolling taste of bile in my throat threatens to choke the wind out of me. He's got Lucian in there.

And Molly Bell has betrayed us.

Terror grips me in fierce claws, but it's wrapped in a skin of rage that this monster of a man holds my life—and those of my friends—in his hands yet again.

No. Not this time.

Before I even realize what I'm doing, I'm in the room, hurtling through the open window to land upon the thick carpet. Lucian pales when he sees me, but he can't do more than groan behind the rag stuffed into his mouth. It's a moment of crystal clarity, my vision narrowing so I only see the lieutenant. He's taken off the sharply pressed suit jacket, and his sleeves are rolled up. A thick cigar hangs between his fingers, a halo of ash and smoke wafting from it.

Lucian's glasses are shattered and his nose bloodied, his fine clothes ripped and torn. I don't stop to think beyond snatching up the poker from the fireplace, and my boot scrapes on the hearth. The lieutenant turns, his mouth dropping wide to shout or gasp.

Whichever it is, I'll never know, because I'm thrusting the poker forward into the tiny target, lancing his head upon the point.

Later I might think on this night's events and remember how easy it is to kill a man. How the flesh parts before the iron, or the way the bone and viscera shatter beneath the force of my arm. In the end, an Inquestor is merely a man, after all.

Crimson splatters my gloves, and my ears are bludgeoned with the wet gurgle of his lungs as they fill with blood. The cigar drops from nerveless fingers, his arms flailing at me. I kick him, the hook of the poker catching on his cheek as I attempt to withdraw it.

He shrieks, eyes bulging as he claws at his throat. He slumps to the floor, breath hissing from between his lips.

It's a feeble, quiet sound, and it fills me with fierce satisfaction. "Sparrow sends her regards."

His legs twitch once and then go still, his chest ceasing to move. I drop the poker and rush to Lucian's side to remove the gag.

"What have you done, Mags? What have you done?" His voice is little more than a harsh wheeze, but there's a thump at the door and shouts from the other side.

"No time." I haul him to his feet. "Can you climb? Down, I mean?"

"What?"

"Ghost is waiting for us below. He's been hurt, and I can't get him to safety alone. But the two of you should do for each other while I create a distraction."

"You heard what he said," Lucian says, full of despair. "This whole thing was a setup. They know, Mags. They *know.*"

"Then you better get moving," I counter. "Go on. There's a trellis there. Even a flatfoot like you should have no trouble." I pick the poker up in my hand again, feeling the comforting weight of it in my palm.

He stares at me as though he can't quite understand who I am. I don't allow myself to think on it too hard. I'm no hero, but if I'm going to go out, it's going to be on my terms.

"You all wanted me in the Pits, right?" I try to smile at him, but it's halfhearted at best. "They find out what I am, and that's where they'll send me. I'm sure of it."

"Not like this, Mags. Never like this." He reaches out to stroke my cheek, but I'm backing away. There's no time for this sort of nonsense.

"Go. Find Ghost and get out. Don't let me give myself up for nothing." I turn toward the door, unable to look him in the face. I'll lose my nerve if I do.

The pounding on the door pops sharply; it's about to break open. Lucian doesn't hesitate any longer and I hear him scoot out over the ledge, yelping when he slips on something. "We'll find a way to get you out, Mags. I promise."

"You better." He grunts in affirmation, and I turn to watch him stiffly toward the trellis, gripping the gutters with white knuckles. I close the curtains behind him and look to the body of the lieutenant lying prone in a puddle of dark scarlet, his stare glassy.

No time to cover up the evidence. Might as well use surprise as my weapon.

I wipe the tip of the poker on his jacket and flatten myself behind a convenient tapestry beside the door. A small horde of Lord Balthazaar's guards spill into the room a half second later, gasping when they see what's left of the Inquestor.

At least one of them noses around the drawn curtains, and I squeeze my poker tighter. Time to give Ghost and Lucian a chance to escape.

Before the guards can investigate any further, I poke my head out from behind the tapestry and cough politely. "I believe you're looking for me?"

The guard directly in front of me stares, his jaw dropping. "You did this?"

I blow him a kiss and bolt for the hallway. A startled cry echoes in my wake, but I don't look behind me to see if they follow. The thud of heavy boots is answer enough on that account.

The hallway wraps around the entire floor in a large rectangle, the ornately carved banister giving way to a view of what appears to be a library. I don't catch much more than some carved statues and shelves upon shelves of books. I duck past a screaming servant girl, shoving her out of the way before the guards can trample her, but I can already see some of them are doubling back to try to trap me on the other side.

No hope for escape but down, I realize. It's only one level to the floor below. I've fallen farther than that on the rooftops without injury, and this will be no different.

I hurl the poker at the nearest guard, buying me a few extra seconds. Then I throw myself forward over the banister, twisting as I fall to grab the rungs. I hang the few seconds needed to pick a landing spot, dropping onto the top of the nearest bookshelf. From there it's an easy somersault to the black-and-white checkered marble floor, and I roll to my feet.

Shouts and cries of alarm fill my ears, but I skitter across the floor. Have Ghost and Lucian managed to get away? I can only spare the briefest of thoughts on them, concentrating on dashing down the hallway.

But a distraction, a large one, could be just the thing. After all, who would count a couple of staggering gentlemen in a wave of panicked, drunken people?

Mind made up, I weave and duck past startled servants and scandalized dinner guests. My shift is torn and bloodied, and I can only imagine what my face must look like as I run into the ballroom. A small part of me nearly snatches a carving knife from the roast beef on the serving table, but bloody or not, I doubt I look like much of a threat.

No, better to hit everyone where it hurts the most.

"I've got the Rot!" I shriek, lunging forward as I smear my crimson fingers over my mouth.

There's a singular moment where it's almost as though I'm moving in slow motion, captured in the tiniest of details. A woman dropping her fork. Pie hitting the floor. Coats and dresses tangled mid-dance, guests with lips parted in surprise as their brains do a mad scramble to interpret what they are seeing. And then they scatter like leaves in a winter storm, eyes filled with raw terror as they shove one another out of the way in an effort to escape.

A solitary giggle bubbles out of me, and I make a halfhearted effort to give chase, but my antics have had the desired effect. Guards dash about, trying to stay out of the way of the mob. From the foyer I see carriages streaming from the estate, tires kicking up gravel. With any luck Lucian and Ghost will have found their way into one of them.

A flash of red catches my attention, and I flinch away from a bird-masked Inquestor who lingers in the doorway. Lightning sparks in his hand. "You have a great deal to answer for," he says, electricity erupting from the Tithe wand again.

The pain drives me to the floor in a white oblivion. Seconds or hours, I can't actually tell how long it goes on, but when it lets up, I'm left gasping, curled in upon myself.

When the guards drag me from the room, I don't bother fighting it. I've nowhere left to go.

Bitter lies and sweet truth
Fall upon my tongue
Like berries made of frost and blood
And words that taste of dung.

— CHAPTER FIFTEEN —

Lord Balthazaar stares at me from the other side of the bars. My eyes are nearly swollen shut, but the reek of his perfume hangs in the air. I can always tell when he's been here to watch me because the stink of him lingers. He never speaks, and I can only imagine what delight he takes in watching a Moon Child wither before him. Perhaps he only seeks to take out his anger out on me.

Somewhere along the way my head was shaved when they were unable to remove the ink completely from my hair. Arms bound behind my back, my wrists ache worse than anything I've ever felt, fire licking up my bones until they're numb with it. I cannot get comfortable; I merely lie upon the brick floor, shivering as the chill creeps into my limbs.

This time there are others with Balthazaar. Dark shadows waver in the corners of my vision, whispers tickling my consciousness. Bleary, I wriggle into a semblance of a sitting position, trying to focus on the people before me. My gaze draws low over the fine cut of their red robes, and I cough behind my gag.

Inquestors. Tithers with their bird-face masks.

They've come to take me to the Pits. A thin line of terror spins its way into my guts, but I haven't been fed in at least two days and it's hard to come up with the strength to care.

One Inquestor studies me from beneath a tall hat and puffs on a cigarillo. Even with blurry vision, I can't mistake him for anyone but the High Inquestor. From this distance, I catch a glimpse of ice-blue eyes set in a bearded face, a scarred cheek, and a sensuous mouth that he wets with a careful tongue. "What a loathsome creature. But the brand is unmistakable. The Tithe roster indicates she's already dead. We should find out how she managed such a deceit."

Balthazaar puffs on his own pipe, tapping on the bars to catch my attention. "Forgive me for not caring in the slightest." He stoops down to my level, his voice shaking in fury. "Do you have any idea of what you've done, you stupid girl? How many people I've had to bribe to keep quiet about your little stunt? The amount of money I've had to spend?"

"Pish on your money. It's not like you don't have enough of it." The red cloaks part to reveal Molly Bell, swathed in an elegant dress and coat, a plucky feathered hat perched upon her curls. Her lushness only serves to remind me of the filth I'm caked in, but the illusion is destroyed a moment later when her mouth splits to reveal the pointed, gleaming teeth.

Fury shunts through me at her appearance, but I've nothing to show for it but a grunting mumble through my gag. She ignores me, glancing up at the High Inquestor with a saucy smile, but I've lived with her long enough to know it's an act. Somewhere beneath the lace and rouge, Molly Bell is very, very afraid.

"I've already told you how it was done: unbeknownst to me at the time, the doctor living beneath my roof found her and took her in. By the time I realized it, the girl had already healed." Her tongue flicks out to run over her lower lip. "It would have been a waste to turn her over to you."

"And just where is this doctor now?" The High Inquestor continues to watch me, paying no attention to Molly's simpering. I try not to register my surprise at her words, torn between helping her play whatever game this is and simply hoping I manage to survive. "I find it hard to believe you had no knowledge of planned conspiracy beneath your very roof!"

"I'm not omnipotent," she retorts. "I hired what I thought was a well-educated bonewitch to see to my girls. He never gave any indication he was working against the Inquestors. Or that he was from Meridion. The moment I had my suspicions, I made sure to communicate them to you, as per our working agreement." She shrugs. "As to where he is, I haven't the faintest. I have had no contact with him, but should that change, of course…"

Relief skitters through me, though it's tinged with fear.

"No doubt." The High Inquestor lets out a long-suffering sigh before turning to bark orders at one of the Inquestors behind him.

Molly approaches the bars and squats down to my level. To her credit, her face doesn't wrinkle in disgust, but her nostrils flare ever so slightly. "Where is the dragon, Mags?" I sneer something rude at her from behind my gag, and her eyes narrow. "Don't be a prat. I'm trying to save your damn life. If you tell them where it is, I'll arrange for your freedom."

I see it then, echoed in the shadows of her eyes. Molly's like a spider so tangled up in her own web that even she has no way out of it. Dr. Barrows had been wrong to trust her, but I doubt he'd had any options given his circumstances. And maybe her intentions really had been good at one point. But fear makes betrayers out of the best of us, and Molly isn't anywhere close to that.

Not that I really give two shits about her reasoning at the moment. I have no idea where the dragon is, so any attempt at bargaining is less than futile. I close my eyes and ignore whatever entreaties she makes.

"The Hells take you, then," she mutters.

The creak of the opening door whines in agonizing clarity, and the clang of keys and booted heels approach. Molly retreats to the far side of the room as the door to my cell is opened.

I wriggle away from it, a worm struggling through mud. My legs drag through something wet, but I don't stop to think on it. My breath wheezes around the gag; it's damp with my spit and cuts into the corners of my mouth, burning my lips wherever it touches.

Head down, Mags. Breathe. Slow. Slow.

But it's laughable. Exhaustion sets my limbs to trembling, and I gag, dry heaving as coughs rack my lungs.

"Well done." The High Inquestor grunts in disgust when I lash out with my foot, kicking piss-soaked straw at his boots as I continue to hack. He snatches me by the neck, gloved fingers nearly twisting to pull my face up as he removes the gag. He ignores my coughing fit, waiting until I go silent.

Sour drool ropes from my lips, but my hands are still tied so there's nothing for it but to let it drip onto my shift. I turn toward Balthazaar. My voice is a hoarse rattle, and it takes me three tries before words form. "Why do you hate us so?"

His brows raise at my audacity. "I don't. You're simply a means to an end, no different from breeding sheep for wool."

"Breeding Moon Children to find a cure for your wife, you mean," I mutter, an angry sneer burning its way through my mouth. "Too bad for us you didn't try becoming immortal, too."

Lord Balthazaar pales. "How dare you!"

I should hold my tongue and safeguard what I know, but freed from my gag, my words are careless and sharp, the only weapons I possess. "She asked me to suffocate her. I just thought you should know."

The High Inquestor slaps me hard across the face. "Lord Balthazaar showed remarkable restraint in not having you killed upon discovery, a fact for which he will be commended. Such restraint will not be shown to your fellow conspirators once we find them." He shoves me away. "And we *will* find them."

Relief floods through my muddled head at this final confirmation. They're safe. *Ghost* is safe. A flutter of giddiness makes me bold, and I roll my eyes at the man. "Not likely. I doubt the Inquestors will be any better at finding imaginary conspirators than they are at finding imaginary clockwork dragons."

The High Inquestor grows very still, and I know the barb has hit. But for that one moment I don't care, and I stare up at him, unflinching. Let *them* be afraid for once.

"Get her cleaned up," the High Inquestor snaps, kicking me in the side so that I'm left gasping like a fish. "An example must be made, and I intend to use her."

My consciousness is already beginning to fade, and I catch one last glimpse of Molly, her mouth pinched tight and terrible, before I slip into darkness.

People line the streets, judging me with bold, curious eyes. My vision is fogged and blurry, and the street jolts beneath my feet, threatening to upend me with mischievous intent. Why is the ground moving?

Somewhere, a bell is jingling madly, and the tinny sound fills my ears until I'm sure they're about to burst. The more I attempt to cover my head, the louder they ring. But it drowns out the jeers and the cries of disgust being hurled in my direction, punctuated by the occasional rock or rotting vegetable.

And so I let them ring, watching my boots as they slip over the mud-encrusted cobblestones. I've been allowed to keep the shift, though the corset is long gone.

The Inquestors do not even pretend to make this act sacred as they have the others. I'm going out of turn. Not as a blessed sacrifice but as a criminal.

The path to the Pits has never seemed so long, but before I realize it, the procession has halted and I stand before the thick metal gates where the High Inquestor waits. I can barely focus through my fever haze. The hood of my cloak has blown off, exposing my nearly bald scalp. Behind me, the wretched sobs of the Rotters hang quiet. The High Inquestor raises his gloved hand to silence the crowd, but it isn't necessary. One look at me has turned this from procession to spectacle.

There are Moon Children in the crowd, mostly hidden, but my eyes are drawn to them. The townsfolk will not meet my gaze, but the Moon Children do, and it satisfies me that they, at least, understand. A sudden movement attracts my attention, revealing Josephine upon the nearest rooftop. She raises her fist to her heart, but we both know she won't risk her people for me. Not when this was the plan all along. Of Rory there is no sign at all.

I bite my lip when I see Lucian by the gates, his face shadowed beneath his cloak. He leans heavily upon a cane, and I glance away quickly, though all I want to do is shout at him, *Where is Ghost?* and beg him to save me despite everything.

But no answers are forthcoming. The Tithers prod me forward, separating me from the group. Will they shove me inside without preamble?

Ah, but no. The show is not finished without drawing at least some blood. My arms are lifted above me and tied to the pole in front of the gates. I look beyond the metal bars, but all I see are shadows. I stare at them as the charges against me are read.

Murderer. Conspirator. Disturber of the peace. Thief. Forger.

There's no point in contesting the charges. They're true, after all. The High Inquestor makes a show of inspecting the brand on my neck, scratching the number down in the Tithe roster. I cannot help but wonder how many Moon Children are on there, how many numbers.

I barely register the chill in the air when my shift is torn open to hang from my waist, exposing my flesh to the gawkers. Some turn from me. In pity or disgust, I don't know. Others make eager sounds as the whip is uncoiled.

The High Inquestor pauses as he glances down at me, his eyes narrowing when he sees the panel upon my chest. "And just what is this?"

My upper lip curls, and for a moment I don't know if I'm going to spit at him or sob, but it doesn't matter because the familiar singsong voice of Mad Brianna cuts through the crowd like a crooked knife.

"The sparrow's flown the coop and left the fox behind, a hidden mask wrapped in bitterness and brine…" The old woman hunches her way into the space before us, her eyes rolling wildly until they land on me. "The key," she mumbles. "The key in the lee of the lock of the note. He'll break your heart to give us hope. When the Mother Clock sings, the dragon takes wing."

I stare at her in confusion, her words sliding past me in a haze.

The High Inquestor motions impatiently at the Tithers, their wands crackling with sudden power. "Enough of this nonsense. Begone or suffer her fate, as well."

Mad Brianna cackles and whirls upon him, laughing even as she is dragged away. "Meridion will fall if you bury the moon. IronHeart's flight is Meridion's doo—"

Her words cut off with a gurgle as one of the Tithers slams her into the cobblestones. Her legs twitch once and she doesn't move again.

I let out a scream, an ugly sound of rage and horror and pure spite as I struggle against my bindings. Adoptive or not, she's the only mother I've ever known.

The High Inquestor prods at the panel with a meaty finger, smirking when I try to bite him. "IronHeart? Is that what you fancy yourself? How quaintly pathetic." He waves his hand as though nothing even happened. "Ten lashes for murder. Two for each additional charge."

The silence bites me with its quiet anticipation.

Crack.

It starts with a sting. A biting fly. A pinprick of tiny focus, nearly negligible in its importance. My breath hitches, and exquisite fire spreads between my shoulder blades.

Crack.

Crack.

I whimper.

Crack.

My skin splits. I am a chrysalis of flesh, a butterfly of bones ready to escape.

Crack.

My body spasms, and the bells at my wrist jingle, discordant and brittle. A hot flush of tears waters in my eyes.

Crack.

By the end of it, blood fills my mouth from where I've bitten through my lower lip. I've retreated into myself, standing outside my own body, watching the crimson stripes ooze over my back.

From within my chest, the clockwork heart thrums, stuttering with each impact. Out of the corner of my weeping eyes, I see Ghost, struggling in Lucian's arms, his mouth contorted in fury.

"...ags...will...come for you..."

And then he's gone, swept away in the crowd.

Not forgotten. I'm not forgotten.

The words repeat themselves in a litany in my mind, breaking the cadence of the whip like the rhythmic rush of the sea as it speeds toward the shore before pulling away again to leave me aching and hollow.

Somehow that small bit of knowledge that he's here makes the rest of it easier to bear. Everything we've done has not been in vain. Josephine. Chancellor Davis. Lucian. Ghost. The actors are onstage, and they know their parts, just as I know mine.

The jeers of the crowd have grown quiet, and the only sound is the low moan escaping my throat. The High Inquestor gives me a satisfied nod. I'm roughly untied from the pole, but I make no move to cover myself.

He barks something at the other bird-faced Inquestors. Their batons crackle with electricity, and the airship above us roars to life as the cranks and pulleys are rotated at the top of the gates. The crowd behind us backs away before the gates are opened; only the boldest remain when the Tithers snap at them to leave.

The High Inquestor has me pulled to the side, allowing the procession to enter first. The newly diagnosed hide behind their masks, their porcelain faces serene, eyes darting with fear. One of them shivers, her shoulders shaking with quiet sobs. They file through the gates, the white of their cloaks turning orange in the guttering sconces lining the tunnel wall beyond the gates. The flames illuminate their passage with solid certainty.

When the last of them disappears into the maw of the Pits, the High Inquestor turns toward me. I expect him to say something snide and smug. Inquestor Caskers surely would have.

His gaze alights upon my half-naked form, but he doesn't leer. He merely removes his crimson cloak to drape it over my shoulders. I yelp as the heavy wool slides over my open wounds. Sinking to my knees, I vomit at his feet.

The Inquestor helps me up, his fingers rubbing over my stubbled scalp as though I am some sort of pet dog. His hand lingers at the nape of my neck, twisting at Sparrow's necklace. Without a word, he snaps it.

The crystals scatter upon the cobblestones like green glass tears, bouncing with sad sighs. The fight drains out of me as this last connection with the surface is severed.

Now he smirks, his mouth lowering to my ear mockingly. "I hope my cloak comes in handy down there. I shall enjoy the thought of you keeping yourself warm with it, *IronHeart*."

I think of Sparrow lying dead in the alley behind the Conundrum. Archivist Chaunders burned and broken in the Salt Temple. Mad Brianna, still and cold upon the cobblestones. Lady Lydia staring at me from behind her corpse-like eyes. Moon Children hiding in the shadows with hollow faces and hollow futures.

A soft laugh escapes my lips, but it carries through the quiet like a hammer against an anvil, the heated promise of a blade being forged. For them, I will carry this burden. For them, I will find the truth of it all.

"It's not your cloak that will keep me warm," I say softly, and the truth behind the words rings with a fierce clarity, a secret hope burning beneath my breast giving me new strength.

He stares, eyes shuttering at my insolence as though he doesn't know what to make of it. And then he shoves me through the gates, closing them swiftly behind me.

— ACKNOWLEDGMENTS —

Well, it's a been a longer ride than I would have liked to get us here, but here we are at last.

Special thanks to Danielle Poiesz, editor par excellence and one of my dear friends. I'm so happy to have the privilege of working with you.

To my family. I'm not sure what else really needs to be said. I'd be lost without you, and I'm beyond grateful for your presence in my life.

In no particular order, thanks to the following people who have helped me out over the last several years, both with this book and other assorted shenanigans: PJ Schnyder, for advice and comforting conversations; Debbie Bliemel, for her continued support and less comforting (but just as important) conversations; Jim Moore, for taking my phone calls and talking me down off ledges that none of us should have to tread; Tonia Laird, for beta reading and being an overall awesome person; Staci Myers, because we have an angel and a vampire story to write one day and I miss them terribly; Jess Haines, for a massive amount of advice selflessly shared; Jaime Wyman Reddy, fellow author spoonie and supporter; and of course, Aimo, my dearest partner in crime and a constant source of support, amusement, and dirty pictures.

—◖●◗—

KEEP READING FOR A SPECIAL SNEAK PEEK
OF *MAGPIE'S FALL*, THE SECOND BOOK IN *THE
IRONHEART CHRONICLES* BY ALLISON PANG.

—◖●◗—

Sing a song of sixpence, a penny for your thoughts.
Roll a ball of red thread, to untangle all the knots.
Tie me up and tie me down, the better for which to hang.
Let me dangle without regret, like no song I ever sang.

— CHAPTER ONE —

I am in the Pits.

This narrow thought fills me until I'm shaking so hard I can hardly stand upright as I stumble along the dark passage. My breath compresses with each numb step, and I hold it in even though my lungs burn. I'll shatter if I let it out.

Part of me aches with the need to turn around, to throw myself at the gates in search of clemency, but that's beyond foolish. Besides, isn't the point of this entire charade to get me down here?

I blink past the tremors, trying not to let the fear sweep me up into a sea of despair. The rest of the Tithe was forced through before me, and I can see no sign of them in the darkness ahead. Behind me, the sound of the gates locking rings through the passage with an utterance of finality that cannot be disputed. I shut it out, the crowd outside becoming a muffled rumble. I take a few more steps, and the bells strapped to my wrist jangle wildly with each movement.

One step. Two. Three.

The floor disappears with a whoosh, and I realize I've stepped off a ledge. My vision grays out in a haze, and I violently dig my fingers into the wall to keep from falling. If only that might somehow stop me from being swallowed down the gullet of the bitterest of my nightmares...

Only my years of dancing upon the rooftops of BrightStone lends me the instinctive edge to tuck and roll when I hit the ground. Pain racks my shoulders in fire, and my newly flayed skin splits beneath the impact, leaving me whimpering upon the rocky floor.

Breathe, Mags.

I lie there, mechanical heart clicking away in its usual fashion behind the panel on my chest. I take comfort in its familiarity as I take stock of myself, a mental tabulation. I wiggle my toes to ensure they still work.

The last several days are nothing but a blur in my memory: Allowing myself to be captured by Lord Balthazaar and turned over to the Inquestors. My head shaved. The Tithe procession. Whipped as *part* of the Tithe procession. The discovery that the Rot wasn't simply a punishment from the gods, but a plague deliberately spread among the people of BrightStone for reasons unknown. It's a plot I am in the process of unraveling, though to what end I couldn't say yet.

The image of Josephine and the other Moon Children saluting me from the rooftops flashes in my mind. The sharp-tongued leader of the Twisted Tumblers granted me that last bit of respect even as I allowed myself to be sacrificed in a final effort to find out what secrets lie beneath the city of BrightStone—secrets that might grant us access to Meridion and a destiny beyond what we'd become.

And then there's Ghost... Despite the rest of it, one perfect moment is etched in my mind: him fighting to get to me through the crowd, Lucian holding him back for his own good. Whether Ghost will truly come for me as he said he would or not...well, it isn't something I can rely on. There is no one to save me except myself.

For all my brave words and bold proclamations about what I hoped to accomplish down here, the reality is already far grimmer than I expected. That I volunteered for such a thing is my fault, I suppose, but knowing that at least Ghost didn't see me as merely a means to an end is comforting beyond measure. And now here I am.

Wherever *here* is...

I glance up at the spot I fell from. It's at least fifteen feet above me, maybe more. It's hard to tell. Something digs into my side. Bells, I think numbly, realizing the strap broke during my fall. I recoil from their brassy sound, shaking my wrist free as though it's coated in cobwebs.

A soft moaning echoes up the passageway, and I shift until I'm kneeling, though I've got nowhere else to go. The flickering of torchlight in the distance brushes over the edges of my vision, and I stagger toward it, the light drawing me in with a terrible need to *see*.

The passage takes a sharp turn, the sudden illumination of the torches blinding me briefly until my vision adjusts. I've found the source of the moaning in the form of the rest of the Tithe, their white robes bedraggled and torn. At least one of them is stained with blood—they undoubtedly had been caught unawares by the same fall I had been. Their masks are mostly still in place, though, the eerie serenity at odds with the miserable sounds from underneath them.

I let out a half sob. "Keep it together, Mags," I mumble. My survival depends on not losing my head.

A few of the Rotters huddle together, their terror evident in the way they shake. "Moon Child...help us... Where do we go?"

"Only one way *to* go." I struggle to get the words out as I limp past them to take a closer look down the tunnel. I have no answers. Moon Child or not, I've certainly never been here before, and no Moon Child has ever returned from the Pits to tell us what happens once the Tithe passes through the gates. I have the advantage of having studied a few old maps of the original salt mines that are now the Pits, but my brain is jumbled, the pain of my wounds making it hard to remember.

I strain to see beyond the few torches lining the walls ahead of us. I'm not sure what else I was expecting, but the only sound is the pulse of my blood pounding rabbit-quick in my ears and the panting breaths of the Rotters somehow thunderous.

And still, I see nothing but stretch after stretch of pale rock and a slanting tunnel leading deeper underground. Whatever natural light the gates let in has long since vanished, so these meager torches are all we have to guide us.

Which begs the question, who lit these torches to begin with? It's clear we are at least somewhat expected, but if so, where is this would-be proprietor of ours? And for that matter, why couldn't they have lit up that ledge we all fell down?

The very air presses down upon me, the stone closing in with an awful finality and no answers at all. As someone who has spent most of her life upon the rooftops, I can't help but whimper.

"Hello?" I try to call into the darkness, but my voice is a scratchy shadow of itself, hardly more than a whisper. My tongue sticks to the roof of my mouth, and the stink of fear hangs heavy on my skin.

I attempt to shrug out of the High Inquestor's cloak, but it's stuck. No kindness there. He'd meant to inflict as much pain upon me as possible, and the shiver of agony that rewards me when I give an experimental wriggle indicates I'll most likely black out if I keep trying to rid myself of it. I take a slow, deep breath. The fabric has the acrid stench of salt on it, but it masks the perfumed scent of the Inquestor. I'm grateful for that much, even if the dust sets me to sneezing.

Mayhap it's all a dream and you'll wake up in your bed at Molly's, a fine supper and a warm fireplace waiting.

The memory is near enough to make me weep.

"Moon Child?"

The voice startles me out of my woolgathering. On instinct, I grab the nearest torch, heedless of the way the hot oil leaks from the cloth to slicken my hand.

One of the Rotters moves beside me. "Are you all right?" She pulls her mask off to reveal a face clearly struck by the Rot—light bruising around the young woman's eyes and lips cracked with sores. She had been pretty once, I can tell, her bone structure delicate and fragile and oddly familiar.

I blink, suddenly recognizing her from the Salt Temple. She is the girl who'd been with the bird-masked Inquestor when Lucian and I went to see Archivist Chaunders. If she remembers me, I cannot tell.

She reaches out to take my arm and then seems to think better of it. "If we can find some water…"

"Why does it matter?" one of the others snaps. "We're all dead anyway."

Another moan arises from the group, someone giving voice to a coughing fit that leaves them curled upon the ground.

"That doesn't mean we should give up," the girl says. "Surely there must be a way…" She looks at me with a hopeful sort of despair. "Is it true what the fortune-teller said? Are you IronHeart?"

I shake my head, sighing inwardly. Damn Mad Brianna and her dockside prophecies. A river of grief runs through me then, remembering the way her body twitched when the Inquestors killed her, though part of me wonders if that had been the fate she'd wanted. She certainly had made no bones about her hope for Meridion's downfall.

"Do I seem like a dragon to you? Some 'Chosen One' intended to break down Meridion rule? I'm a scapegoat for a herd of sacrificial cows, eating their so-called sins," I say, shuddering against the fire licking over my shoulders when the cloak slips slightly, pulling on the wounds from the Inquestor's lashing. They've been oozing something awful, I know it.

My throat, swollen and hoarse, bobs as I struggle to swallow, and my thoughts patter like rain in my head. How do I tell them? *What* do I tell them? That the Rot has nothing more to do with sin than the wind? That the Inquestors have been purposely injecting innocent citizens with a plague so virulent that the city has been forced to quarantine the infected belowground? That the floating city of Meridion may be the source of the plague in the first place?

I've been keeping secrets for so long that I'm not sure it even matters anymore. Dead men tell no tales and all that. Besides, the truth isn't usually kind. The whole reason I am down here is to gather evidence of all those things, and I am in no shape to field questions from the others.

"Who's there?" A new voice sounds from an unseen passage before I can gather enough of my wits to give the girl a real answer. The shadows part to reveal an elderly woman, her pale hair glowing in the torchlight. I frown at her. Moon Children all have white hair—something about our half-breed lineage makes us so. Most of us are Tithed to the Pits before we reach twenty-five, but the Tithes have only been running for about twenty years. Even if one of the original Moon Children had survived down here that long, she still seems far too old for that.

A shabbily dressed man in loose-fitting trousers and a patchwork coat lingers behind her. He's younger than she is—maybe late thirties or so, though it's hard to tell. Dark hair frames a pleasant face and a scruffy chin, and his expression appears compassionate. A bonewitch, perhaps.

That doesn't mean I intend to trust either of them. In my experience, friendly faces often hide something far more sinister.

"Who are you?" I wave the torch in front of me in warning. I push the young Rotter behind me without thinking; I had protected my clanmate Sparrow for so long in such a way that it's nearly instinct now. The Rotter may not be a Moon Child like Sparrow had been, but there is something about this girl's innocence makes me want to hide her, all the same.

The two strangers squint at the harshness of the light but make no sudden moves other than to turn their heads away. The old woman smiles gently despite the glare. "Be still, child. You're safe now."

I'm lying on my stomach on a musty mattress in an actual room with real walls and a stone floor. A table laden with medical supplies stands beside the bed, topped with rolls of bandages and a tray of an odd blue liquid. The old woman kneels nearby, her head bowed.

In the distance, the moans of the Rotters have quieted some— the bonewitch had seen to them before me, but they're in another room. Not that it matters. I've got bigger things to worry about.

"Bite down on this." The bonewitch shoves a piece of rope into my mouth. I jerk away when it brushes my lips, the memories of being gagged still a little too fresh, but he sits there calmly until I relax.

I give him a nod, bracing myself for what comes next.

His movements are gentle as he dampens the wool with warm water, but it burns despite the careful treatment. He begins to remove the cloak from my back, and my shriek whistles past the rope.

"Easy now," he says. "It's stuck in the wounds. Stay still."

I have no choice but to do what he says, and I pretend not to hear the wet sounds of my skin pulling apart. I grind my teeth into the rope, my entire body shivering violently as I grip the table with trembling fingers. My guts churn, and I briefly wish he'd rip the whole thing off in one go, just to get it over with. But even I know that's foolish if I hope to make it out of this with any skin at all.

The old lady hasn't moved this entire time, and I attempt to distract myself by studying her with unabashed curiosity. I still can't tell her age, but her face is a maze of dark, craggy skin and crow's feet, and her pale hair hangs in myriad braids fastened by...seashells? They gleam in the lamplight, their spiral beauty drawing my attention.

"There now." The bonewitch lays the bloody cloak on the ground beside me. I fight the urge to spit on it. "That's an Inquestor garment," he observes, removing the rope. There's a slight tone of censure in his voice.

"Well it's obviously not my wedding gown, aye?" I mutter, unable to keep the anger from bubbling out.

"I meant no offense." He dips a series of bandages into the blue liquid before laying them upon my wounds. A soothing tingle spreads over my skin, and I exhale one long, shaky puff of air as the tension slips out of me.

My mind whirls with relief. "Well, you have to forgive me, then. I was a bit ill-used before I arrived here. My manners aren't what they ought to be." It's all I can think of to say, though I know it's not the right thing. "How long will it last? The numbing stuff, I mean." The sudden absence of pain is nearly mind-boggling in its sweetness, and I almost forget where I am.

Almost.

"Several hours, at least. Long enough to get you fed and settled." He shifts beside me. "A moment—I need to clean this up, and then I'll see about getting you something to drink."

"I did not expect the Pits to be so...hospitable," I admit wryly. Though *hospitable* might not be the right word. Regardless, it will do me no good to cross swords with my hosts, at least not until I get my bearings.

I narrow my gaze at him as he stands up and begins collecting his supplies. "Settled where?" With the pain receding, my wits have begun to return, reminding me exactly what situation I'm in. My stomach pipes up, too, growling to be noticed. Food would be a welcome distraction, but... "And where is everyone? The other Moon Children? The Rotters? Who are you people?"

The old woman lifts her head finally, a shadow crossing her proud features. "Perhaps it would be easier if we simply showed you," she says, her tone surprisingly soothing. "Whatever false-hoods you were raised to believe must be unlearned. Rest assured, everyone is properly seen to down here."

The bonewitch pats my shoulder. " Lie down awhile first... Do you have a name, lass?"

I pause, unsure which name to give him. If there are other Moon Children about, my Banshee clan name would make the most sense. I've earned more than my fair share of notoriety as "Raggy Maggy"—supposedly having been killed by Inquestors several months ago didn't help—but I'm edging toward caution over honesty now. The events of the last few weeks have left me a little gun-shy, and rightfully so. Besides, I'd been kicked out of the Banshee clan, and Moon Child clan grudges are nothing to sneer at. I'd rather not be shanked for my trouble before I even get a chance to figure out what's what. I'm not sure I want to give my real name, either, though.

"More than I care to list," I say. "Call me Magpie." I decide on the nickname only a few would know me by.

"Well, Miss Magpie, let these strips sit awhile. When the bleeding stops, you'll be able to move around some. You were lucky; most of the wounds aren't too deep. You should heal up right quick." He sits back down in his chair, wiping his hands on a damp rag. "You can call me Georges, if you like."

"Georges," I repeat. The name is familiar, but I can't place it. I turn toward the old lady to mask my frustration at my lack of memory. "And you?"

"Tanith." She gets to her feet with a gentle grace that belies her age, the seashells tinkling in her hair and pours me a mug of water from a nearby pitcher. She sets it on the table beside the bed. "Rest. I'll get you some new clothes."

The two of them duck behind a thin curtain drawn in front of the room's entrance. I shift carefully on the mattress, relieved when the pain is minimal. Whatever that blue stuff is, it certainly works well.

The room I'm in appears to be a makeshift infirmary, judging by the additional empty cots. Bottles of concoctions line the shelves, which are built into the stone walls, and a surgical table claims the center of the space. A tray of scalpels and a bucket of plaster sit beside it. It's clean in here, too, and smells faintly of lavender, which is strange considering where we are. The bonewitch must be kept busy with the Rotters, yet somehow the odor of blood and other less pleasant things is nearly nonexistent.

Which begs the question...If only Moon Children and Meridians are immune to the Rot, how are Georges and Tanith surviving it? The salt priests always insisted that only the sinful could catch it, and while my time with Lucian and Ghost had taught me that none of that was true, I'd never dreamed that people were somehow *surviving* down here. Perhaps miracles did exist. If so, my task to discover the actual source of the Rot—whether the Meridians are spreading the plague themselves or it's being done through some other mechanism—would be that much simpler. Surely, I would find answers...

I reach for the mug of water next to me, and I sip it slowly, ignoring the bitter aftertaste. None of this is how it should be. Lucian, Ghost, and I were betrayed by our fellow conspirator, Molly Bell. My clockwork dragon disappeared. I split the skull of an Inquestor to protect Lucian and Ghost. I was whipped in front of the entire town of BrightStone for my crimes.

And Lucian just stood there at the gates and let me be taken. But what right do I have to be angry about that? After all, how many times have *I* stood by and watched one of my fellow Moon Children be subjected to the Tithe? There is nothing he could have done to stop it anyway.

It stings nonetheless. For Lucian, maybe it really is all about protecting his brother.

Oh, Ghost…

I sigh. *I* started this chain of events: finding the dragon, Sparrow's death, leading the Inquestors to the Archivist, letting Ghost get captured. And then everything had fallen by the wayside in my decidedly rash impulse to let Lord Balthazaar capture me, forcing me to be Tithed. In the end, I've no one to blame but myself.

A gleam at the foot of my bed catches my eye, and I shift so I can get a better look at the marks etched into the wooden footboard.

I run a finger over the lines, sounding out the letters. "Suck-tit." I trace the letters again and am struck by a cold certainty. Penny has been here. Of course she has. I watched my former clanmate be Tithed weeks ago, taking my place when the clan thought I'd been killed. But where is she now?

As much as I want to bolt from the room and demand answers, I soon find myself dozing off into a fitful sleep. I've been thrust into the underworld like the hero from one of those tales Mad Brianna used to tell me, Sparrow, and rest of the orphans she had taken under her wing. I will need to rest and regain my strength if I'm to have any chance of finding the other Moon Children and learning the secrets of the Pits.

In the end, you do what you do best. Hide in plain sight, and hope they do not discover you, Mags.

I have no magic sword or shining armor, but I do have a quest. And that will have to do.

The curtain flutters and Tanith reappears, holding a set of clothing similar to her own—clean trousers and a linen shirt. She eases the shirt over my head so I don't have to strain the skin on my back by stretching, and belts it at my hips. It hangs loose off my shoulders, but I get the feeling it's less about modesty and more about comfort. Without any friction, my wounds won't stick to the cloth.

She nudges my feet. "You'll have to make do with your shoes. Or go barefoot, if you prefer, but I don't recommend it."

My thoughts turn to Ghost and the toughened soles of his feet. He might not have a problem down here, but I don't need to lose a toe in some sharp-edged crevasse. I lace up my old boots, their once fine shine now quite dull.

Tanith helps me stand. "I'll take you down to meet the others. We'll be in time for supper."

"Others?" My mind races with the thought of seeing Penny and the rest of the Moon Children. Or did Tanith mean the Rotters? Or both? The casual way she speaks of mundane things such as supper makes my head hurt. But Penny was my clanmate. She's smarter than the rest of us. She can read and write, and if there was any chance of her finding a way out of this place, I don't believe she would have passed it up, supper or no.

"I'll show you. Come along." Tanith waves at me to follow her through the curtain.

She leads me down a maze of dimly lit passages lined with glowing lanterns. There's a bluish hue to them, and I resist the urge to run my fingers over the glass. Unlike the earlier tunnels made of rock above, these ones are clearly the well-used remnants of the salt mines from earlier days. The walls are flat and smooth and white, the turns following an obvious route. Side passages scatter into the darkness toward some distant destination.

It's all so *empty*.

"Where is everyone else?" The question seems to hang in the air, with no breeze to move it along.

"Below. Most of us don't care for the light up here. It's too bright. Gives us headaches."

I frown. "I can barely see past the shadows."

"Not yet. But you will." She pats me on the shoulder. I'm sure she means to be reassuring, but I'm more confused than ever.

"What about Georges? Where did he go?"

"He's a Rotter himself. He led the rest of the infected to a separate living facility. Everyone who isn't a Moon Child or a Meridian carries the disease, and their needs are different as a result. Not all are fully affected by it right away."

My mouth goes dry. "He's a Rotter? But I thought the Rotters... I don't know...just decayed away down here. Isn't that why Moon Children are Tithed? To help them die?"

Amusement flickers on her face. "You all think that when you first get here. But I'm a Meridian myself; the last thing I want to do is let these poor people die. Come along—let me show you."

I don't understand any of this. Everything I've ever been told is a lie—an incredibly intricate one. Apparently not even Lucian, with all his learned doctor's ways, has any idea how things are here.

I have no time to ask another question before the passage opens wide, a silvery glow illuminating what appears to be a village.

The light is gentle, whatever its source, not as glaring as the torches lining the walls up in the upper tunnels. Everything is bathed in a soft haze. If I wasn't so terribly awake I'd think I was dreaming my way into a fairy tale.

But fairy tales are peculiar. All the ones Mad Brianna used to tell me and Sparrow ended with beautiful monsters eating the children, so fair warning.

And this village is nothing if not beautiful. Excessively so. Hundreds of softly lit domes have been arranged in clusters far below with spiral pathways looping throughout. Small groups of people slowly walk along the paths as they go about their business in a seemingly casual fashion. I catch the chatter of laughter and low conversation.

Normalcy. Or whatever passes for that here. It's like a utopia built in the darkest part of the underground, somehow only serving to draw attention to how drab and awful everything else is.

I glance up, though certainly there is nothing to see except the ceiling of the cave we're in. But the village has the same ambiance as the floating city of Meridion that hovers mockingly above BrightStone, a beacon of everything I've ever wanted and would never have.

Tanith hasn't said it in so many words, but I have no doubt this village was built by Meridians. That she herself doesn't glow like they are known to do doesn't mean much. Ghost once told me the electrical current that seems to flow beneath a Meridian's skin fades away if they are away from their city for too long.

So how long has she been down here?

The trail to the village is made up of a series of steep switch-backs, the stairs carved directly into the rock, but Tanith leads us to an enormous basket attached to a roped pulley system. A small door is latched shut on its side, and she opens it with a quick pull. "Normally, we would walk down, but my old bones prefer a little less impact." Ushering me through the door, she pats my hand and then gets in after me.

The basket creaks as we are slowly lowered into the canyon. "There used to be mechanical lifts many years ago," Tanith says. "But they fell into disrepair, so we are forced to use more primitive measures these days."

Fell into disrepair? Or were destroyed?

I don't voice the words aloud, but Ghost and I had researched the Pits as much as we were able and the working theory was that the Meridians had blown up a portion of the mines, for some reason only known to them.

And soon, perhaps to me, as well.

A man and a woman in hooded blue robes meet us at the bottom, bowing respectfully to Tanith.

"Ah, Tanith. You've arrived." The younger one, a man who appears to be in his forties, gives me a nod. He pushes his hood down, and his dark hair falls in a loose queue to his shoulders. His features are sharp and handsome, brows artfully arched and eyes half-lidded and languid as they flick over me, taking my measure the way a rat sizes up a piece of cheese.

But this man is different from the others. Like the dead architect I found who'd fallen directly from the floating city, his skin ripples as though myriad stars are trapped beneath it, beaming softly. I stumble, and his teeth flash as he grins, clearly aware of the effect he has on people. But more importantly, the fact that he still has that glow at all must mean he's been on Meridion recently. And if he's not using the gates to the Pits to get there, then there must be another way…

I file this piece of information away for later. No sense in tipping my hand too quickly.

Caught up in my thoughts, I startle as Tanith puts her arm around my shoulders. The sensation is oddly intimate, and I want to shake her away. "Prepare a dwelling for Magpie. There is an empty one in the third quad that will suit."

"As you say." He bows again and retreats swiftly, leaving the three of us beside the basket. Tanith gestures in his direction. "That's Buceph. He runs security here."

"And I'm Rinna." The woman removes her hood, revealing a mop of curly brown tresses, decorated with the same sort of seashells as those in Tanith's hair. "I see to most of the scheduling and the day-to-day tasks. Once you've recovered from your wounds, you'll get a rotation on the roster."

I blink at her. "Roster? For what? Last time I was on a roster it was to be sent down here," I say, my tone perhaps too blunt.

"Ah…yes," she says carefully. "Well, we all work to survive down here. If you have any particular trade skills, let me know your preference and I'll make sure you get that."

"Not unless you count murder," I say sourly. In truth, I've only killed one person, and Inquestor Caskers had deserved it, but still, honest work intrigues me. The concept, however, is almost beyond my comprehension. Their easy acceptance of me into their ranks seems a tad suspicious, but I'm not some innocent Moon Child anymore. And if the work allows me access to their records or a chance to snoop around without notice, I'll take it.

Rinna smiles weakly. "Don't worry, Magpie. We understand. Most of the lost ones who find their way here require a few lessons in civilization before they fit in."

I bristle, but Tanith squeezes my shoulder. "Very good, Rinna. That will be all."

"As you will, mistress." Rinna bows and heads up the path, her hair flowing behind her in soft ringlets. I cannot help but run a finger over my baldness with a twinge of envy. I've spent my entire life hiding my hair beneath a cap, and it's ironic that I might wear it so freely here when I have no hair at all.

Tanith's wrinkled hand reaches out to run over the stubble upon my scalp, something like pity in her expression. "Tsk. It will grow back, little one."

I snort, brimming with impatience. "I'm sure it will. It's only hair."

"Indeed." The two of us follow the path the others took, albeit more slowly. Tanith's pace is deliberate, with a hint of stiffness that suggests joint issues. It's noticeably pronounced on her left side in particular.

I study the others walking around us, looking for something or someone familiar. A Moon Child's hair is a peculiar shade of white—almost silver—and with all the soft light illuminating the space around us, Moon Children would stand out like beacons. But I do not see a single one.

From this distance, I can't tell exactly what the dwellings are made of—some sort of metal, perhaps—but they reflect the bluish light captured in the small glass lanterns hanging from nearby lampposts. Most of the houses are single stories with round windows. They are clearly meant for one or two people, with barely enough room for a bed and not much else, so village or not, it doesn't seem like there are any families here. No children that I've seen, at any rate.

"So, I don't understand," I say finally. "If there's a whole settlement down here, why does Georges have a surgery above? Where are the other Rotters? Where are the Moon Children?" Once it's freed, my tongue unleashes a torrent of questions with my need to understand why I've been betrayed and lied to for most of my life.

Tanith sighs. "It wasn't always this way. In the beginning, we stayed in the upper chambers simply because we were afraid to venture any farther. But when the plague didn't respond to our early attempts at a cure, we expanded our operations down here where we had more room. That said, all newcomers are checked out in the upper chambers to assess possible threats, as well as to see to injuries."

I raise a brow. "Why would you come down to the Pits at all?"

She shakes her head, and the shells jingle. "When the plague first erupted in BrightStone, a group of Meridian scientists, including myself, was tasked with finding a solution. We originally worked out of a facility in BrightStone—close to the Salt Temple, in fact." She curls her upper lip. "But before the Inquestors were able to quell the riots and fear in BrightStone, fires began to break out regularly, and we lost a number of labs that way. Frankly, we made people nervous, and it was decided it would be best to send everyone down below—both infected and our Meridian science team—to keep the other citizens safe."

The timeline Archivist Chaunders showed me and Ghost flashes into my memory. "So you've been down here for *twenty years*?"

"Nearly seventeen, actually. And we're still not much closer to a cure than when we started."

I nod. It makes sense, but I can't help wondering how easily everything is explained away. It hasn't escaped me that she didn't answer my question about the Moon Children, either.

"It's a lot to take in," she murmurs. "When you've had a chance to eat, rest, and become accustomed to how things work down here, you'll be more comfortable. Can you read, Magpie?"

Tanith asks it kindly, and I answer without thinking.   "A bit here and there, but nothing too hard?"

She's clearly surprised at my answer, but maybe feigning ignorance is better. I decide to keep my thoughts to myself for a while longer. Besides, the spiral paths are diverging; one leads to a cluster of dwelling pods and one to a...

"A greenhouse?" I ask, incredulous. It's squat, with one wall made of thick glass panes, and a purplish glow emanates from within.

Tanith makes an approving sound as we approach it. "Yes. A small miracle—one of many, in fact."

"But without the sun, how do you grow anything?" Not that I'm an expert on greenhouses. But the ones I'd seen on Lord Balthazaar's estate were completely made of glass to let the light in. Down here, though...

"Would you like a quick tour? Here." She taps on the glass, and someone moves inside to open a small door on the far side. A skinny beanpole of a man emerges and stands aside as Tanith ushers me in. His wiry frame reminds me somewhat of Ghost. His hair is bound beneath a cap, and he wears a discolored apron.

"This is Joseph, one of our expert underground farmers," she says.

There's something sad about Joseph, his gaze resting upon my shaved head with a slightly furrowed brow. But then I'm inside the greenhouse proper and any thoughts about him fade away as I'm embraced by the purplish lights and the scents of dirt and growing things.

I'm half-starved for color already, even in this short amount of time. Beneath the purple light, the green leaves don't seem quite right, but there's a certain brilliance to the way they shine. Not that I can recognize one from the other, but there are pictures in front of several plants that indicate various vegetables or herbs.

"Using different shades of blue or red light allows us to determine levels of growth so we can maximize the space we use and ensure the best harvest," Tanith drones from behind me.

I leave her and walk down the rows, unable to restrain my fingers from drifting through the soil in one of the trays. In the far corner of the greenhouse is a small table covered with potted flowers. It's hard to tell exactly what color they are beneath the purple illumination, but it doesn't really matter. Flowers are hard to come by even in BrightStone. Only those who lived in the Upper Tier would have the money for something so frivolous.

Living underground for as long as they have, perhaps these Meridians are just as hungry for things other than food.

"The others find me foolish for this particular hobby," Joseph says, walking toward me.

"Sometimes foolishness is all that's left." I bend over to sniff one of the flowers, sighing at the sweetness.

"Too true." He reaches over and plucks a flower from a pot. "Here. Have a daisy." He hands it to me and then bows his head, heading for one of the other tables. I touch the flower bemusedly, my fingers slightly trembling. I'd never actually held a flower before. Not one from a hothouse.

Deathflower weeds are common enough in the BrightStone Warrens, where my clan makes its home, but they are ragged plants, tough and built for survival. The only purpose for something like this is beauty. What does one do with a such a thing? In the end, I tuck it carefully into one of the pockets of my trousers and head to where Tanith waits by the door.

Her mouth quirks in amusement as we leave the greenhouse. "Meridian technology is a wondrous thing, isn't it?"

I chew on it, sure whatever's showing on my face is not particularly pleasant. After all, such technology has been dangled in front of me for the entirety of my life. Luckily, I don't have to respond aloud, though, because the other villagers are emerging from their dwellings.

I'm greeted with open curiosity and friendly waves, and yet, I recognize none of them. Not that I have ever been particularly close to anyone but Sparrow, but shouldn't there be Moon Children here? What of Penny? She was sent here only weeks ago.

Watch your step, Mags. A society that eats its children is not interested in protecting the young.

My gut twists, uneasy. I catch a hint of pipe music nearby, but it's nearly drowned out in the excited chatter.

Tanith claps her hands, silencing the others. "Prepare the table for our guest. Tonight we shall feast and welcome our sister, Magpie. Bid her good and gentle welcome, but be careful, for she is weary and her wounds are many."

I'd nearly forgotten the lashes upon my back, but thinking about them now, I feel exhausted beyond measure and my stomach rumbles at the mere thought of food. It's stranger still to feel like I'm welcome at a banquet like a person and not some piece of street trash.

Tanith points out the various buildings as we continue walking the main path through the village. They are all squat with slight domed shapes at the tops. Some have symbols carved into the domes, noting what they are. There is a baker and a butcher, a blacksmith and a tallower, and other signs I don't recognize at all. An herbalist, perhaps, and a metalsmith.

My mind reels as doubt continues to creep into my mind. Things were starting to look too good to be true. And yet...

Where does the meat come from, Mags? What are they eating down here in the depths?

With the lack of Moon Children about, the thought chills me, squelching much of my appetite. I don't *really* think they're eating Moon Children, but I will withhold judgment until I know for sure. And perhaps I'll stick to less carnivorous fare until then.

Before long, we pass a dome larger than any other we've seen so far. "The main hall," Tanith points out. A glance through its pillared entrance shows several long tables and benches. "Wait here and rest while everything is prepared."

There is a bench outside the entrance, and I gratefully sag into it.

"Welcome home, Magpie." Tanith gives my shoulder one last squeeze before retreating into the great hall.

"Aye," I breathe, but dread sweeps over me all the same. Where are the other Moon Children?

— ABOUT THE AUTHOR —

ALLISON PANG is the author of the urban fantasy *Abby Sinclair* series, as well as the writer for the webcomic *Fox & Willow*. She likes LEGOS, elves, LEGO elves…and bacon.

She spends her days in Northern Virginia working as a cube grunt and her nights waiting on her kids and her obnoxious northern-breed dog, punctuated by the occasional husbandly serenade. Sometimes she even manages to write. Mostly she just makes it up as she goes…